# DEATH'S EDGE

## JOHN ORTEGA

SMASH BEAR
-PUBLISHING-

First published in Great Britain in 2021 by SMASHBEAR PUBLISHING.

Office 6945, London, W1A 6US, United Kingdom

www.smashbearpublishing.com

This paperback edition published 2021

Copyright © John Ortega, 2021

All rights reserved. No part of this publication may be reproduced, distributed, or transmitted in any form or by any means, including photocopying, recording, or other electronic or mechanical methods, without the prior written permission of the publisher, except in the case of brief quotations embodied in critical reviews and certain other noncommercial use permitted by copyright law.

The right of John Ortega to be identified as author of this work has been asserted by them in accordance with the Copyright, Designs and Patents Act 1988.

This is a work of fiction. Names, places, events and incidents are either the product of the author's imagination of used fictionally. Any resemblance to actual persons, living or dead, is purely coincidental.

ISBN: 978-1-8382561-5-9

*Also available as an ebook.*

*To my mother, who has always stood by me and encouraged me to follow my dreams. This one's for you, mom.*

# 1

The penguin glared at me with big black plastic eyes. I held it up in the air by one of its green wings and frowned back at its fuzzy yellow belly. How could normies find such dreadful creatures cute? I had faced the largely terrifying fae equivalent once before – cute and fuzzy were the last descriptors that came to mind. I shuddered, picturing the face of the piranha-like monsters superimposed over the soft toy. In reality, the Gob Reoites loved to lure young children into frozen lakes so they could eat them – not the friendliest of guardians to be watching over the twins. 'You're not buying this.'

A hand reached out, swiping the penguin from my grasp and dumping it into the shopping cart full of other questionably coloured stuffed animals. 'This is perfect for the kids. Besides, you have no taste,' said the man next to me.

I looked over at my thirty-seven-year-old best friend and let out an exasperated sigh. His messy sandy-blond hair was in dire need of a haircut, and dark circles surrounded his pale blue eyes, giving him a tired panda look behind his lopsided glasses. His gray polo shirt and black jacket had pink glitter sprayed across the left sleeve, probably from his daughter Margie. She was going through an artistic phase, and everything had to have glitter.

'You do realize that Alice texted me the list of the things she *actually* needs for my nephews' room and gave me explicit instructions not to let you go overboard?' I pulled out my phone and scrolled through the small list of items, pausing at the bottom.

*Don't let my Mad Hatter buy the entire store. Just the items above are NEEDED!*

Devon shot me a rueful grin, rubbing at his jeans absently and shaking his head at the cascade of green and yellow glitter that fell to the floor. He looked as if he had spent the whole night at a gentlemen's club rather than performing two autopsies back to back. It wasn't enough that Portland had one of the most culturally rich magical communities in the United States, now apparently, we had our own serial killer.

I looked down at the shopping cart bursting with baby things. 'None of this is on her list, so we're going to put it back,' I said firmly.

'The boys need cute and fluffy toys to decorate their room. How can you say no to these lovely faces?' Devon scowled mockingly and picked up a purple giraffe with a pair of magenta-coloured gossamer wings and a glowing silver horn. He held up the abomination of a green penguin in the other hand, and I shuddered when its eyes fixed on me. Alice was right. It really was like shopping with the Mad Hatter.

I snorted, thinking about the real Mad Hatter, then found myself frowning when I remembered he still owed me a hundred gold coins. Bastard liked to cheat at chess. At least he didn't have a penchant for stuffed animals, unlike some people.

I held my phone up to show Devon the text, and a smile bloomed across his haggard face. It was his funeral if he decided to ignore his wife.

'Firstly, the boys aren't here yet,' I pointed out. Given that Alice was due to give birth in February, the boys wouldn't need anything but diapers and milk for the foreseeable future. Let alone an army of cuddly toys. 'Secondly, you bought about twenty stuffed animals of all shapes and sizes just last week.' His eyes widened, and he opened his mouth to speak, but I continued. 'Alice can barely walk into the room without tripping over a red lion or blue triceratops. Thirdly, we are *supposed* to be getting the cribs, which you currently seem to be missing. And finally ... get rid of that penguin. It's unnatural.'

Devon dropped the toys into the shopping cart, crossed his arms and glared at me. 'How do you know about those? You haven't been to the house since Margie's birthday at the beginning of October.'

I ignored the look he was giving me and stuffed my hands into my jacket pockets. 'Alice told me when she found out that I was coming with you.' I gave the mountain of toys another look. 'But if I knew we were going to buy the whole toy aisle, I would've stayed at home.'

'After all the begging and groveling I had to do to get you to come out of the inn.' He wagged his finger at me, pink glitter floating through the air in small waves. 'You were coming whether you liked it or not.'

I snorted and arched an eyebrow at him. 'Begging and groveling? More like demanding and threatening.' I dropped my voice in a close imitation of Devon's. "You've got five minutes to get ready. I'm picking you up, and if you're not ready by the time I get there, I'll summon a horde of zombie dogs to piss on your precious flowers."

Devon blinked innocently at me. 'Well, what the hell was I supposed to do to get you to show your face?' He gave me a concerned look and stepped forward, putting his hand on my shoulder. 'Nathan, no one has seen you, really seen you, since what happened at the Lighthouse. We're worried about you. Margie asks about you constantly, and not for nothing – you look like crap.'

I gave him a once over. 'Have you seen yourself recently?'

He picked up a toy mirror in the shape of a hippo and held it to my face. 'Have you? I've been dealing with back to back autopsies and a serial killer on the loose. Not to mention Alice stressing over the baby prep, and obviously, Margie's magic could awaken any day now. Things are a little tense. What's your excuse?' He wasn't wrong. The killings were seriously taking their toll on him – hell, on the whole community. Devon, like all of the Portland P.D., felt responsible for each death that had occurred since October. It was December now, and the body count had reached eight, with the cops nowhere close to catching this monster. Baby shopping was not my usual idea of fun, but I needed to help Devon take his mind off the case.

A worn-out face stared back at me from the toy mirror. The man in the reflection had long unkempt dark hair that fell below a bearded chin. Exhausted gray eyes peered back at me above hollow cheekbones. While the bruises had faded and the wounds had healed, the emotional scars from my last encounter with the Fae were still fresh and bleeding. 'So we both look like crap.' I took the mirror and put it in the cart. 'But you're still ignoring Alice's orders, and you know how she gets.'

'Nathaniel Mercer,' he growled. 'I swear by all that is dead and holy that I will beat you within an inch of your life if that's what it takes for you to talk to me.'

I looked around and noticed several mothers with their kids giving us weird looks. A plump elderly woman with dark hair streaked with gray shook her head at me. 'Honey, take advice from an old soul: communication is the key to any relationship. You don't want to make your husband feel like he can't connect with you.'

Devon and I blinked at each other before a laugh began to curve his mouth. I started to correct her but stopped short as Devon cut me off.

He turned to the woman and gave her a grateful smile. 'Thank you, ma'am, finally someone who understands. You don't know how hard it is to please a man that has the emotional capacity of a platypus.' I stared at him, stunned. He continued, 'We have two lovely daughters, and he can't even make the time to go to their ballet recitals, and now we're expecting twins!'

Now everyone in the aisle was giving me the stink eye – even the employees. I rolled my eyes at Devon. *If that's how you wanna play it, fine.*

I let my Irish accent grow thick. 'If you didn't spend all hours of the night with your clients and leave the girls with me, then I wouldn't be the way I am now, would I? I'm sick of it.'

A mischievous glint sparked in his eyes as he stomped his foot. 'I'm providing for our family, and what are you doing? Sitting on the couch all day eating nachos, drinking beer and watching figure skating.'

One of the employees, a young man in his mid-twenties with short dark hair, walked towards us from the other end of the aisle, frowning. 'Sirs, could you please lower your voices and discuss your problems at home? If not, I'm going to have to ask you to leave.'

I raised my eyebrows at Devon and poked him in the chest with the damn penguin I had picked up from the mountain of accessories. This whole theatre was his doing. 'You see what you did? Now you've got' – I looked at the employee's name tag – 'Ron here asking us to leave before we can buy half the stuff we need. I hope you're happy.' I grabbed the overstuffed cart and walked away.

A few seconds passed before Devon found me in the maternity clothes section. As soon as he saw me, he started laughing his ass off. I smacked him on the arm with a maternity gown. 'Yeah, sure, laugh it up. You know we can never shop here again now the whole store thinks I'm a scumbag dad?'

Devon kept laughing, holding his stomach as tears flowed from his eyes. 'Since when are you going to come back to *My Bella Mama* anyway?' He stopped laughing and picked up a red gown cut in a provocative style. It had a deep V-line that was supposed to curve around the breasts before opening up around the belly and falling towards the back like a wedding dress. 'Unless you're finally planning on making me an uncle. So far, I got you beat three to none.'

I rolled my eyes at him and checked the list again.

*Soft maternity gowns, no pants and nothing too shocking. It's for doctor's appointments.*

I considered the clothes that Devon picked up. They were certainly soft. I'd give him that, but that was it. 'You do know that Alice plans on going outside in these, right? It's not just to wear in your bedroom.'

Devon paused with a deep sapphire one in his hands. 'What do you mean?'

I gave the dress another glance. 'It's lace and has a zipper from the chest to just above the thigh. Though, I guess that'll definitely make it easier for the doctor to perform a check-up.'

He looked at the gown again. A flash of green light sparked in his

5

eyes and his cheeks turned a rosy colour. 'Ah, right. Doctor-appropriate it is.'

I shook my head and swallowed a laugh. 'I'll leave you to shop for clothes. What else do we need?' I checked the list and nodded. 'I'll gather the rest of the stuff. You finish here and then look for the cribs. Also, you do know there's this thing called baby showers, right? I'm told they are used by expecting parents to pawn the really expensive stuff off on friends and family. Why are you buying all of this?'

He gave me an incredulous look and put the gown back on the rack. 'I'm not going to let someone put a wonky spell on something my boys will be sleeping in. Automated rocking beds that vibrate through walls? Self-feeding bibs that nearly choke the poor kids? No, thank you.' He shuddered visibly, and I fought the urge to smack him on the back of the head. 'As for my family ... let's not get into that. If I let them, my dad would get me a crib made of twenty-four-carat gold because anything less is for plebeians, and my mom would fill the nursery with so many flowers my kids would be asthmatic before they turned a day old.'

I laughed at his overprotectiveness and clapped him on the shoulder. 'And I thought I was the paranoid one. Fine, go and get the cribs. I'll settle the rest of the stuff. You get the clothes, and then we can go have something to eat. I'm starving.'

Devon nodded, still eyeing the plethora of nightgowns available with a small crease between his brows. I sighed and grabbed a cosy looking one. 'How about this one? If there's one thing I know, it's comfy clothes.'

'It's not just comfort I'm worried about. It's the style,' Devon replied with a quick glance at me. I looked down at the blue and red flannel shirt beneath my jacket and smacked him on the back of the head. You can only fight an urge for so long. It's like eating nachos; you can't just stop at one.

'What's wrong with this? It's soft and warm, and I can buy them in bulk because apparently running an inn for the supernatural is detrimental to your wardrobe.'

Devon's eyes were skeptical as they darted from the gown on the rack to me. My hand twitched from the effort of not smacking him again.

'Fine, I'll see you in twenty minutes,' I said with a huff, and he hummed noncommittally before putting the dress he'd held earlier in the cart as well as two other more modest gowns. I rolled my eyes as I walked away and pulled out my phone, texting Alice:

*Mission semi-accomplished.*

A reply came back with a facepalming emoji.

*He bought the entire store, didn't he?*

I pushed the cart towards the newborn clothes and replied,

*Half, and according to everyone, we make a cute couple. See you later.*

My phone chimed again as Alice replied with a confused emoji. I grinned to myself as I put my phone away. I picked up some clothes for the boys and managed to dump the hideous penguin in an aisle nearby. Time had flown by since last September when Devon and Alice had found out they were having another baby. Remembering the crazy grin on Devon's face when he told me the news made me smile even now. While I was recuperating from my injuries after stopping a crazy fae bent on drowning the city, they went to their first appointment and discovered that Alice was four months pregnant with not one but two babies.

Half an hour went by without Devon reappearing. I decided to play Nancy Drew and look for him before he could make his way back to the toy section. Raised voices snagged my attention, and I sighed, recognizing Devon's voice as he argued with an employee over why they didn't have twin baby cribs. He was demanding to speak with a manager. I turned my cart around and walked away. There was no way I was getting in the middle of *that*. I texted Alice again, hoping she could provide me with an excuse to get out of here before her husband sent a zombie after the poor employee.

I don't know what she said to him, but he returned ten minutes later with two similar-sized cribs, a rocking chair, a large playpen, and that damn green penguin. I picked up the offending toy and placed it on a rack next to us. Devon didn't even blink; he simply put it back in the cart with a smile. I sighed in defeat. I would just have to teach the boys how to kill Fae while they were still in diapers. Who said being an uncle was easy?

We paid for our purchases – penguin included – and went to have lunch at the food court. I ordered two double bacon cheeseburgers with fries and a chocolate shake for me and a grilled chicken salad for Devon.

I eyed his food and offered him one of my burgers. 'Here, have some decent food. It pains me to see you eating that.'

Devon looked at the burger mournfully and reached out for it before his hand stopped several inches away. 'No, I can't.' He retracted his hand and speared his salad leaves, eyeing them with distaste.

'Come on. I won't tell Alice. Have a bite. It even has lettuce and tomato in it, so you're technically eating an upgraded salad.' I put the burger on his tray and started on the other one. After hours of shopping, it tasted heavenly, especially the crispy bacon between the layers of cheese and meat.

Devon chewed on his salad and moved the burger away. 'I promised Alice I would follow her diet during the pregnancy. She's been on this whole food regime for months, but the babies made it worse. Whenever I sneaked a burger here or there, she can smell it on my breath.'

I gave him an incredulous stare. 'You do realize there's something called mouthwash, right? It's something the normies invented for guess what? Bad breath.'

He put his chicken down and leaned back, crossed his arms and matched his voice into a close impersonation of his wife. "Why does your mouth smell like mouthwash, dear? Did you eat something you weren't supposed to? What did you eat? How could you? You promised you were going to support me? You don't love me anymore, and you want me as fat as the cow you ate!"

I choked on a fry and took a big slurp of my shake. 'That sounds oddly specific.'

He went back to his salad. 'You don't know the half of it. I slept in the guest room for two nights after my little slip-up. Even if the mouthwash hadn't blown up in my face – well, when your wife's a telepath with mood swings, you learn what hell is really like.'

I shrugged but gladly removed the temptation by eating the burger he was eyeing. I was such a great friend. 'Devon, I lived among the Fae for years, possibly centuries. I've seen pregnant Fae before, and trust me, as scary as Alice was with Margie, she doesn't hold a candle to Sidhe women. You haven't known true fear until you've been screamed at by one of them.' Devon looked doubtful but didn't argue as I munched through my second burger.

We finished our food and walked outside to my old black pick-up truck, our purchases in hand. The cold December air sucker-punched me after the toasty warmth of the mall, and the sky had become an amalgamation of purples and oranges as the sun began to set. The truck was parked only a couple of feet away from the entrance, which was a miracle in itself. I opened the back and raised the cover. Half the truck bed was filled with saplings, which left a small amount of space for the clothes and furniture.

Devon eyed the saplings warily. 'What's with the trees?' he asked as we started loading the cribs inside.

'The attack on the inn wrecked a good chunk of the woods, so Julia wanted to reforest the area. But we've been so busy dealing with ... stuff that there just hasn't been time. So with Yule coming up, I went and picked up a few apple, peach and western hemlock trees. I just didn't have time to unload them before you showed up,' I said as we picked up the rocking chair and loaded it up. Alice was going to kill him for buying yet another one, but I'd learned it was pointless trying to tell him what he shouldn't buy, so I kept my mouth shut.

I climbed inside the truck and turned on the heater as soon as the engine started. The blast of hot air felt good against my cold skin as I pulled out of the parking lot and headed for Devon's house. A couple of minutes into the drive, Devon's favorite song played through the radio, and instead of busting out into an off-key tune, he sighed. His eyes were glazed over, staring out the window at the waters of the Willamette River without really seeing it.

Ever since the media gave the killer the moniker of 'The Woodland Ripper', the entire police force had been under the national spotlight. The cops had found two more bodies, and there was no telling who the killer would go after next or how many bodies they might find next week. If they didn't catch this guy soon, going by his previous actions in six days, another body would turn up. Nobody felt safe anymore.

'Worrying what Alice is going to say about that third rocking chair?' I asked tentatively.

Out of the corner of my eye, I saw Devon's lips twitch into a brief smile before settling back into a worried frown. 'Things are bad, Nathan, really bad. I was the medical examiner that performed the autopsy on the first victim. She was a kid, only just turned eighteen the week before she died. When the cops declared a serial killer was active, Jason stepped in and took over all the autopsies. Pompous asshole. He barred me from even coming near the bodies. Then last night happened. They found the two bodies, and Jason decided he needed me after all.'

Jason was Devon's boss and the Chief ME for the city. I'd never met the man in person, but the picture that my friend had painted of him over the years was less than flattering. To use Devon's own words: he was 'a glory-seeking, arrogant, brilliant, pompous asshole.'

Devon rubbed his tired face with his hand as if he could wipe the memories from his mind. We had both seen our share of death. While I was living among the Fae, there were days where I was up to my neck in blood, and Devon, being a necromancer, walked with death every day and invited it to tea. I tried not to think about how my life was slowly falling back into familiar and unwanted patterns since the Fae came back into my life. I had escaped the blood and turmoil of court life, and yet, sometimes, it felt like I never left.

'What is it about these killings that can haunt even the most powerful necromancer in the country?' I asked him.

'People, even other necromancers, think the dead don't speak. That they don't feel.' He shook his head. 'They're wrong, Nathan. The dead do care. I feel their emotions every day at work. Right now, they're disturbed. It's unlike anything I've ever seen before. I'll have to ask my dad if he's ever experienced this before.'

'Think he can help from Europe?' Devon came from a line of necromancers, but he had never told me which parent he inherited his powers from. Guess I now knew.

Devon nodded confidently. 'If anyone knows, it'll be him.'

'The more information you have, the higher the chance of catching that sick son of a bitch,' I said as we passed into a more heavily wooded area.

Devon sighed. 'I raised last night's victim,' he said mournfully, pulling up the sleeve of his jacket. There was a multitude of scars along his forearm, a bright purple band-aid with smiley faces covered his most recent addition.

That must've been hell for both the victim and Devon. 'What did she say?' I asked.

'Nothing, she just screamed.' His hands clenched, knuckles turning white. 'It was like something was missing; her eyes were so blank, Nathan.' I reached over and squeezed his shoulder. 'I've raised murder victims before, they know they're dead, and they can usually relay the last moments of their lives, but this time...' He shook his head, his eyes shining with unshed tears. 'It was as if everything that made her alive had been stripped away along with some of her organs. She screamed and begged on my table for five minutes. I tried coaxing her to calm down, but she kept going. Nothing about it was natural; there wasn't anything left inside her to communicate with. In the end, I had to lay her to rest.'

Worry gnawed at me, for Devon and any future victim this animal might set its sights on. I tried thinking of something that would give him the slightest bit of hope, but my mind was blank. I didn't do well with hope. Call me a cynic, but my years with the Fae taught me it's a fleeting thing that kills more often than it saves.

I shook my head. Now I was bumming myself out. 'You think the killer is from the community?'

Devon rubbed his eyes beneath his glasses and laid his head against the seat. 'I don't know. Humans can be just as monstrous to each other, if not more so, than the magical community. Her corpse was mutilated with almost surgical precision. That could mean anything from medical training to an experienced hunter, or Gods knows how many other things.'

A thick gray blanket of fog rolled from the woods to the left, shrouding the entire road in darkness. I could barely make out the car in front of us. I heard several car tires screeching ahead of us before the unmistakable sound of two vehicles crashing into each other. The minivan in front of us swerved from side to side. A dark silhouette burst through the fog and crashed into the side of the van, driving it off the road until it vanished into the woods.

## 2

'What the hell?' Devon cursed.

I jerked the wheel instinctively, missing an oncoming Prius by the skin of my teeth.

'What are you doing?' Devon swore again, hanging onto the door handle.

I stopped the car at the edge of the road and saw a trail of broken branches that led deep into the foggy woods. 'You saw whatever that thing was, right? Whoever is in that car needs help.'

'All I saw was a dark ball of fur. I know that you can't just sit on your ass, but give a guy some warning next time.' He shook his head and squinted into the fog. 'It's going to be difficult to see anything.'

I nodded and turned the headlights to full beam, improving our vision slightly. 'Better than nothing.' I pointed to the glove compartment. 'Pass me the pair of gloves in there, will you?'

Devon opened it and handed me a pair of fingerless gloves with steel knuckles embedded into the black leather. I had carved a pair of runes into them – two intersecting lightning bolts and a tongue of flame on the palms. Unlike Devon, I couldn't summon an army of undead to fight my battles.

'What happened to your morningstar?' Devon asked as we jumped out of the car and entered the woods. The musky scent of pine surrounded us and mixed with the stink of burnt rubber. Normal forest sounds were absent as we made our way deeper. As I pulled the gloves on, the familiar soft leather gave me a boost of confidence.

A twig snapped next to me in the eerie quiet. I whirled with my fist held high, magic gathering inside me to strike. I could barely make out Devon's profile at my side, and at the last second, I twisted my torso, barely missing him with my fist. I let out a breath but tensed again as the shadows from the trees behind him seemed to grow longer, reaching further. At least Devon hadn't noticed I had almost clocked him.

'I lost it along with my shield and dagger after the battle last September, and since you can't just walk into Costco and pick up a magical weapon off the shelves' – I rolled my eyes – 'I bought these to make do until my weapons guy comes through for me.' I missed my morningstar, but at least I wasn't defenseless. An orange light cut through the fog ahead of us, casting a sickly glow over the floor. With a nod exchanged, we began walking in the direction the light seemed brightest. The closer we got, the louder the static from the van's radio became.

The canopy of trees partially obscured the sky, and the winter clouds covered the moon in a dark embrace, letting no light through. Memories flooded me of a different forest, one filled with monsters far more terrifying than anything this world had to offer – even the Woodland Ripper. I clenched my fists tightly, magic brimming beneath my skin, ready to be unleashed. Tonight wouldn't end the same way.

'How long will it take to get your new weapons? I don't like the thought of you having nothing to protect yourself with but gloves,' Devon asked quietly as they continued together through the fog.

These gloves packed quite the punch. Devon meant well, but his worry still stung. I could take care of myself. 'Sadly, he lives on another plane of existence and only comes to the inn during Yule. I did manage to mirror him a request, and he said he would have something for me.' I smirked. 'Don't worry, bud. I made some upgrades.' My smile died as the orange rear light cut out, and we were left standing in dense gray fog. I could barely see five steps ahead of me. Even Devon next to me was obscured by it.

Darkness closed in around me like a hungry predator. My heart pounded in my chest. Adrenaline shot through my veins, making me hyper-aware of my surroundings. Not that it did me any good through the thickness of the fog. I strained my ears, trying to catch the slightest hint of noise, but the only sound was the static from a radio. My pulse throbbed in my head until a small breeze stirred the mist, revealing Devon to my right.

Devon opened his jacket and pulled out a knife about eighteen inches long. Black with a large belly towards the edge, like a kukri. I could've sworn a small, almost inaudible growl emitted from it. If I hadn't been paying attention, I would've thought it was my imagination. Every time I saw that blade, it sent a shiver of fear down my spine. Even so, I was glad Devon had it with him. It could cut through or kill anything – or so I'd heard. The temperature around us dropped, raising the hairs on the back of my neck. My magic prickled beneath my skin in silent warning.

A loud wrenching sound came from somewhere ahead of us, like metal scraping against itself. I winced, covering my ears. My stomach churned at what that could mean for the passengers in the car. Devon and I took off towards the source of the sound, the radio static having stopped when the metal had screeched. I stumbled, my leg catching on an errant log that I just about managed to leap over in time. The thickness of the fog made it difficult to see more than a couple of feet in front of us. If not for the training I'd taken up again with Travis over the last couple of months to get my body back into fighting shape like how I was when I lived among the Fae, I might have stumbled more seriously over the uneven ground. Shaking off ten years of rust couldn't be done overnight.

The fog parted before us, revealing a small clearing with a couple of trees that had been knocked down, presumably from the car speeding through here. My heart lurched in my throat as I looked ahead and saw the minivan. It had wrapped itself almost completely against a tree, like a grotesque C. The metal twisted around the trunk; the hood had flown completely off and landed several feet away. I covered my mouth with my hand as the smell of gasoline permeated the air. Next to me, Devon didn't seem to mind the smell – he was probably used to worse, working on corpses all day. Smoke rose from the engine, and one of the back tires was missing.

But the car on fire was the least of my worries. Standing over the wreckage was a hulking creature, snuffling around the carcass of the vehicle. It had to be at least seven feet tall with coarse, dark brown fur and a wide, unnatural head that sat on top of a muscular neck. Round bulky shoulders gave way to arms longer than its short but broad legs that ended – were those hooves? I knew if I wasn't careful, those meaty palms would snap me in half like a twig. Silver hair shaped like a saddle course from its back to its waist and legs. Gods above and below, this wasn't going to be an easy fight. I wet my dried lips, trying to look for a weakness. The beast stood hunched forward on bulging arms. A noticeable lump rose from its muscular back. I shuddered. What corner of hell had this thing crawled out of?

So far, the beast hadn't noticed us. I didn't know if this thing hunted by scent, sight or sound, but we were lucky it was too caught up in its search to notice us. I signaled Devon to walk around and get to the car. He tilted his head to the side and raised his eyebrows. I palmed my face and pulled him to me.

'Get to the car. See if anyone is in there and if they're okay. I'll distract him for you,' I whispered into his ear.

Devon nodded and started sneaking around in a wide circle, stepping carefully over the broken branches and glass that littered the ground. My heart stopped as he nearly fell over the tire that had flown away from the car. I turned to the monster to see if it noticed. The creature's back was to me as it thrust a hand through the car's skylight, rummaging around and giving a squeal when an audible groan emerged from the passenger seat. It started rummaging in earnest. The car reached its waist while it was hunched over. Paint flaked from the car as it crumpled under the weight of the creature's arms. Then the unmistakable cry of a child split the air. The creature stilled for a moment before making its way to the back of the vehicle.

I felt my chest tighten, and out of the corner of my eye saw Devon pause mid-step. A child's cry rose in a crescendo of fear and desperation, calling out to its parents. My heart quickened, thundering in my ears as my palms grew slick with sweat inside my gloves. We needed to act. Now.

I dove into the well of my magic, revelling in the familiar rush of electricity coursing through my veins. My last battle with the Fae left me powerless for almost a month. I'd called the Head of Portland's Mage Assembly, and she had assured me not to worry and that it would return with rest. Still, being so defenseless for so long was an experience I didn't care to repeat.

My magic rushed like a raging river toward my hands. The flame runes on the palm of my gloved hand glowed with intense red light through the leather, illuminating the foggy woods. The creature stopped in its tracks and turned to look at me. I paused, getting my first good look at its face. Deep-set amber eyes stared at me from below a bony ridge and a large pig snout where six nostrils flared, taking in the scents around it.

'Step away from the car, you pig, boar, gorilla ... thing, or this is going to get nasty,' I said to keep his attention and give Devon enough time to get to the child.

*Yes, you big ugly bastard, focus on the noisy red caster and ignore the necromancer.*

His wide jaw hung open, revealing a forest of sharp yellow teeth meant for tearing into flesh and crushing bone. Two large incisors rose from his bottom jaw like tusks, and he snapped them fiercely at my words. Ice spiked along my spine. Never in all my years had I seen such a creature. Brown light flashed in its eyes, and for a moment, they looked almost human before they faded back to amber.

The pig-gorilla rose to his full height, and I realised he was taller than I'd originally guessed. He pounded his chest, letting out an enraged roar reminiscent of a boar or hog. Fear coursed through my body, and I fought to shake it off, letting adrenaline drive me instead. 'I warned you, Swinekong,' I said, naming it the first thing I could think of, and lifted my palm towards the creature. 'Dóiteán,' I called out as the heat licked the side of my face, chasing away the winter cold. A burst of light shone in front of me, and a baseball-sized orb of bright orange flame shot out from my hand and streaked through the air. The beast swung a big meaty fist towards the fireball. I smirked and lifted two of my fingers, raising the ball a few inches above his arm and crashed straight into his chest, igniting the shaggy fur.

Panicking, the monster began to beat his chest, trying to put out the flames. Singed fur clogged the air and scratched at the back of my throat, making my stomach churn. A loud shriek of pain, more akin to a pig than a gorilla, filled the stillness of the air, making me wince. I glanced at Devon as he waited for his opportunity to get inside the van before looking back to the creature. It had beaten the flames away and had its amber eyes filled with unbridled, animalistic rage trained on me.

It charged towards me, pounding its heavy fists into the ground and making the dirt tremble. As soon as it stepped away from the van, Devon made a run for it. Great, now all I had to do was deal with the five-hundred-pound monstrosity and we were set.

It covered the distance between us in a couple of steps, swinging its long arms in a wide arc. I dove underneath the strike and punched it in the gut. It felt like punching a wall. My fist shook from the strain, and I rolled to the side before it could swing at me again.

Fire and steel didn't do much but anger the bastard, so it wasn't Fae. I looked for any signs of damage but didn't see so much as a scratch, which meant I was nowhere near close to figuring out how to kill this thing. Punching it to death was a stupid plan, sadly. I was fresh out of ideas.

With a resounding bellow, it grabbed a large pine. Its sausage fingers closed around the trunk completely, and with barely any effort, it uprooted the tree and swung it at me. My eyes widened as it sailed through the air, and I threw myself forward, dirt and leaves filling my mouth with an earthy taste as I crashed to the ground. A boom sounded somewhere behind me then pine needles showered my back. The creature was on top of me before I could jump back to my feet, slamming its fist down with all its might. I automatically rolled to the side, but the beast kept coming at me as I kept rolling for my life. Twigs and rocks dug into my skin, but I barely felt it as I dodged another strike.

I let my magic flow through me and into the lightning bolt runes on top of my gloves as the Swinekong loomed above me. 'Tintreach!' I roared, and the runes lit up with a silver radiance that turned into sparks of electricity coursing through my hands. I stopped rolling and swung my arm towards the Swinekong's jewels, smacking them like a bell with the back of my fist.

The creature let out a high pitched noise that echoed through the forest before it fell forward onto its knees, its hands reaching for the burning section below his waist. No matter what kind of beastie you were, a hit to the balls hurt like hell. The acrid stench of scorched meat and musk hit me like a battering ram, and I fought the urge to hurl.

I turned back for a second to look at Devon, who had managed to pry open the driver's door and was administering CPR to an unconscious woman on the grass. A hint of movement behind me was all the warning I had before the creature rose and charged at me. I took a step back and bumped into a large tree.

*One little pixie, two little pixies, three little – now!*

I jumped to the side, rolling over my shoulder while the Swinekong smashed headfirst into the tree. In my head, the monster hit the trunk and was dazed enough for me to fireball his ass. In reality, trees make for terrible stopgaps to enraged supernatural creatures. The monster hit the bark, splintering it in half, and kept going.

I channeled my magic into my palms, and two volleyball-sized fireballs ignited in the air. I lobbed both of them at the creature, who stopped in its tracks as it realized that the pesky human hurting it wasn't a pile of mush on the floor.

As a loud cry came from inside the car, panic boiled inside me. *Come on, little one. I need you to be quiet, please.* But sadly, telepathy wasn't in my toolkit.

The monster turned around just in time to catch the spell in its face, the fireballs exploding on impact. Flames spread across its dark fur, and the beast roared in pain as it tried to put the fire out again. I thought that would keep it busy for a moment, but the monster stopped and, in a very human fashion, dropped to the ground and started rolling from side to side to extinguish its burning fur.

What the hell was this thing? That took some level of reasoning and intelligence – most creatures on fire would just run for the nearest source of water. Inside the car, the baby's cry grew louder, pulling my attention away from the still-thrashing creature to cast a worried eye at Devon, who was still trying to save the woman. 'Devon, not to rush you or anything, but *hurry*. I don't know how much longer I can hold this thing's attention.'

'Her heart stopped! I need a defibrillator, or she's going to die – damn it!' Devon paused to give the woman mouth to mouth, then resumed compressions. 'Come on! You got a baby girl waiting for you.'

I looked at my gloved hands and rushed towards him while the Swinekong kept trying to put out the flames. If I was going to do this, I needed to do it fast. Devon looked at me with hopelessness in his eyes. 'There was a passenger, but—' He shook his head.

'Give me space and keep an eye on that thing.' When Devon moved his hands, I placed mine under her shirt, over her heart and focused, letting my magic flow. Lightning sparked from the gloves into the woman. Her body jumped an inch off the floor, but nothing else happened.

Devon moved in to check on her. 'Give her another jolt, stronger this time.'

'I could kill her.' I shook my head. 'I didn't exactly calibrate these for saving people when I designed the rune.'

Devon looked at me, his blue eyes flashing with green intensity. 'Nathan, I can feel her soul slipping away.' His eyes darted between me and the woman. 'We need to jump-start her heart now, or else we'll *really* lose her!'

A loud bellow filled with pain and rage sounded from the creature's direction, and I turned to see the Swinekong swaying as it rose from the ground. Devon looked behind me, and his eyes widened. 'Now, Nathan!'

Another louder cry came from the car, a scared child crying out for its mother. Anger sizzled inside me. No, not again. I won't let it end like last time.

I placed my hands back over the woman's chest and channeled a smidge more magic into my hands. Out of the corner of my eye, I could hear the lumbering footsteps of the creature and the cry of the baby. *Gods, please guide me and don't let me kill her. Dian Cécht, let this work. Morrígan, don't take her soul away.*

Lightning sparked beneath my hands with more intensity, and the woman's body jumped a solid foot off the floor. Damn it! Had I used too much? I gazed at her still form, my heart beating in my throat, desperation swelling in my stomach like poison. I turned to Devon helplessly when she suddenly gasped in a breath and opened her eyes. Relief washed over me, and I nearly collapsed. *Thank the Gods!*

I jumped to my feet. 'Devon, make sure she's okay. I'll take care of the big ugly over there.' I rushed forward, pouring all my frustration and relief into my gloves. If that had gone any other way ... I didn't want to think about it.

Fire and lightning enveloped my gloves, crackling with power and illuminating the darkness, swirling through the remaining fog in a psychedelic haze. Magic coursed through me like a raging river, undaunted and full of fury.

The Swinekong squealed as it ran to meet me. I moved to the side in an effort to get behind it, but the creature didn't want a repeat of what had happened earlier with the tree. It spread its hands to the side, catching me by the waist and holding me up to its eye level in a crushing grip.

It growled in my face, the putrid breath hot against my cheeks, making my eyes water. I didn't waste any time and grabbed its tusks, pouring all my magic into my gloves; raw determination flowed within me like a warm current. Fire and lightning coursed through my hands into the creature, and the monster's grip tightened as it let out a soul-wrenching howl. Fire engulfed the creature's head, and electricity flowed through its body, causing its muscles to contract.

The monster's hold on my ribs strengthened, and a roar erupted from my throat. I felt a jolt run through me that made my muscles tense

JOHN ORTEGA

up, and I immediately let go of the tusks. The Swinekong released me, and I fell to the ground. Pain flared through my back as my body spasmed, legs flailing beyond my control, and it took all of my will not to bite my tongue. *Not again.*

I looked up at the creature and tried to rise, but the electricity had locked my body in place, and I couldn't move. The Swinekong opened its eyes and looked at me on the floor. It was fighting through the flames on its head that were slowly spreading to the lump on its back. It raised its large muscular arms and brought them down on me.

'No!' I heard Devon scream behind me.

I closed my eyes and waited for the pain to hit, but it never came. Something wet fell onto my cheek, and I opened one eye to see the creature impaled by thick roots from the nearby trees. Dark gray blood was dripping down from the wounds, and the creature was struggling to breathe. For a moment, I thought Julia had come to save me, but that was stupid. She was back at the inn. I focused on the well of magic in my lightning bolt runes and urged them to absorb the electricity coursing inside me. A rush of relief waved through me as my muscles relaxed.

I looked back to see Devon holding the woman by her shoulders. Her hand was stretched towards the Swinekong, and next to them was a majestic looking stag. Its fur was green, with patches of brown bark that covered its powerful chest. Bright white and pink lotuses curled themselves around its antlers like a floral crown. The stag clawed at the ground with its hoof, and a dozen flowers of all shapes and sizes suddenly sprouted from it: purple daisies, pink roses, blue violets, black dahlias and even a sunflower, all creating a wave of color that spread across the ground. The sweet scent of a dozen flowers permeated the air. A familiar – the woman was a witch.

A sound caught my attention, and I turned back to the monster. It was looking at the stag with such intensity that it didn't seem to notice its wounds. The creature opened its wide mouth, and a thick pink tongue pushed its way out of his mouth and darted impossibly fast towards the woman. The witch screamed and sagged in Devon's arms as the tongue slammed into her chest before darting back inside the creature's mouth. The floral stag let out a mournful cry, its body turning translucent as a black mark appeared on his front. Dark veins spread all over him like a spiderweb, the lotuses around its crown wilted into ash and swept into the air by a gust of wind. The mark was pulsing with angry light, shrouding the familiar in darkness. The symbol grew bigger, the light from the familiar dimming until its form vanished completely.

The lump on the Swinekong's back was pulsing, extending and contracting like it was filled with snakes. Before I could do anything, it burst in an explosion of gray blood, drenching me. Two enormous leathery wings sprouted from the creature's back. The Swinekong grabbed onto the tree roots pinning him to the ground and ripped them apart. The huge wings flapped several times before it lifted into the sky. The massive form broke through the canopy of the trees and darted away.

## 3

Devon let out a long breath as he lay the woman on the ground and leaned back. 'She's alive.'

I turned to the woman, finally able to really look at her. Short, in her late twenties, with light brown skin and dark hair streaked with shades of blue. Her brown winter coat was stained with dirt, and her green top and flowing pink skirt had soaked up the blood. Recognition suddenly flared within me, and I cursed myself for not recognizing her sooner. I had seen her several times before. Her name was Maria, one of the witches in the Portland coven who used to provide the cleaning service for my inn. I could feel the beginnings of a headache pound at the back of my skull. Even if this wasn't my fault and all I had been trying to do was help, the coven would surely blame me for this. I wasn't exactly their most favorite person at the moment. Witches weren't the most rational bunch, and they carried grudges like no tomorrow.

'Should we be concerned?' I pointed to her chest.

There was a hole in her shirt above her heart. Devon carefully undid the top two buttons and pulled the shirt to the side. Instead of a wound, her skin was marred by a black tattoo that matched the stag's. The ink was shaped like a mouth with crooked teeth and two spears crossed beneath it, it wasn't anything I recognised, and Devon looked just as perplexed.

'What the hell?' Devon said as he inspected the tattoo.

'I don't understand. Why would that thing target Maria?'

Devon shook his head. 'She's out cold, but at least she's stable.' He looked as confused as I felt. 'You said her name was Maria?'

I nodded. 'Yeah, I didn't recognize her at first, but she's part of the local coven.' I rubbed my face trying to expel the memories of another mother fighting for her daughter, only to be brutally killed in front of her. 'After the head priestess died, the coven named me persona non grata and cut all ties with me.'

Devon frowned and turned to me. 'Why? From what you told me, it wasn't your fault.'

I shrugged. 'Somehow, they found out about my past with the Fae, and since it was a fae that killed their priestess, they see me as a guilty party.' I rubbed the back of my neck, trying to ease some of the tension. 'Also, the fact that I didn't give up Roel to the witches from out of town didn't endear me to them.'

'That's stupid. They can't blame you for something you couldn't prevent.' Devon shook his head. 'What were you supposed to do? Hell, you barely made it out of there alive!'

It was true. Last September was touch and go for everyone involved. I had made it out, but I was lucky. To say that relations with the local coven were now 'strained' would be the understatement of the year. Luckily, my magic had finally replenished itself. If they tried to retaliate, I would be ready.

'Someone has to bear the blame. I'm okay with it.' I gave him a strained smile. 'Though finding a new cleaning crew has been a bitch, to be honest. The moment you mention the word 'dragon', they flee faster than vampires avoiding the dawn. I mean, the guy isn't that bad ... just eternally ornery.'

Devon opened his mouth to say something, then closed it and frowned. 'Isn't it a little quiet here?'

I looked around. After the Swinekong left, the woods had slowly started to come back to life. My eyes flew wide as I realized what we had forgotten. 'The baby!'

I rushed over to the car, broken glass crunching beneath my boots. The passenger side of the van was covered in blood. I looked inside and saw a woman with dark blonde hair slumped forward. One of the tree branches had struck the windshield and pierced her in the chest. A soft growl emanated from the back seat and caught my attention, raising the hair on the back of my neck. I frowned and tried to open the back door, but it was jammed. I walked to the other side of the car. Due to the crash, the door was popped towards the outside. I grabbed the handle, and after struggling for a moment, it became clear that the bloody thing wouldn't open by normal means.

Magic rushed towards the tip of my finger, and I carved a keyhole-shaped rune. 'Oscaíl.'

The rune flared with white light and the door vibrated for a moment before it slid all the way open with a loud screeching sound of metal against metal.

The toys scattered over the back seat were covered in leaves, and an open box of Lucky Charms had spilled its contents all over the floor. A bright pink car seat was secured in the middle. Its pink cushions were ripped open, the foam exploding everywhere. A green froggy onesie lay in tatters next to the seat.

'What the...' A loud thunk came from the back.

Devon peered out from behind me. 'Nathan, where's the baby?' he asked, voice shaking.

I held up a finger for him to wait, walked towards the back and popped the trunk open, my eyes flying wide as I looked inside. 'Devon, earlier you yelled something about a little girl, right?'

'Yeah, she was wearing a cute little frog onesie. Why do you - oh. Wow.' Devon's eyes grew comically big.

Batting her paws against a neon orange plastic container was a baby mountain lion. She was about the size of a house cat, with dark brown fur, black spots and bright blue eyes. Her tail swished back and forth as she lay low to the ground before pouncing on the container, missing by a mile and smacking her little head against the side of the car. She looked up, noticed us for the first time and opened her little mouth to hiss at us, showcasing a row of tiny teeth.

I fought not to smile, but it took a lot of effort. She was so adorable. I looked at Devon. 'So this is a problem,' I stated the obvious. We needed to call the paramedics and there was no way we could do that with a baby mountain lion running around.

Devon nodded his head as the cub padded her way towards us. 'Do you have any way to change her back?' he asked as he reached out with his hand. The cub smelled it for a couple of seconds before she sneezed and backed away.

I gave him an incredulous look. 'Why would I have a way to forcibly change back a shifter?'

He gave me a steady look. 'You're the swiss army knife of magic, Nathan. If you don't know something, you come up with it on the spot. Do I have to remind you of the incident with the nymphs?'

I glared at him. 'Hey, you were sworn to secrecy, and I was under pressure at the time.' I turned back to the cub and shook my head. 'Besides, shifters have a natural resistance to magic. The best I can do is make her go to sleep and pray to the gods she changes back. She's young, so it shouldn't take that much.'

Devon frowned, crossing his arms. 'So what you're saying is that either it works, or we end up with a sleeping mountain lion.' He shook his head. 'Not sure I like those odds, it's basically all or nothing.'

'Well, unless you have a better idea...' The cub ignored our squabbling and went back to batting the container with her paws.

'What would make her change?' Devon asked, scratching the back of his head.

I didn't have much experience with their kind. Out-of-town shifters stayed at the inn from time to time, and on the full moon, they shed their skin to run in the surrounding woods. I'd never really been around their young before. 'Well, the full moon can make them shift. It's not forced like in the movies or books, but the compulsion to change is greater under its influence.' I counted with my fingers. 'Fear or stress can make them change, which is what I think happened to this little one. I'm guessing she'll eventually change back on her own. '

'You know that doesn't help us at all, right?' Devon remarked, running his hands through his hair in frustration.

I sighed, turning to the back seat and searching for something that would make a mountain lion want to become human. 'Why can't my life ever be normal?' I muttered underneath my breath as I pushed aside a diaper bag. My eyes set on the box of Lucky Charms, and I picked it up slowly. Half the contents were spilled on the car floor, but it was better than nothing.

I walked back to Devon as he eyed the box in my hand and arched an eyebrow. 'Hungry are we?'

I handed him the box with a roll of my eyes. 'You're going to use your dad-voice and tell that cute cub that if she doesn't shift back, she won't get the delicious half-moons and rainbows.'

He grabbed the box, looked at the cub doubtfully and raised an eyebrow at me. 'Cats don't eat cereal, you know.'

I crossed my arms and waited. Devon turned towards the cub with a smile on his face and shook the box. The cub turned towards us, her blue gaze turned predatory as she eyed the bright red box. I looked at the cartoon depiction of one of the most heinous and dangerous creatures to roam the lands of Faerie and couldn't help but wince. Only humans would make leprechauns cute.

The cub padded softly over to us and batted at the air with her paws, hissing at the box. It was so cute, I wanted to take a picture. Devon drew the box back out of reach and steeled his expression. The kitten's eyes questioningly rose to meet his gaze. 'No, this is for baby girls, not kitties. If you want it, change back,' he said in his best dad voice, and I fought hard not to laugh at the ridiculousness of the whole thing.

The cub sat on her butt and actually glared at us with all-too-human emotion in her feline eyes. She opened her mouth to let out a threatening roar, but it came out as a raspy purr, and she batted at the air again with her paws. Devon shook his head, his voice gaining the edge he used when Margie raided the fridge for the last cup of chocolate fudge. 'Change or no snacks.' He picked up a colorful rainbow marshmallow, making loud chewing noises as he ate it. 'Mmm yummy-yummy delicious.'

A laugh trembled on my lips, and I held my breath to hold it back. The cub dropped, laid on the floor of the car and turned her head, ignoring us. Devon shook the box louder and made even more of a show. 'So much yummy cereal that I get to eat all by myself.'

The cub's fluffy ears twitched and she turned back to us, her eyes mournful as she looked at the box and let out a soft mewling sound. I slowly took my phone out, turned off the flash and snapped a picture. Devon, the heartless monster, shook his head. 'Change and you can eat all of it.'

The sad expression vanished as she hissed. Then ripples coursed through her fur, bones shifted underneath the skin, and suddenly, a beautiful baby girl, about a year old, sat on the floor with tears in her light blue eyes. She had light brown skin and a mop of chocolate curls that framed her cherubic face. She reached for the box, and Devon handed it to her. The baby girl stopped crying and was about to dig into her prize when she let out a long, drawn-out yawn, closed her eyes and promptly fell forward. Devon moved with cat-like reflexes and caught her before she hit her head.

'Huh, I guess shifting took a lot out of her,' I said.

Devon carried her with such care, his whole face lit up before turning to look at me. 'This whole ordeal wouldn't have been easy for her, but kids are resilient.'

I patted him on the shoulder, careful not to wake the baby. 'Thanks for the sage advice super-dad, now go find somewhere to put her while I call this in.'

'Oh sure, leave me with the dirty work while you go and make the call. Really, Nathan? Just because I'm a dad doesn't make me an expert on babies. It's been a while, you know,' he whispered urgently.

I smirked, turning around and left him to his own devices. Fighting giant Swinekongs I could do without blinking an eye – dealing with babies not so much.

Calling 9-1-1 was out of the question. The normies couldn't help with the situation, and I ran the risk of exposing the supernatural

JOHN ORTEGA

community if I involved them. Luckily, in Oregon and other Mage controlled states, the Assemblies had set-up a private helpline: 9-1-3. The Mages who formed the governing body of the assembly were not the most creative bunch. Once you've dialed, a mage on the other line would send the cavalry – EMT's, cops and firefighters – if need be. Depending on the situation, most of them would still be mortals, but at least one responder would be part of the community and could help deal with the things that went bump in the night.

It took the paramedics eight minutes to arrive. I was waiting for them by my truck at the side of the road and as soon as they jumped out, I extended my magical senses towards them, and noticed that both of them were brimming with magic. Good.

I led them towards the crash site. 'We got a baby shifter about a year old, she's unharmed. A witch that survived the crash was attacked by some sort of magical creature. We fought it off but not before he marked her with some sort of tattoo – then she fell unconscious. The third passenger didn't make it,' I said, bringing them up to speed.

Devon held the sleeping baby that was now dressed in a blue onesie he must've found in the car. One of the EMT's, a burly man with a head of red hair and a beard, gestured towards his partner, who was diminutive in comparison with her dark hair pulled into a professional pony-tail. 'Hernandez, I got the witch – you go and make sure the baby is alright,' he said in a rough voice.

Hernandez nodded and moved over to Devon, smiling as she took the baby from him. I turned to the other one and read the name Lane on his nametag. He knelt beside Maria and started administering first aid. I thought he was going to work some magic, so I offered to help, but he shook his head. 'I can't perform more than standard care at the moment since we were notified that a normie detective is riding with one of our people. But don't worry, we will perform a more thorough evaluation once we get her to Ohsu Hospital.'

Before I could say anything, a yell from somewhere in the trees cut me off. 'Hello! Anyone there?'

'We're here!' Lane barked so suddenly that it made me jump. A loud cry came from the baby.

30

Hernandez glared at her partner. 'You stupid oaf, you scared her,' she cradled the baby and started making shushing noises, but the shifter continued bawling. 'Do your thing on her, Lane.' Her voice sounded soft as she tried unsuccessfully to calm the baby.

Lane looked from his work to the baby, his green eyes flashed with pink light, and I could feel the traces of a calming presence descend on me before the bulk of it moved forward. The baby girl suddenly stopped crying, put her thumb in her mouth, and promptly went back to sleep. An empath mage – a high-level one at that to be able to calm a shapeshifter child in a second. Before I could inquire more about Maria's health, a branch broke behind us. I turned and recognized the detective right away.

A tall middle-aged man with dark skin, short graying hair and hardened blue eyes that seemed to take in every detail around him and file it away for future reference. Those eyes turned to me, and I saw recognition and suspicion flare behind the mask of professional neutrality he projected.

Detective Richard Kane. Great, just my luck. Of all the normies in the Portland PD, it had to be him. During my encounter with the fae, the Detective's partner had gotten caught in the crossfire. She had paid for it with her life. The Assembly had cooked up a cover; the official story was that she had died while trying to stop an animal trafficking ring. But Detective Kane didn't believe it, and he had been keeping a close eye on me ever since.

Walking alongside him was a woman in her early thirties with short brown hair and sharp almond-shaped eyes hidden behind a pair of sensible glasses. She walked with a confidence that belied her small stature and a swagger that all law enforcement acquired after a few years on the job.

I extended my senses towards her and almost recoiled in shock. She was bursting with power, more than the two EMTs put together. I had only witnessed that level of power from High Circle mages who were the ruling members of their respective Assemblies. What was a mage of her caliber doing riding shotgun with a normie like Kane?

'Mr Mercer, what a surprise to find you here,' said Detective Kane in his rich baritone voice as they reached us.

I nodded towards him. 'Evening, detective.'

Detective Kane looked from me towards Lane. 'Lane, what do we have?'

Lane motioned towards Maria. 'Female, late twenties, she has cuts and bruises all over her face, chest and arms, but her pulse is steady. I won't know more until we get her to the hospital for a full workup.'

Kane nodded, pulled out a small notepad and started writing something in it. Hernandez made her way toward us carrying the baby with Devon following behind her. 'We also have a one-year-old baby girl that looks relatively unharmed and one female passenger in her thirties. She was dead when we got here.'

Detective Kane looked up and noticed Devon. 'Dr Othonos, I think this is the first time the ME has arrived before the cops.'

Devon gave him a small smile. 'It was a coincidence, Detective. We were driving home when we saw the car go off the road.' He looked back towards the minivan. 'Sadly, we didn't get here in time to save all of them.'

The female detective's face softened a little. 'You saved two lives, Devon. Sometimes you've got to take your victories in small doses.' She spoke with a commanding voice tinged with a Welsh lilt.

Devon nodded and readjusted the baby on his other shoulder. 'Thanks, Elaine.'

I looked at the female detective again. So this was the infamous Elaine. I'd heard a lot about her over the years from Alice, but our paths hadn't crossed yet.

'So, can you tell us what happened?' Detective Kane asked, his pen hovering over the notepad.

I gave them a condensed version. 'Like Devon said, we were driving home when suddenly we saw the car in front of us lose control and drive into the woods. We parked on the side of the road and came upon the crash. Devon administered CPR to Maria while I checked on the passenger and the baby.'

Detective Kane paused and looked at me. 'You know the victims?'

I shook my head and motioned to Maria as Hernandez and Lane were getting her ready to move her. 'Not personally. Maria worked for a cleaning service that used to come to my inn three times a week.'

Detective Elaine rubbed her hands together; the night was getting colder. 'What's the name of the cleaning service?'

'Magical Hands. Their base is near South Tabor. I have their number if you need it,' I said, and Hughes nodded.

Detective Kane gave me a once over. 'Mr Mercer, I have to ask what happened to you. You don't look like you were just out for a drive.'

I looked down and realised that I was covered in dirt, broken twigs and leaves, not to mention the gunk that exploded from the Swinekong had hardened into a sticky goo. My gloves were wrecked, the leather ripped and singed in some places, pieces of them flaking off with every movement. Damn it – I needed my new weapons from Kathour like yesterday.

I nodded towards the site of the wreck. 'I guess I must've gotten some blood and dirt on me when I was trying to help Maria's friend while Dr. Othonos performed CPR. That's why I asked Devon to take care of the baby. I didn't want to get her dirty.'

Detective Kane opened his mouth, looking skeptical, but Elaine cut him off by stepping forward and taking the baby from my friend. 'Thanks for your help, gentlemen. We'll contact you later for an official statement, have a good night. And Devon, say hi to Alice for me.'

# 4

D evon lived in Lake Oswego, a beautiful part of the city that the locals described as the place where Oregon hid their rich folk – and they would be right. It was beautiful, and the sunsets that caught on the surface of the lake were breathtaking. The first time I visited Devon, I'd asked if he'd robbed a tomb to afford it, which made him laugh. I parked my truck on the drive of the modest – by the neighborhood's standards – single-story house. 'So that was Elaine? Her magic was off the charts.' I opened the back of the truck and started unloading the boxes with Devon.

He caught the other end of the rocking/nursing chair and helped me carry it to the front door. 'She's one of the Assembly's top Sentinels. From what Alice tells me, she's a high-level summoner.'

'That thing we fought, the Swinekong, it didn't feel like a summon,' I finally said what had been bothering me since we first saw the creature.

'Summons don't have what we consider a soul. At least, every summon I've ever encountered didn't have one.' Devon nodded and grabbed one of the cribs from one side, and I took the other. 'They always feel apart from this reality, and that thing, whatever it was, had something ... alive and tethered to this world powering it. It felt dark, not alien.'

I shuddered as we finished unloading everything except my trees. 'So you're saying somebody out there is making these monsters artificially? To what end?'

He shrugged, clearly as disturbed as I was. 'I don't know, Nathan, but whoever they are, they're packing serious power. Also, Swinekong? Really? Was that the best you could come up with?'

I opened the door and glared at him. 'It was either that or Baconbits. You have to admit, that's not something you see everyday.' Muffled voices came from inside the house as I wiped the snow from my shoes on the welcome mat. 'If I'm careful and do some really good marketing with a blurred out picture and shaky video, I could create the Legend of the Swinekong, Bigfoot's cousin.'

Devon snorted and shook his head. 'Smartass.'

I shrugged and smiled. 'Better than a dumbass.'

We laughed, and I felt the dregs of tension and adrenaline from the fight leave me as I walked into the house. Arms full of various baby paraphernalia, I neatly dodged a side table before I could knock the crystal bowl from it. Ooof, that was a close one. Alice would've killed me if I'd broken her bowl. The hallway opened up into a large, wide-open space, to the left was the living room where the muffled voices were emanating from. At the centre of the room stood two large teal-colored couches placed in an L shape behind an oak coffee table that had a tray of half-eaten lasagna on top of it.

Sitting on one of them was a woman reading a book. She pushed her dark brown hair away from her face and rested a hand absently on her belly as she looked up at us.

At the far side of the room above a lit fireplace, a large flat-screen TV played some cartoon about a purple unicorn fighting the forces of darkness with the power of friendship. I smiled, shaking my head at the little girl lying on top of the big fluffy beige carpet. She was working on her homework while the television played her favorite program. She had long brown hair that fell to her lower back and wore a similar dress to her mother, only hers was a darker shade of purple. I looked at the TV and saw the unicorn blast the dastardly lions with a rainbow beam from her horn.

I sighed. If only real unicorns weren't such assholes.

Devon paused next to me, his eyes glued to the lasagna, and I bit back a laugh. 'Didn't you say she was health-conscious now?' I said, nodding to the food.

*I'm also a pregnant woman with cravings, Nathan.* Alice said in my head while she grinned unrepentantly. Her whole face was lit up with the glow that some pregnant women seemed to develop, which had nothing to do with magic, and everything to do with the knowledge that they were carrying a new life inside them.

'There are my two favorite guys. How did the shopping go?' Alice's hazel eyes sparkled with mirth as her gaze landed on the packages behind us. 'Also, it's just a vegetable lasagna, thank you very much. Julia's recipe – everything is organic and delicious, so hush.'

Margie had torn herself away from the program at the sound of my voice and let out a shout of joy. 'Uncle Nathan!'

She got up, ran towards us and Devon intercepted her like a professional football player, raising her in the air and making raspberry noises into her neck. 'You say hi to your Uncle before your Dad?'

Margie groaned, trying to escape her dad's hold as she inadvertently giggled. 'Dad get *off*! I'm not a baby anymore.'

Devon rolled his eyes at me. 'You'll always be my baby.'

Margie squirmed in Devon's arms before finally hugging him. 'Fine, Dad, but I see you every day, and I haven't seen Uncle Nathan in forever.'

I crossed my arms and shook my head. Alice rose from the couch and gave Devon a peck on the cheek before smiling at Margie. 'Sweetie, it's only been a couple of months.'

Margie looked at her mom with a serious expression. 'That's like, forever, Mom.'

I lost it and laughed. 'I'm sorry, my little treasure. I've been busy, but I promise to come over more often.'

Margie gave her version of a death glare, which made her look like a puffed-out kitten. 'You said that on my birthday and look what happened.'

I feigned a hit on my chest. 'Ouch, the distrust – it hurts, it hurts so much.'

Margie didn't seem amused and folded her arms. 'It wouldn't hurt if you kept your promise, Uncle Nathan.'

I winced. I had really hurt her by not showing up these last couple of months. I nodded at Devon and he put her down. I knelt, placed a hand on her shoulder, and looked into her eyes. 'I'm sorry for not being around as much recently Margie.' I swallowed, pushing back the memories of what happened last September. 'Things happened that I needed to take care of, but I promise to spend more time with you again.' I gave her a shaky smile. 'Am I forgiven?'

Margie scowled for a moment before she nodded. 'Okay.'

I opened my arms and she ran to me. I hugged her tightly feeling a warmth spread through my chest. Gods, I'd missed her – Devon and Alice too. My worries about the Fae could take a backseat for a day. Tonight was for family.

I kissed the top of her head and laughed when she looked down at her now dirt-smeared clothes with a wrinkled nose. 'Uncle Nathan, why are you so dirty?' She pulled on my beard. 'And you're so scruffy too.'

'I was trying a new look, what do you think? Am I more handsome than your dad?' I said the first thing that came to mind. She didn't need to know that I had been too preoccupied prepping for a Fae attack to care about grooming.

She scrutinized my face and looked from me to Devon. 'I don't know. Dad would need to get whiskers of his own for me to tell, but mommy won't let him. She says it tickles her when they kiss.'

Alice grabbed Margie and led her to the sofa. 'Come on, sweetie, you still have to finish your homework. Let your Dad and Nathan take the stuff to the babies' room.'

Devon looked for a long moment, his eyes flashing with something I couldn't quite make out.

I shook my head and went to move the rest of the stuff we bought upstairs.

We dumped most of the baby stuff on the floor of Devon's guest-room-turned-nursery. The large bed that usually occupied the space was missing, the only other place it could be was the basement, and I thanked the Gods they hadn't asked me to help move it. The nursery walls had already been painted a soft mint color, with drawings of baby elephants and tigers wearing diapers scattered around. I shook my head, smiled, and started pulling things out of boxes before putting them next to the large white wooden dresser with a diaper changing station on top of it.

It was around midnight by the time we finished putting the cribs together and positioning them into the only gaps left in the room. Whoever made the instructions needed to be shot, stabbed and then shot again before getting dumped into a pit full of vipers. It didn't matter if you knew several languages, were magically powerful and used to complex requests from supernatural creatures – furniture instructions made you feel dumber than a rock troll.

In the end, Alice had come up to help us and single handedly assembled both cribs while Devon loaded them up with so many stuffed animals I was left wondering where the kids would sleep. While we were working, we brought Alice up to speed, and she assured me that Elaine would keep Detective Kane in check.

I yawned and stretched when Devon looked from the cribs to me with a smile on his face as Alice stepped outside. 'Thanks for this, man. It was good spending time together again, evil flying monkeys aside. Why don't you stay the night?' He rubbed his tired eyes and stifled a yawn. 'It's late, we're both tired, and you could really use a shower.'

The prospect of driving back into the city was an unwelcome one, so I was tempted to agree. I was sore, dirty and ready to crash on the nearest bed. Sadly, for me, the closest one was about four feet long and filled to the brim with toys. 'Your car is still at my place,' I said even as my mind drifted to that shower he had mentioned.

Alice entered the room with a bundle of Devon's clothes in her hands. 'You'll pick it up tomorrow. Right now, shower and go to bed.'

Knowing when I was beaten, I gave her a small smile and kissed her on the cheek. 'Gods bless you, Alice.'

She smiled as she handed me the clothes. 'Besides, you'll need the truck to take back that extra rocking chair,' she said, giving Devon a pointed look.

He opened his mouth, and I shook my head. 'Let it go, bud. You're not going to win this one, and for the record, I told you so.' I grinned.

Devon glared at me. 'Go shower, Monkey Butt, before I decide to finish what the Swinekong started.'

'Children, enough. Nathan, go shower and rest. I'll contact the Assembly to see if there are any records of the creature you described.' Alice turned to Devon. 'And you get *your* monkey butt to bed. We need to have a talk about following instructions and discuss some of the questionable purchases you made today.'

I beat a tactical retreat and made my way to the guest bathroom, stripped off my filthy clothes, and turned on the shower. The hot water flowed over my skin, taking the fatigue from the fight away, and my tense muscles relaxed under the spray. It took me almost half an hour to get all the grime and dirt off me. I had forgotten how much of a pain in the ass taking care of long hair was. As soon as I finished drying myself, I looked in the mirror and was pleased with the marginal improvement.

My reflection showed a fresh collection of purple bruises up my sides where the Swinekong had grabbed me. I examined my left arm, where a network of barely visible scars ran all the way down from my shoulder, starting with a more pronounced circular one. It was a parting gift from a fae spirit that had blasted me with lightning. Below that was a starburst mark where a witch had shot me. I traced my fingers along a particularly nasty mark along my ribs, another present from the Fae but this one was more personal, and I intended to collect on it. Magical healing could only do so much. I was lucky to come out with only this much damage after that particular incident.

I shook my head, picked up a spare razor from the cabinet and got to work – the grungy look had to go. Twenty minutes later I was looking at an all-around cleaner version of myself, bruises and bags under my eyes notwithstanding. I threw my clothes in the nearest wastebasket, there was no saving them, and pulled on the ones Alice had given me. Clean and dressed, I headed to the basement. It had once been Devon's man cave where he kept a pool table, mini-fridge, two leather couches and a large flat-screen TV. Now everything had been pushed against the walls to make room for the king-size bed from the guest room. I threw myself on it, the pillows exquisitely soft and fluffy, and darkness soon took me.

~

*T*he high noon sun was blistering, and I could feel droplets of sweat falling down my forehead. I covered my eyes with my hand and looked out at a sea of grass, stretching over hills and mountains. To my right was a long pebbled road and coming towards me was a cart with three men riding in it. I looked down and found myself wearing a strange set of long, loose black garments that covered me from head to toe. The strangers were wearing the same type of garments but in different colors. Their features were so similar they had to be related, broad oval-shaped faces with high cheekbones, dark slanted eyes and ruddy tan skin.

The cart stopped, and I waved at them hesitantly. They looked past me, their attention focused on something in front of them. I turned to look at what had caught their eye, and my eyes grew wide. Walking down the road was a giant of a man at least seven feet tall, wearing a long tattered cloak that did nothing to hide his muscular build. His face was ruggedly handsome: dark brown eyes the color of freshly plowed earth were set deep in his brow, a pointed nose and square chin were framed by a large beard. He seemed to be carrying someone on his back, and, as he walked, he sang at the top of his lungs. What surprised me the most was that he was singing in Gaelic, a sad song about the grief of a father whose son was struck down in front of him.

'...And among the eternal isles, we shall meet again to sing and dance once more.' The man ended his song as he saw the cart stop a dozen feet in front of him. He raised a hand and smiled at the three men.

'Morning to ye,' the giant man said in a thick Irish accent.

The man in the middle of the cart was a short and stocky fellow with dark hair wearing a vibrant yellow garment that reflected the light of the sun. He returned the giant man's smile and waved. 'Morning, what brings you to these parts?' He spoke in a language I didn't know but that I could somehow understand.

The man nodded to the person he was carrying. 'My son had a little too much to drink, and I had to go pick him up.'

The man on the left was tall and lanky with long dark hair that fell in waves around his face, his cloak appeared to be a dark shade of blue, almost as deep as the ocean. He nodded wistfully. 'Ah, to be young and carefree. I enjoyed the song you were singing. Are you a bard?'

The giant man shook his head, smiling. 'Nothing of the sort, just a humble traveler that sings when he's sad, sings when he's happy and sings when he is furious. Where are you headed?'

The man on the right was neither short nor tall, slim nor bulky, he was the most average of the lot, clad in a soft green set of clothes. He thumbed his finger at the cart. 'Our father just passed away, and we were going into town to trade his treasure. He was a great man in life and even greater in death.'

The giant man raised an eyebrow. 'Oh, really? What have ye there?' The man put down his son on the grass, he was covered in a shroud weaved of herbs that made him blend in with the greenery.

The brothers got down from the cart and went to the back with the giant man. 'We have this old staff.'

Even from dozens of feet away, I could feel the raw magic emanating from the cart.

The stocky man grabbed the staff. It was about as long as the giant man and seemed to be made of two types of wood fused in the middle. One side was pale, almost white with a smooth end at the tip, and the other was a darker shade with small needles sticking out of its end. 'A staff made from rowan' – he pointed to the smooth side – 'and yew. One side ends a life, and the other brings it back.' He indicated to the rough end of the staff.

A light sparked in the giant man's eyes, and he laughed suddenly, a full belly laugh that somehow made the world around him brighter and filled with life. 'That's a fine gift ye have there, friends. May I see it? Never have my eyes witnessed such craftsmanship.'

The stocky man nodded, putting the staff in the other man's hand. Swift as lightning, the giant man closed his fingers around the staff and struck all three brothers at once with the dark end. Surprise flickered in their eyes before the brothers fell to the ground, dead.

I tried to run to them, but my feet wouldn't move. I opened my mouth to yell at the man, but no sound came.

The giant man turned around and went to his son, his previously jovial face now mournful. 'My son, I hope this works.'

He removed the herbal shroud to reveal a slimmer, younger version of himself. I focused on the son and noticed a nasty wound on his chest, the young man's heart had been pierced by some kind of spear. The father turned the staff around and touched his son's chest with the white end. He waited.

For a second, nothing happened. Then the wound on the chest closed, and the young man's eyes opened as he took a deep breath. The father gazed at his son, tears falling from his eyes. They held each other for a long moment before they broke apart.

'Father, how could ye do this?' The young man pointed to the three dead men lying on the ground.

The giant man held the staff towards his son. 'They claimed that this staff could both kill with a single touch as well as bring back the dead. I needed to see if their claims were true.' Happiness shone in his eyes, and the ground around him seemed to glow with vibrant life as if it too was happy for the man. The wooden cart suddenly sprouted flowers from its boards, covering the vehicle in a myriad of colors. 'And it worked, my son, yer back among the living! Let us rejoice because today Cermait walks the Earth.'

Cermait walked towards the dead, then looked at his father. 'How could I celebrate when these men have been denied the gift that was bestowed upon me. Please, father.'

The bearded man nodded and touched each man with the staff's thorns. The men all woke up, gasping for breath before slowly getting up.

'You tricked us.'

'I did no such thing, friend,' the bearded man said, shaking his head. 'I merely put the knowledge ye gifted me to use and thus have given ye lives back.'

The stocky man looked at his brothers then at the man. 'You have created an imbalance between life and death, make no mistake, there will be consequences for what you have done. There's a reason why we didn't use the staff to bring our father back. We were not prepared to pay the cost.'

The giant man grinned and held the staff tightly in his hand. 'Let me take the staff back home for a year and a day, and I swear to put it to good use and right this imbalance. To slay my enemies and give life to my friends so that we may all be merry. At the end of that time, I'll return it to ye.'

The stocky man frowned before slowly shaking his head. 'Keep it. One day the cost will strike you – we want nothing further to do with the staff. Or you.'

Cermait walked next to his father, and the giant man observed the brothers for a moment before nodding solemnly. 'Then I thank ye for the gift.' Without another word, Cermait and his father turned into birds and flew towards the horizon. The brothers watched them depart with clenched fists.

'It is no gift,' said the stocky brother as the birds swept out of sight.

# 5

I woke up to a loud screeching noise followed by someone jumping on my bed. I sat up straight, trying to get my bearings, ready for an attack. It took me a second to remember I wasn't at the inn. I rubbed my eyes and focused on the excited jumping bean on my bed. 'Morning to you too, A Stóirín.'

'Uncle Nathan, wake up!' Every word was followed by a jump as Margie looked at me behind a curtain of bed hair that was flying all over the place.

I pulled my phone from under the pillow and checked the time. 'Sweetheart, it's six thirteen in the morning. Don't you sleep in on Saturdays?' I had gone to bed at around one. I needed at least a couple more hours before I could function properly.

'Nope,' Margie said, bouncing with more force – if she bounced any higher, she was going to hit the ceiling.

I groaned and threw myself back on the pillows and closed my eyes. Maybe I could catch a few more winks. The bed grew suspiciously still, and then Margie landed on top of me. 'Okay, okay, I'm up, my treasure.' I raised my hands in defeat.

Margie grinned. 'You shaved your whiskers!'

'They were beginning to itch.' I cracked open one eye and looked at her. 'What do you think?'

Margie grabbed me by the chin and started moving my face around for a minute before finally letting go. 'You looked better with them.'

I sighed and closed my eyes. Everyone was a critic.

Margie started poking my cheek with her finger. 'Uncle Nathan, are you asleep?'

I started to snore loudly. She began to poke harder, digging her finger all the way into my cheek. 'Uncle Nathan, stop it! I know you're faking. Get up! It's time for breakfast.'

'Oh good, you're awake,' Devon said from the foot of the basement stairs. He was wearing a dark blue long sleeved shirt and dark gray pants. In his hands were two mugs, and I could smell the sweet delicious aroma of freshly-brewed coffee.

'Yeah, the Margie-alarm is full-proof,' I said as Devon shook his head at me and took a sip from one of the mugs.

He smiled at Margie. 'Sweetie, one of these days you're going to learn how to sleep in.'

Margie rolled her eyes. 'I'm going to find Mom.'

Devon watched his daughter stomp her way up the stairs. 'I shudder to think what she's going to be like when she reaches her teens. The world isn't ready for that kind of power.' He smirked and handed me one of the mugs as I laughed. 'Here, you need this after Hurricane Margie went through you.'

I took the hot mug gratefully, blowing the steam rising from the rim. I sighed at the first sip. The coffee tasted heavenly and washed away the last remnants of sleep. I looked up to see Devon staring at me. 'Is there something on my face?'

He shook his head. 'No, but you don't look like you got much rest.'

I snorted. 'Yeah, well you can thank Margie for that.' I thought about my dream and couldn't make heads or tails of it. 'I had weird dreams, that's all.'

Devon raised an eyebrow. 'Weird prophetic dreams or waking up naked in school dreams?'

I shook my head. 'Jury's still out.' I took another sip from my mug. 'Coffee,' I sighed happily. 'Bless you.'

Devon nodded and was about to say something when Margie came running down the stairs again, a fresh pile of clothes in her arms. She dumped them on the bed. 'Mom said that you can borrow some more of Dad's clothes.' She stuck her tongue out at me and bolted right back up the stairs.

I laughed, finishing the last of my coffee and went to shower and dress. I came out of the bathroom feeling refreshed and surprisingly full of energy. The wonders of caffeine. Devon had lent me a long sleeve button-down red shirt and some worn out black jeans. I pushed the shirt's sleeves to my elbows. Everyone was already sitting at the dining table where a massive breakfast of eggs, bacon, toast and waffles lay. Alice was trying to braid Margie's hair, but she was huffing and squirming in her chair so it kept coming loose. Devon was eating a piece of buttered toast and listening to the news, and I grabbed a plate and piled it with food as the TV blared in the background.

'...the survivors of the accident were twenty-six-year-old Maria Collins and fourteen-month-old Allison Davis. Sadly, baby Allison's mother, thirty-five-year-old Angela Davis, was pronounced dead at the scene. Police are still nowhere close to catching the Woodland Ripper, who has taken the lives of ten victims, we can now confirm. Citizens are advised to remain home after dark and not to travel alone through wooded areas—'

Devon turned the broadcast off and shook his head. 'They're ruling last night an accident caused by slippery roads.'

I shrugged. 'It makes sense, you can't very well say a Swinekong is on the loose.'

'Yeah, I know,' Devon said with a noncommittal shrug, finishing his toast and taking a sip from a glass of apple juice.

Alice looked up from her work, hands still maneuvering Margie's hair. 'While your naming ability is as charming as ever, Nathan, I checked the Assembly's database, and there isn't any record of the creature you fought. It could be something new, something so old we've forgotten, or simply something we haven't encountered before.' She shrugged as Margie's braid came loose again. 'As for that brand you showed me, there weren't any mentions of it according to my replacement, but she's only filling in for me, and I have this nagging feeling that I've seen it somewhere. I might have to drop by to check myself.' She smiled helplessly. 'Linda is a sweet girl, but she has her head in the clouds most of the time.'

The Oregon Assembly had several different departments that dealt with all sorts of issues. Sentinels, who were its law enforcement division, people dedicated to hunting down and safeguarding dangerous magical artifacts, and then those responsible for keeping meticulous records of every spell, creature and event known to man. Before her maternity leave, Alice worked for the Records Keeper division. If the Assembly didn't know what the hell the Swinekong was, then it was unlikely anybody did.

I swallowed a mouthful of bacon and smiled at her. 'Thanks, Alice, it was worth checking.'

Margie moved her head to the side, making the braid come loose. Alice sighed, giving up. She pulled her daughter's hair into a ponytail then went back to her food. I fought back a laugh. 'Uncle Nathan, is it true you fought a pig-monkey monster last night and lost, and that's why you're eating bacon as revenge?'

Alice choked on her toast, and Devon put his mug down and tried to keep a straight face. I looked down at the piece of bacon in my hand. 'Am I only allowed to eat bacon if I lose to a pig?'

Margie chewed on her toast for a moment before nodding. I popped the bacon strip into my mouth and chewed on its crunchy goodness, smiling. 'Well, I better enjoy it because I'm never losing to another pig ever again.'

'Don't worry Uncle Nathan, if you lose again I'll make you some muffins with pink-pig icing to cheer you up,' Margie said with a smile.

Alice grinned at her daughter. 'Sweetie, you don't know how to bake.'

Margie looked at her mom before turning back at me. 'Don't worry Uncle Nathan, if you lose again, *Mom* will make you some muffins to cheer you up – and I'll help.'

I couldn't hold it in anymore and a laugh burst through my lips. I leaned to the side and gave her a peck on the cheek. 'I'm sure they will be the best muffins ever.'

Devon cleared his throat. 'No muffins for me?'

Margie rolled her eyes. 'Don't be jealous, Dad.'

I wiggled my eyebrows at him. 'She loves me more.'

Devon glared at me. 'Those are fighting words, sir. Care to take it outside?'

'Anytime, Zombie Breath, any time.' I raised my fists in a mock fighting stance, a piece of toast in one hand and a glass of grape juice in the other.

Alice shook her head, laughing. 'Alright, children, that's enough. No fighting at the table.' I popped the food into my mouth and winked at her. 'Nathan, what are your plans for today?'

I swallowed my food before I replied, 'I was considering talking to the coven to see if they knew anything about the Swinekong. I need as much information as I can in case that thing pops into the inn for round two.'

'I'll go with you then,' Devon said from his side of the table. 'Maybe we can swing by the hospital and check on Maria before picking up my car from your place.'

Having a necromancer with me would definitely come in handy if that thing showed up again. 'Don't you have to go to work?'

He shook his head and stood up. 'Not today. I knew you would try to make some sense of what happened last night so I called in sick.'

'But you're not sick, Dad,' Margie mumbled through a mouthful of eggs.

He smiled at her. 'I know, sweetie. I only said that so I could help Uncle Nathan.'

She thought about it and nodded slowly. 'I'll bake the muffins with Mom then, just in case.'

I laughed at her lack of faith and helped Devon clear the table before we headed out. Alice was going to visit Elaine today, so maybe together we could find out what the hell was happening to this city.

~

T he Coven lived in the Belmont Apartments just across the river from Downtown Portland and south of Lone Fir Cemetery. We circled the block a couple of times, waiting for a parking spot to open up and finally managed to find one right in front of the entrance next to a *park for fifteen minutes* sign.

The apartment building was four stories tall with a gray brick exterior peppered with large square windows. Given the early morning, not many people were around, just a couple of joggers, a lady with a stroller across the street and an old couple walking their golden retriever.

I got out of the truck and stared at Lone Fir Cemetery, which sat behind a black iron fence. The cemetery had been in operation since the late 1800s. Named Lone Fir for its solitary Fir tree amongst the other oaks in the plot of land, and it is still standing to this day. They hosted an annual Halloween Tour that I used to accompany Devon and the girls to every year and the place brought back fond memories.

Devon caught me looking at the cemetery and placed his hands over the hood of my truck. 'We missed you this year, bud.'

I gave him a rueful smile. 'I'm sorry, who was she this year?'

Devon grinned. 'Wicked Witch of the West. I was Dorothy and Alice was the scarecrow.'

I faked a shudder. 'I don't know what's worse, imagining Margie as a fae or you in pigtails.'

He cocked his head to the side. 'Wait? Is the Wicked Witch real? And I looked damn fine in my pigtails. Besides, it was either that or explain to every kid why the scarecrow knocked up Dorothy.'

I tapped my fingers on the hood and nodded. 'Yeah that would lead to some interesting conversations. The witch is real alright, she's part of the Winter Queen's inner circle, not someone you want to mess with or owe money to. Trust me.'

Devon opened his mouth to reply when a loud crash came from above us. I looked up to see a fourth story window explode, shards of glass raining down in front of us. A figure flew out the broken window towards the cemetery. The few pedestrians that were on the street stopped in their tracks to look at what was going on. A thunderous roar came from the depths of the apartment, and a huge beast leapt from the building, landing on the cemetery grounds in a single bound, too fast for me to get a good look at it.

Devon and I shared a look. 'We need to call this in, there are too many witnesses around.'

If that was the Swinekong we were in big trouble. I raised my hands and drew the pedestrians' attention. 'Sorry, folks, we need you to clear the area as we're shooting a movie here.'

An older gentleman walking a retriever glared at me. 'Yeah? What movie? And why didn't you warn people, there's children around.' His wife was trying to calm the dog who had pissed itself.

I gave him a warm smile, hoping to mask my rising panic. The last thing we needed was a bunch of normies screaming bloody murder. 'I'm sorry, sir, this section was supposed to be blocked off. I'll talk to the director about it.'

The man flipped me the finger and left, the mother with her stroller just shook her head and beat a hasty retreat. Devon gave me a weird look. 'A movie?'

'If you have a better idea please share with the class.'

I ran towards the back of the truck and looked for anything that could be used as a weapon. Sadly, I suspected tree saplings weren't this thing's kryptonite. Finally, I settled on a tire iron and prayed to the gods for Kathour to move his dwarven ass already. I was getting sick and tired of being weaponless.

We took off across the street towards the twelve-foot iron fence. On the other side, a loud battle was taking place behind a cluster of trees and tombstones, making it hard to see what was going on.

I threw the tire iron over the fence and braced my back against it, making a step with my palms. 'We have to jump it. There's not enough time to run around and look for the entrance.'

Devon grimaced and nodded. He took a couple of steps back and took a running start. As soon as his boot touched my hands, I heaved him up with all strength. Devon flew into the air and over the fence, landing in a crouch on the other side. I had seen a few martial arts movies with Devon and was particularly impressed with how they would run up walls or jump from roof to roof. We had practiced a bit one night while Margie cheered us on.

I took a few steps back and ran at the wall in my best Jackie Chan impression. My boot connected with the fence, and I pushed up to catch the top of it, hauling myself over to the other side.

'We gotta stop watching so many kung-fu movies,' Devon said as I got to my feet.

I rolled my eyes at him and picked up the tire iron from where it lay on the ground. 'They come in handy, now shut up and run.'

We ran across the cemetery, passing tombstones and oak trees until we came upon a clearing where a young woman was battling it out with the creature. Good news – it wasn't the Swinekong. Bad news – it was something that looked worse.

The creature jumped back, several tombstones crumbling in its wake. At least twelve feet at the shoulder and six feet long from muzzle to tail. It had the body of a goat, large curling horns on the side of its head, but its face was that of a snarling feline, neither lion nor tiger but a blend of both. Around its neck, sprouting like a massive mane, was a nest of black cobras hissing at the woman.

Startled, I recognised her, Leann, the daughter of the former head priestess of the coven. Her dark eyes flashed with cerulean light as they darted from the creature to us. I hadn't seen her in months, and she had changed a lot since then; there was an air of confidence to her now that countered her obvious youth. The beast opened its maw and roared into the air. The nest of cobras, their crown heads in full display, hissed in tandem, giving birth to an eerie sound that grated on my ears like nails on a chalkboard. The cobras opened their mouths, spitting a shower of bright yellow venom towards Leann.

Leann raised her hands palms forward in the telling sign of casting a spell. 'Kourtína neroú!' she yelled, and a thick curtain of water fell from the sky, shielding her. The venom hit the water and disappeared within its depths. 'Get out of here, I got this!' she snarled at us.

As if we were going to let her fight this creature alone. I nodded towards Devon, and we split apart to corner the beast. I could only hope my tire iron fared better than my gloves.

# 6

I twirled my paltry weapon in my hands while stepping between the tombstones. Adrenaline pumped through my veins, my body coiled, ready for the upcoming battle. Devon had taken his kukri blade out and was eyeing the large goat-lion-cobra thing. The beast was laser-focused on Leann, the hissing rattling through the cemetery. We needed to do something fast, before the mortals got an eyeful of the supernatural world.

'Leann, can you generate some mist or something? We're a little exposed at the moment,' I said, making my way towards her.

She glanced at me, her face curling in anger and exasperation when she noticed Devon had stuck around too. Before she could say anything, the creature pawed at the earth with its hoof and charged, the mane of cobras writhing as it moved. *Oh, no you don't.* Leann glared at the incoming monster and cupped her hands, her eyes blazing like two azure stars. 'Cheímaros.' I raced past Leann and saw Devon do the same on my other side, flanking me as we prepared to cut the creature off in the middle of the clearing.

A torrent of water shot from Leann's palms, gushing towards the creature straight between the eyes. Devon and I jerked to a stop and glanced at her with wide eyes. For a moment, the creature struggled onward until finally, it couldn't withstand the force. The water pushed it onto its back, and the creature skidded backwards, crashing into a nearby oak tree that splintered under the weight and fell. I blinked, looked at my tire iron then at the creature.

*Alrighty then, sure, that works too.*

Leann spun her arms in front of her chest and a small gray cloud condensed between her palms. 'Omíchli!' her voice rang with power, and a curtain of mist exploded outwards from her hands, circling the clearing to obscure our battleground from view.

'That should keep the mortals out,' she said, before she turned to me, her eyes blazing with fury. 'What are you doing here, Nathaniel?'

The creature roared as it slowly got back to its feet. Its fur was soaking wet and its slit eyes were focused on us with unwavering tenacity. 'We'll talk about it after we deal with this ... whatever the fuck this is.' I swore. What the hell did you call something made up of three animals? A Snoaklon? Gionake? Loarpent?

Devon kept pace with me while frowning at the beast. 'It looks like a chimera, but the placement of the bodies are wrong.' We scattered to the side as the monster released another stream of venom towards us.

'What do you mean the bodies are wrong? What part of this is right, Devon?' I yelled, running towards the beast.

'Chimeras usually have the body of a lion, a head of a goat and a snake for a tail. This is a messed-up version of that. Hopefully, it doesn't spit fire,' he chimed helpfully from my side. Right, no spitting fire would be good.

I was about to hit the chimera with my tire iron when the cobras around its neck swerved towards me, mouths wide. The musky acrid scent of reptile mixed with wet fur clawed at the back of my throat making me gag. I didn't have time to think and threw myself forward. I landed in a crouch beneath its body as the spray of venom hit where I had been a moment ago. There on its torso, I saw the same mark that was branded into Maria.

With no time to consider the implications, I jabbed the iron spike upwards, stabbing it into its ribs. I felt it hit bone and the creature roared in pain. Blood poured down from the wound, drenching me and the taste of rotten eggs flooded my mouth. I spat a mouthful of blood, cursing my stupidity for not keeping my mouth shut. Out of the corner of my eye, I saw Devon rush past me towards the back of the creature.

The chimera raised itself on its hind legs, wrenching the tire iron from my hand and reared in the air before stomping on the ground with its hooves. I rolled to the side and missed getting my head smashed like a watermelon by an inch. I jumped to my feet and saw Devon slicing at the beast's back leg, cutting a long line from the thigh to the knee, then stabbing the joint where the flesh parted. The kukri flashed with eerie green light, and the wound began to ooze with yellow puss as the surrounding tissue blackened and decayed right before my eyes. The stench of decomposition floated through the air. I fought a shudder. Nasty weapon.

Devon tore the kukri out and stepped back before the cobras had a chance to bite him. The monster let out a roaring hiss that sent shivers down my spine. It turned to Devon, but before it could move towards him, Leann snapped her fingers. 'Klósi Vélos!' she screamed, and a dozen spinning arrows made of water formed a perfect arch around her, coursing through the air like a raging river and piercing the chimera's body.

Gray blood flowed from the monstrosity as the arrows lined its side and face. One of them protruded from its eye socket and turned my stomach. The beast snarled and swayed on its hooves but then a brown light shone in its remaining five eyes, glaring menacingly at us. The black scales of the cobras began to glow with obsidian light. It was the same light that had come over the Swinekong's eyes. There was an intelligence in that gaze that wasn't there before.

I took a few steps back and stood next to Leann and Devon.

'Any idea what the hell is wrong with this thing?' Leann asked as she raised her hands to her chest.

Devon shook his head before looking at me with worry. 'I don't know, but it feels the same as the Swinekong. Alive but not. Corrupted.'

'Other one? How many of these things are there?' Leann asked between breaths.

Hundreds of cobras sprouted from its mane and fell to the floor like a flood as the light flared intensely, and the feeling of *wrongness* grew. They swarmed over each other, slithering over the grass and broken tombstones until they coalesced in a grotesque looking mound of black scales and flesh. I craned my head up at what was now a giant black cobra, weaving its body awkwardly between the tombstones. It raised itself fifteen feet in the air and opened its mouth, revealing razor-sharp fangs as it spat. Three pairs of slitted eyes glowed ruby light.

*Great, just freaking great!*

'Okay, well, that's just not fair at all.' I said, looking between the chimera and the giant snake that had split away from it as fear began to burn in my chest. The giant cobra's mouth filled with a strange amber liquid and it spat a globule in our direction that we quickly dodged. The amber orb crashed against a tree behind us. It began to emit steam as it melted into a puddle of goo within seconds. Of course it could shoot acid. Naturally.

'Okay, divide and conquer. The chimera is half-dead – I think. Devon, you take the snake. Your blade can handle it better than my tire iron or Leann's magic and if not ... well you have friends that won't mind a bit of acid right? We'll deal with the other beastie.'

Devon looked around with a frown on his face, he knew what I was asking him and he didn't like it. 'I need a second to prepare.'

I clapped him on the shoulder supportively as another dollop of acid hissed off to our right. At least the creature had a terrible aim. 'Sure. I just reached my quota of weekly monster workouts so let's shut this down ASAP.'

'Are you seriously making jokes right now?' Leann cursed under her breath as the cobra slithered its way towards us. Her hands began to glow with intense cerulean light. 'Emfanízomai!'

'Well, when else would I make them? I am seemingly always fighting, and I need to do it sometimes,' I responded as a geyser erupted in front of us. Cold water sprayed my cheek as it transformed into a fox – if foxes were the size of ponies, had emerald eyes, and their whole body was made of coursing water. The animal glided towards Leann and nuzzled its watery neck against her chin. She smiled at her familiar, and nodded towards the cobra. 'Kill.'

The fox's eyes flared with power as it leapt into the air and transformed into a torrent of water that attacked the cobra's eyes, clearly a weak spot. The snake reeled back with a hiss and the powerful blast of water pushed it back against a small mausoleum. The building crumbled under the cobra's weight, scraping along its scales, and the surge of water flowed into the air, turning back into a fox.

Seeing its partner go down, the chimera roared at the fox and pounced, twelve-inch fangs poised for the kill.

'Talamh!' I roared. The magic pulsed from the rune I had drawn in mid-air and fell into the earth below me. It was my most powerful one to date, a gift from a friend. The first two times I had used it I had been able to raise a thirty-foot tall obsidian spire and control a crumbling island, but that was with an infusion of external power. When I tried the rune on my own, the amount of earth I could move was related to how much of my own magic I poured into it. As it sunk into the air, I felt a tether form between the tips of my fingers and the ground below me like a puppet master pulling on the strings.

Out of the corner of my eye, I saw the crumbled mausoleum explode outwards, sending pieces of stone flying as the cobra rose twenty feet in the air. Its crimson eyes trained on me. Anxiety spiked through me, but I pushed it down and focused. 'Devon, hurry it up!'

I jerked my hands upwards, and a column made of earth and stone rose from beneath the chimera, punching it in the stomach. The chimera tried pouncing into the air, but instead fell on its side, letting out a miserable sound. Finally, some real damage. I turned to Devon, praying I had made the right choice. I couldn't summon magic like that twice in quick succession. 'Whenever you're ready, bud. We could really use the help.'

The snake hacked and coughed like a cat trying to spit up a hairball and a dozen smaller snakes bled from its mouth and raced towards us. My eyelid twitched. This thing had more tricks than me, what's next? Laser beams from its eyes.

Devon had pushed his sleeves up, revealing a network of scars. Some were old, while others were still scabbing. He used his kukri to cut a horizontal line from his elbow to his wrist. Black blood gushed out of the cut like a stream and fell into the earth. His eyes shone with every shade of green from jade to emerald, and mist emanated from his body. He opened his mouth, the mist clinging to him like a cloak, and spoke in a language I didn't understand. I had never seen him summon like this before, how many hidden talents did Devon have?

'Sikotheite! O gios tou Adi sas diatazei!'

Leann whirled towards him, her eyes widening in fear. A giant acid-spitting snake didn't phase her, but my best friend says something undecipherable and she freaks out? Devon and I were going to be having a long talk soon.

The ground shook as the earth absorbed Devon's blood. An eerie pressure began to spread from him, like looking into the eyes of a wild tiger and knowing that if you made the wrong move, you would become its prey. My whole body became tense, and I was suddenly ready to run as far away as I could. I bit my cheek, and the momentary pain brought me back to my senses. This was Devon, my best friend. I mentally shook myself. What did I have to be scared of?

From all around us, the ground exploded outwards as dozens of decayed hands burst forth, awakened from their eternal slumber by the call of the necromancer. The permanent residents of Lone Fir Cemetery arrived to do battle. Unlike the zombies in movies, the real deal didn't make any moaning sounds while shambling forward in slow motion. They rose from their graves with an effortless grace that didn't belong to the living and made their way towards their master. Dressed in clothing from every era from the late nineteenth century to some more modern styles, the zombies were in various states of decay; some were nothing more than a pile of moving bones, while others seemed no different than Leann or me. The only way to tell them apart was through the eyes that glowed with opaque emerald light. Thankfully the smell emanating from them wasn't rot and decomposition, but a lingering pine scent mixed with mint.

I had seen Devon raise corpses before in the morgue, but never on this scale. There were at least two dozen zombies gathered next to him. I fought to keep my heart under control, there was no way I was going to run screaming from my friend, no matter how disturbed I was feeling. He raised his kukri in the air, and when he spoke, his voice echoed with the power of the grave. He stood like a king demanding obedience from his subjects as waves of cold magic slithered across my skin. 'Kill them.'

The zombies all turned in unison towards the monsters and surged forward like an impending wave. The cobra hissed, spatting a globule of acid at the incoming horde, but the zombies broke away into two separate lines, evading the attack, and jumped on top of its scaly body. The cobra began to shake from side to side, throwing them off, but the undead were relentless, and as soon as they fell, they began their climb once more. The fox let out a bark and flew into the air, turning itself into a long stream of water that wrapped itself around the cobra and pulled its gargantuan body earthwards.

The cobra crashed into the ground with a loud thud. The zombies began to hammer into it, some with their fists. The skeletons used pieces of their ribs or femurs as improvised daggers, stabbing into the eyes and head. Showing no sign of wavering, the familiar kept the cobra pinned to the ground as it tried to rise. The beast let out a mournful sound and tried to free itself, writhing in place, but it soon stilled.

The snakes that had emerged from its mouth were moving towards us, and I raised my hand, pulling on my tether with the earth. The ground rose around them like sand, capturing them in a granite box.

Leann stepped beside me, her eyes darting from Devon to the snake and swore, before waving her hands in front of her chest and spitting out a spell. 'Neró lepída.' A screen of water shaped like a guillotine blade formed above the snake's head and came down with lightning speed, severing the head from its body.

The chimera let out a thunderous roar, and I turned to see the scales around its body falling away like dead leaves. I sent more magic into my tether with the earth and pulled with all my strength. The earth rumbled like a roaring dragon and opened itself up beneath the running chimera. It tried to move out of the way, but its own momentum carried it forward, and it fell. It was too big for me to bury it and its ass rose above the ground, hooves kicking in the air. I clapped my hands together, closing the earth and slicing its bottom completely off.

The large goat butt fell to the ground, and I had a moment to think that perhaps I hadn't thought this through when the body of the snake suddenly melted into a gray puddle, followed by the bottom half of the chimera. 'Well shit, there goes any evidence we could have given to the Assembly.'

Next to me, Devon raised his blade again. 'Thank you for your help. You may rest once more.' His voice sounded like a soothing lullaby, charming the undead to sleep. The horde of zombies turned to him in unison and then slowly began to make their way back to their resting places. One by one, they jumped into the holes they came from, and I used a smidgen more magic to smooth the earth back over their graves.

I released the magic and felt like I had finished a marathon wearing a full suit of armor. My body was sore, and there was an insatiable itch on the back of my neck. I moved to scratch it and came away with a twig. Out of the corner of my eye, I saw Devon wiping the sweat off his brow and taking a deep breath on unsteady feet. The mist that Leann had conjured up dissipated into the air, giving us a clear view of the rest of the cemetery. I looked around, if it weren't for the broken mausoleum and a couple of trees, no one would know that a battle had taken place here.

Gods, it wasn't even noon and I desperately wanted a nap. I was getting too old for this shit.

Leann strode towards me, her eyes blazing with fury, her fox familiar floating behind her like a solemn guardian. 'Are you insane, Nathaniel? You dare bring someone like *him* here? To the coven's stronghold?' she pointed towards Devon, who was putting away his kukri and turned to us with a stoic expression.

I crossed my arms and glared at her, I was so not in the mood for this. 'First of all, young lady, *you're* welcome. It was a pleasure saving *your* life, and we gladly would do it again. So, why don't you calm down and tell me what the hell is going on with your coven?'

She poked her finger in my chest, her eyes flashing with azure light. Sweat trailed down her forehead as she swayed on her feet. 'What happens in my coven is none of your damn business, Innkeeper. So why don't you take a hike and leave us alone.'

Devon marched towards us, he had ripped a piece of his shirt and used it as a makeshift bandage. 'Hey, that's no way to talk to someone who just helped you out of a jam, so why don't we take a step back to cool off.'

She spun towards Devon and raised her hand, but before she could speak, I saw the strength leave her body, and she crashed to the floor. We rushed towards her, but her familiar barred our way, watery lips raising to show a hint of fang. I glared at it. 'Save it, you mutt, before I decide to skin you for a hat. And don't think that being a familiar will save you. I have a dog that loves munching on your kind.'

The fox's eyes flashed with emerald light. He lowered his head and let me approach his master. Devon knelt next to me and began checking her pulse.

'What the hell is wrong with her?'

'You do realise I'm a corpse doctor not a people doctor, right?' he muttered as he lifted his finger from her neck. 'Her pulse is weak. It could be magical exhaustion, a hit to the head or any number of things. We need to take her to a hospital before that snake decides to come back for seconds.'

The fox lowered itself to the ground and pressed its nose to Leann's forearm. I frowned and lifted her sleeve to see several red puncture wounds on her skin. The area around the wounds was red and swollen, with dark blood streaming from it. 'Ah, shit. She must have gotten bit before we arrived. How come she didn't collapse until now?'

Devon looked at the wound and swore. 'You'd be surprised at what you can do with adrenaline pumping in your veins.' He turned to me, his eyes worried. 'Nathan, she needs urgent care, but I think they have a pretty strict no pets policy at the hospital.'

I turned to the liquid fox with a frown. 'Yeah, mortals might take issue with that.' I put my hands under Leann's arms and lifted her. 'Let's take her to the inn. Hopefully, Julia can do something to help her.'

Devon rose and looked around. 'Okay, but how are we going to get out of here? It's not like we can toss her over the fence.'

I considered it briefly before shaking my head. 'I think there's an exit back the way we came. We better hurry, though, before someone sees us. Grab her legs.' I side-eyed him. 'Besides, I think we need to have a chat, don't you?'

# 7

Turns out walking away from a cemetery with an unconscious woman, a bleeding medical examiner, and a floating, magical fox is a lot easier than you might think. The security guard at the entrance gave us a weird look, and I just mumbled my movie excuse. He stopped paying attention to us, instead looking about for the cameras. The hard part was walking all the way around the cemetery to the apartments where I had parked my truck. Devon and I were exhausted, and carrying Leann wasn't doing us any favors.

As if battling two oversized monstrosities wasn't enough, there was a ticket pinned to my windshield and one of those stickers on the driver's window stating that this was a no-parking spot. I growled at it as I placed Leann in the truck bed and then crumbled the ticket between my hands. The universe apparently was having a ball messing with me today.

Tír na nÓg sat at the entrance of five hundred acres of wood near Linnton Park. Unlike the actual Tír na nÓg, my inn is not an island paradise where you remain young forever and party with the Celtic gods from dusk to dawn. It is, however, a cozy three-story wooden building surrounded by a forest of Western Hemlock trees. It was rustic and homey, and I loved it. Sometimes it reminded me of escorting the princess through the woods back in Faerie. Just the two of us together. One of the few enjoyable memories I had of my time with the Fae.

As I pulled into the driveway and opened the truck door, the musky scent of the woods and the citrusy smell of the Red Verbena and St. John's Wort filled my lungs. I took in a deep breath as a warm sense of belonging spread through my chest. The flowers surrounded the building in a beautiful landscape of red and yellow colors that spoke to me in a way no castle or palace ever could – it was all mine. I felt the soreness and discomfort from today's battle wash away as a feeling of peace and happiness settled within me.

I was home again.

Nothing had changed since I left yesterday; it was still in one piece. I had an irrational fear that one day I would return and find a smouldering ruin in its place, a fear that only grew stronger in the months after the Fae discovered my survival. Silera had promised me that she wouldn't tell anyone I was alive, but there was a lot of Fae involved in that battle. One of them would talk, someone always did, and I would be hunted again.

Yet, for now, my home was here to welcome me. The stairs that led to the porch housed a wooden table for guests to drink tea and enjoy the scenery were still intact. The balcony that circled the entire second floor where the guest rooms were was in pristine condition.

'Nathan, what's that?' Devon asked as he got out of the car and stood next to me.

I followed his gaze and stared at the column of black smoke rising from the back of the house. I had been too focused on finally being home that I hadn't noticed. Before I could say anything, a ginger and black beagle ran through the wooden wall as if it didn't exist. She landed on the lawn in front of the inn and rubbed her little black nose along the grass, sneezing her lungs out.

Sabine turned her head to look at us and glared at me before going into another sneezing fit.

'What do you mean it's my fault?' I asked incredulously. 'I just got back.'

Sabine laid on the ground and put her nose between her paws. She tried to rub it in a very human-like manner before barking at me.

'Where did you learn that language?' I started walking hurriedly towards the back of the inn with Sabine following close behind me.

An explosion rang from behind the inn, and I stopped in my tracks as pieces of metal flew through the air. I was about to ask Sabine what the hell was going on when a deep vibrating roar shook the entire inn to its foundations. It came from the attic that was reserved for Xaris, my only permanent guest.

Sabine looked up and rolled her eyes before sneezing again. 'Devon, take Leann and find Julia now!' I yelled and took off towards the explosion. Out of the corner of my eye, I saw a red car coming down the driveway, but I had more pressing things to worry about. Whatever the hell was happening was bad enough to wake up the dragon, and that wasn't good. Dragons were notoriously deep sleepers, but Gods help you if you touched their horde or disturbed them. I just hoped he was in his human form, or the inn might not survive this.

I heard a sneeze and turned to see Sabine running next to me. She gave a low whine.

'I'm going to need to wash your mouth with soap if you keep calling me names, young lady.'

Another whine answered me.

'Where's Julia?' I asked.

She sneezed twice. The closer we got to the back, the more she sneezed. Sabine's nose was highly sensitive to magic, a gift for a guardian spectral dog.

We rounded the corner to see a blackened patch of grass surrounded by charred pieces of metal. Next to the debris was a man holding a kid in the air by the throat. My body tensed, and instinctively I reached for my morningstar only to remember that it was gone. Xaris must've teleported from the attic to the backyard and now had Roel in his clutches.

Xaris stood at an impressive six foot eleven of unrestrained fury; his usual mocha color skin glowed with navy veins. Broad, muscular shoulders shook with rage as a deep growl built in his throat. Roel's face was slowly starting to turn purple. The kid was kicking at the air, boot laces flying all over the place as he tried to escape the dragon's vice-like grip. Xaris' long blue hair was tousled to the side as if he had just woken up. I swore softly. A freshly awakened dragon without their first cup of coffee tended to get peckish. A tough lesson Roel was about to learn.

White mist flowed from the dragon's nostrils and wrapped itself around the kid's neck like a noose, and Roel struggled harder. Dragons could easily throw down with the best of them. I was going to have to intervene if I wanted Roel to remain intact. He was usually a hit with the inn's guests, but Xaris found him less than charming, judging by the still-tightening grip he had on his throat. If it wasn't for the hex dampening Roel's magic, maybe the fight would have been a little more even. Maybe.

Roel clawed at Xaris' forearm and managed to choke out a few words.

'Trying....hex....exploded...'

'Xaris, let the boy go! You know humans give you indigestion,' I reminded him reasonably while slowly approaching. I'd learned long ago that slow and steady was the way with dragons, and had the burn marks on the ceiling of the reception to prove it. One wrong move and Roel was ash.

Xaris turned his head to look at me with white reptilian eyes. Ice clawed at my spine; he wasn't looking at me like the man who housed him but as prey. 'You don't intimidate me, Xaris. Or have you forgotten who I am?'

Sapphire scales began to wrap around his fist. I glared at him, gathering my magic around me. 'Let the boy go, Dragon. I won't ask you a third time. You know the laws, Xaris. Release him.'

'And what if I don't? He interrupted my nap, and that deserves punishment.' His voice sounded cool and even with a lyrical accent that I couldn't place even after a decade.

'Then you and I are going to have that rematch you've always wanted.' And that I was so not ready for, not even remotely. Silver and red sparks crackled along my fingertips. 'But need I remind you that if you hurt him, you would be in violation of the inn's laws and banned from my premises for life.'

'What do the laws of men have to do with one such as I?' Roel's eyes were rolling to the back of his head, and he was struggling less and less. A low growl came from behind me, and suddenly, a wolf stood next to me, her fur was wintry white and seemed to glow with ethereal light, but her ears were a deep crimson color as if someone had dipped them in blood.

The dragon regarded Sabine in her natural form with a serious look. His eyes narrowed, and I could see his body tense. If we really went all out, the inn wouldn't survive, neither would the forest or pretty much the whole city. Xaris was a powerful and dangerous bastard, and I was running low on magic. The smart thing would've been to talk things out like civilized beings, but dragons didn't do smart – they did hellstroms and carnage, especially when they were riled up. I had to stand my ground and hope for the best; it wasn't my first time dealing with cranky dragons.

'The laws of men may not hold power over you, but you gave me your word that you would abide by the Compact of Guesthood and wouldn't harm those under my employment.' I released my magic and looked straight into those alabaster predatory eyes. 'I believe you are a dragon of your word.'

Xaris' gaze rooted me to the floor, but I kept a straight face, not showing him how much he scared the crap out of me. He shifted his gaze to Sabine and inclined his head in acknowledgement before releasing Roel. The kid fell to the floor and began coughing and massaging his throat before rushing to get behind me.

Xaris turned to me, his arms crossed over his muscular chest as more sapphire scales covered his entire body. His blue hair rippled in the air as if it had a mind of its own and began to tie itself into a braid that fell to his ankles, its colors shifting from blue to platinum white. Two leathery wings sprang from his back, twelve feet long, the underside of them a beautiful lapis lazuli. They folded over his frame like a cloak. A long segmented tail that ended in a razor-sharp bone spike flailed in the air behind him.

*Oh shit.* I started gathering my magic and felt my eyes glow silver. 'Put my honor into question again, Innkeeper, and nothing will stop me from using your spine as a back scratcher.' His eyes flashed with bright light as he teleported himself away.

I waited for exactly five seconds before sitting down on the grass, legs wobbling. I turned to Sabine, who regarded me with blood-colored eyes. 'Thank you, girl.' I laid my head against her soft fur and took a deep breath, inhaling her familiar scent.

Sabine turned her majestic head and gave me a long sloppy kiss before growling low in her throat.

I laughed and gave her a kiss on the nose. 'Fine, I'll ask Julia to make you your favorite tonight.'

Her form shimmered, and she melted back into a beagle. She gave Roel a death glare, turned around and pawed some dirt at him before running back into the inn.

Roel's skin had returned to its usual ruddy tint that no amount of cold weather could lighten. He had collapsed to the ground and was visibly shaken as he continued to rub his throat. 'Mind telling me what the hell I just walked into?' I leaned back on my arm and looked at him. 'Had to piss off the dragon again, kid? We really need to cultivate a sense of self-preservation into you, or you won't last long.'

'I'm sorry, boss, but I was so excited. I thought I had finally found the one.' Roel gave me a helpless look. 'I found this old ritual last night and spent hours getting the ingredients ready. I followed all the instructions to the letter, in the appropriate order and used the last bit of my magic, but something went wrong and kablooie.' He groaned as he twisted a small silver ring with a sapphire on it.

The ring had lost all remnants of Roel's power. Unless he could break the hex his aunt had placed on him, he would never be able to practice magic again. Witches like Roel and Leann derived their power from their familiars, and since Roel's connection was severed by a hex, he was stuck. No familiar, no magic and no luck, it seemed.

I looked at the blackened patch of grass, kablooie was right. 'What are these metal pieces?'

Roel visibly winced and gave me a sidelong look. 'I needed something big enough to stir the ingredients, so I borrowed the stew pot.'

I was so tired all I wanted to do was scream at him, but after what Xaris put him through, the kid had been punished enough. Plus, delivering a lecture required more energy than I currently had. 'You took Julia's stew cauldron?' I glared at him. 'Are you tired of living?' He certainly had a death wish.

Roel blinked as if the horrifying thought of Julia's reaction had only just occurred to him. He looked at me with pitiful eyes. 'Boss, my mighty and strong boss, won't you help a poor lost soul?'

The urge to kick him was almost too strong, but instead, I gave him my best death stare – anything else took too much energy at this point. 'Your mess, you clean it up.' I got up and brushed off my pants. 'Don't worry, I'll be sure to bury your body under a nice tree.'

The young witch groaned and threw himself back onto the ground. 'What am I going to do now?'

I ignored him and went back inside through the kitchen door. I walked around the island and paused to look at a hunk of meat on the counter. My stomach was growling, but the prospect of cooking was too much for my aching limbs. I opened one of the refrigerators, took out a pitcher of iced tea and served myself a tall glass. Julia was going to be livid when she found out her favorite stew pot was now a lawn ornament. I found myself smirking at the thought that, for once, I wasn't the one in trouble. A long sip of the cold sugary drink washed away the remnants of my fear and perked me up just enough to tackle the rest of the day without falling flat on my ass. Well, assuming nothing else went wrong today.

Between the reception hall and the kitchen lay the dining room, and snuggled in between the rooms was my dark cherry wooden desk, scattered with papers, my laptop and an old fashioned hotel bell Julia had bought me. From here, I could keep an eye out for new guests and the current ones sitting at the wooden dining table, big enough to seat a party of twenty. It often lay unused unless the inn was full. The soft light spilling from the large spiral chandelier threatened to send me to sleep as I eyed the comfy desk chair with longing and was jolted to awareness at the sight of a woman standing before the desk with a small bag.

She was in her mid-twenties with long dark wavy hair that fell to the middle of her back and a soft, peach complexion. I put on my best innkeeper smile and walked towards her. 'Good Morning miss, welcome to Tír na nÓg. My name is Nathan Mercer. How can I help you today?' Tight blue jeans hugged a curvy form, and her piercing green hazel eyes skewered me to the spot as they analysed me. A small braid hung from the side of her face, tied with blue string; her beauty marred only by the fresh bruises that peppered her face, trailing down her neck and disappearing beneath her jacket. Handprints.

'Good morning. I would like to rent a room.' Her voice was soft and soothing, like a velvet caress with a distinctly English accent. She tucked the braid behind her ear and gave the reception hall a once over. 'I was led to believe this was a safe place for people...' She seemed to struggle with the word. 'Of a different nature,' she finally said.

I reached over the desk and offered my hand. She looked at it for a moment before slowly shaking it. A jolt of power rang through my arm; it felt like sticking it into an electric socket. Whoever she was, she was powerful. I felt her magic probing mine before it quickly receded. Her brows furrowed, and I hid a smile. My magic was too unique for people to get a read on me straight away, and given how spent I was, she probably thought I was harmless. Good, I didn't want my guests to feel anything but comfort when they stayed at the inn, and it never hurts to be underestimated.

I sat behind the desk and put my drink down. 'If you're wondering if this place is safe for those with magic, then the answer is yes. So long as our guests abide by the inn's laws, they can enjoy our full protection and service,' I said, pointing to the plaque on the wall where a cartoon version of Sabine was reading the text:

*'Come in peace. Do not harm the other guests. Don't run out on your bill. Be courteous to the staff.'*

She looked towards the plaque, and a small smile appeared on her face before she squashed it, and her face once more a neutral mask. 'I see no problem with them. Where do I check-in?'

I pulled out a form and handed it to her. 'Just fill out your information and sign that you agree to abide by them.' Her eyes narrowed at the paper, and a ripple of magic flowed from her and hovered over it. I waited a second as she called back her magic and reassured her. 'Don't worry, it's not a magical contract. Just a regular pen and paper. The room costs five gold pieces a night. If you know how long you'll be staying, you can pay upfront. If you don't, we do collections on Sundays.'

She took the form as I finished my drink and began to fill it out. Gold was the universal currency of the supernatural world; every gold piece was the size of a Thin Mint and worth a hundred American dollars.

She handed me the paper, took a quick glance to make sure it was alright, then reached into the front pocket of her carry-on bag and pulled out a small velvet pouch. She placed it on the desk with a solid thud. 'There are seventy gold pieces here. That should cover a two-week stay.'

I picked up the bag and put it inside one of my drawers while looking at the cursive signature on the bottom of the form. I grabbed one of the keys to the empty rooms from their hook. At that moment, Roel came out of the dining room, a large plastic bag in his hands that clanged as it moved. He saw the guest, and as if on queue, his eyes widened and a smile formed on his face.

Patrizzia, as the name on the contract had stated, wrinkled her nose and looked at the bag. 'You used too much wormwood and not enough poppy. That's why your cauldron exploded. Next time you should read the recipe before attempting a dispelling hex. Or just don't do it. Your kind is more of the elemental nature – you should stick to that.'

The smile on Roel's face froze, and he zeroed in on her. 'You know how to dispel a hex?'

I turned towards my newest guest and saw her in a different light. A witch, huh? Why did it seem like I was swimming in them all of a sudden? I looked at Roel and gestured towards Patrizzia. 'Roel, this is Ms Patrizzia Roberts. She will be staying with us for a couple of weeks. I was about to show her to her room, but now that you're here...' I motioned towards him before turning to Patrizzia. 'Ms Roberts, this Roel Theron, he is—'

'A mágissa dabbling in things that are beyond his understanding,' she grabbed her bag and lifted it off the floor, ignoring the look of murder on Roel's face. 'If you could please show me to my room, Mr Mercer. I would love to freshen up.'

Roel was a mágissa? Whatever the hell that was. I rubbed my eyes and escorted Patrizzia to her room. Maybe some rest would do me some good and, hopefully, nothing else would turn up.

# 8

I led Patrizzia to the guest quarters and tried to get a read on her. When her magic probed mine, it had felt potent yet murky. Based on my previous encounters with witches, they all carried a hint of the familiar they were bound to, yet my guest's magic didn't give me a clue as to what her familiar could be. I let my magic gather around my thumb and traced a small pentagram on the smooth metallic surface of the key. They were a safety measure for the guests. Each key was linked to a specific person, and no one but them or I could access their rooms. The rune would last until the guests checked out and handed the keys back. It was especially handy when shifters from different species stayed at the same time – never again would I host tiger and lion shifters simultaneously.

I got the sense that Patrizzia liked her privacy, so I led her to the farthest room from the stairs. We stopped in front of the wooden door, and I glanced around for Sabine. Welcoming a guest was one of her favorite things to do; she wouldn't usually miss it.

'This will be your room, Ms Roberts,' I said, opening the door and handing her the key. 'You'll find everything you need to make your stay as pleasant as possible. If I may?' I gestured towards the room, and she nodded, granting me entrance before following me inside. I walked towards the large sandalwood bed in the center of the room, draped in dark green linens, and the small nightstands that stood with brass candle holders atop. 'The matches and candles are in the first drawer. If you fancy reading by candlelight, we have a selection of books downstairs.'

I walked around the soft red lounging chair situated at the foot of the bed and motioned towards the wooden door that led to the second-floor balcony. 'Through here, you can get some fresh air without leaving your room.' I turned around and pointed towards the double doors on the other side of the room. 'Bathroom is through there, and the closet is right next to it.'

When I reached the front door again, I looked back at her. 'Breakfast is at seven, lunch at noon and dinner just after sunset. I hope you have a comfortable stay with us, and if you need anything at all, please don't hesitate to ask. We're at your disposal.'

She put the key away as she gave the room a once over. 'This will be more than enough. Thank you, Mr Mercer.'

I nodded before I closed the door and made my way over to the stairs leading to the third floor, where the staff rooms were located. If Julia was treating Leann, she would've taken her there. I looked at the spiral staircase that led to Xaris's abode and wondered if the dragon had gone back to sleep. I would need to talk to him about today's *incident* eventually, but for now, it could wait.

I stepped onto the third floor and saw Devon leaning against a wall outside one of the rooms. A green glow was coming from beneath the door, and a bitter, spicy scent permeated the air. *Julia.*

I walked towards him and nodded at the door. 'How's it going in there?'

Devon took his glasses off and rubbed his eyes. 'I have no clue. Julia took her inside and kicked me out, said my 'death aura' was making it hard for her to concentrate.' He put his glasses back on and looked at me. 'So, what blew up?'

I leaned against the wall and let out a breath. 'Julia's stew pot and Xaris's temper. You'll know in a minute when Julia comes out and kills Roel.'

Devon chuckled and nodded. We stood there in silence for about a minute before he cleared his throat. 'We need to talk.'

'Devon, are you breaking up with me? I'm hurt, sweetie. What did I do?'

Devon rolled his eyes. 'I mean it. There's something I've needed to tell you for a while now but there just never seemed to be a good time...'

Oh. So we were going to have *that* kind of talk. Got it. I slid myself down to the floor and placed my hands on my knees. 'You have a secret, and it's yours to tell, Devon. You don't owe me anything. Morrigan knows how many secrets I'm still keeping.'

Devon gave me a look but sat down next to me cross-legged and tapped the floor absently with his fingers. 'It's a little complicated, but I want to tell you.'

I simply looked at him expectantly. He was my best friend, and no matter what, he always would be.

'Back in ancient times, when men stopped worshipping the Greek Gods and started pillaging their temples, the Gods were furious. Zeus wanted Apollo and Artemis to send a plague to teach men a lesson. Some of the other Gods agreed; it was a particularly hectic time for them.' He shrugged as if to say, 'what can you do about it' and continued, 'Wise Athena was against it. They didn't need mortal prayers, but to wipe out humanity would make them no better than those who had come before them.'

I looked at him, confused. 'They don't?'

Devon shook his head. 'Common misconception. Yes, prayer gave them a power boost, but it wasn't the main source of their strength. They drew energy from their sphere of influence; Zeus from the sky, Poseidon from the sea, and so on. As long as those things exist, they are as powerful as they were before they created the Greeks.'

'Loving the history lesson, Devon, but why are you telling me this?' I scratched the back of my head, trying – and failing – to connect the dots.

He gestured for me to wait. 'I'm getting there. Gods, you're so impatient.' I rolled my eyes at him. 'Like I said, it's complicated. Athena proposed that they choose one family each and bless them with their bloodline. That would allow them to keep their fingers in the mortal world and restore faith. These scion families would be their agents working in secret, maintaining Olympian influence on the world. The Gods voted and agreed.'

I raised my eyebrow at Devon. 'Are you saying you're descended from one of the Greek Gods?' Given his power over the dead, I had a pretty good idea which God it was. 'So what, Hades is your great-times-a-million grandfather or something?'

Devon gave me a nervous smile. 'Not exactly. To prevent the blood from diluting too much, every couple of generations or so, they would descend from Olympus to renew the bloodline.'

My mind screeched to a halt, and I could only stare at him. 'Devon, if you're screwing with me...'

Devon shrugged a little awkwardly. 'Hades is not my great-times-a-million grandfather. He's my Dad. And he loves his wife too much to ever look at anyone else, so my mom is Persephone. They came down to Earth, took a mortal form and nine months later, I was born.'

My mind didn't just screech – it blew up into a thousand pieces. 'Wait, doesn't that make you a God?'

He shook his head. 'Nope, I was conceived while they were in their human form, so I'm a scion. More powerful than others, given that I have two divine bloodlines in me, but I'm not a God in any way.'

I rubbed my temples, trying to clear the incoming headache. 'So, your parents, who I've met several times, are really Hades and Persephone?' A nod. 'I beat Hades at poker? I'll be going to hell for that.' Devon laughed, and I felt my eyelid twitch. Bastard. 'What does this have to do with Leann flipping out on you?'

He looked at the door that was still emitting a green glow. 'Her flipping out on me has more to do with her being a mágissa than anything. They just don't like scions that much.'

I was about to ask what the term meant when a column of rainbow light tore through the roof and appeared right in front of us. Magic flooded the inn, crashing against my skin in hot waves. The multicolored beam flared with flames that landed on the floor sizzling with heat, and Devon and I jumped to our feet. I mentally checked my wards and found them intact, so I knew this wasn't an attack. A loud sound came from the burning rave show, almost like a war horn.

The column vanished, leaving behind a scorched metal chest. The wooden floor around the chest caught fire, and Devon swore, racing towards the end of the hall and returning with a fire extinguisher. When one of your guests is a dragon, you tend to buy them in bulk.

White foam swallowed the flames as I tried to make sense of what had just happened. I looked up and saw scorch marks on my ceiling that were starting to catch fire as well and directed Devon, brushing errant foam from our shoulders as he went.

Once all the small fires were put out, I extended my magical senses towards the chest. It seemed to contain only trace amounts of magic which felt ... odd after its spectacular entrance.

'Just so we're clear,' Devon mumbled while putting the fire extinguisher on the floor, 'a rainbow just burned down part of your inn, right? I didn't imagine that.'

I shook my head slowly. 'Nope, that is exactly what just happened.'

'Wait. Is that a note?' Devon pointed to the light-blue vellum envelope that had somehow remained undamaged.

'Oh, that's so nice of them. Now I'll know whose ass I need to kick for this little stunt.' Like the chest, it held only the smallest amount of power so I picked it up, confident it wouldn't blow my face off. Probably.

There wasn't any writing on the front, but a white wax seal stamped with the silhouette of an anvil on fire adorned the back. I broke the seal, and the envelope lit up with silvery light. An image appeared. It portrayed a six-inch dwarf with a long bushy black beard that covered most of his face, so I could only see his large bulbous nose and pair of piercing orange eyes. *Kathour*. The figure floated in the air in front of me and slapped its large belly.

'Nathaniel, you crazy bastard, I hope you're doing well.' Kathour's rough voice thundered through the hallway, and I fought the urge to cover my ears. The smaller they were, the louder they sounded. 'If you're seeing this, then it means you got my Bifröst mail, or at least I hope you did. The damn thing is more temperamental than my wife.' I looked from the image of Kathour to Devon, who was staring at it with wide eyes.

Kathour continued, his voice growing louder with each word. 'My apologies for not delivering the items you requested in person, but those two-faced glory-seeking goat-fucking good-for-nothing bastards of clan Ivaldi challenged me to a smith off!' Kathour roared. 'As if they could ever beat me! Bunch of one-hit wonders that stink more than a three-day-old skunk shoved up Fenrir's arse. Ha!' Kathour laughed so loud, I almost jumped. 'I'll show the pampered prissies who's the boss. Now, onto the business at hand, I trashed your old armor. Shoddy workmanship all around, but what can you expect from a bunch of flower-sucking fairies!'

Another booming laugh, but this time I was ready. 'Your new one is a combination of iron, silver and kevlar, the enchantments I put on it are simple ones but they work wonders. The armor absorbs a portion of the kinetic energy you generate as you move and it powers up a shield that comes out from the palm of the glove. As for your new weapon' – the dwarf grinned – 'Fjall, the mountain crusher. Works on the same principle as the armor; it will store energy inside and release it all in one big blast when you hit something.' Kathour seemed to look straight at me, like he could see me. 'Don't you dare lose these ones; they're my finest work yet. If you do, there's nowhere in the Nine Realms you can run without me finding you and cracking your skull like a melon.' With that cheerful send-off, the image vanished.

'What in Demeter's sake is going on out here? I'm *trying* to heal someone!' The door suddenly opened, and Julia stepped out of the room, glaring at us. Her long dark hair was pulled into a high ponytail, and her olive skin glistened with sweat. She looked to be in her late twenties rather than the three-hundred-plus years she actually was. She aimed a finger at me. 'Keep it quiet, or I'll beat the shit out of you both.'

I eyed her carefully. 'Julia, if you beat us up, then you would have to waste your magic to heal us, and that seems like a pointless thing to do.'

She glared at me. 'Besides, you're going to want to save your energy for Roel.'

Devon smirked. 'Poor Roel. Besides, if someone is going to get beat up because of this mess, it will not be me. That rainbow post had your name on it, not mine.'

Julia crossed her arms and looked between Devon and me. 'I don't know what you two are going on about, but someone needs my help in here, so keep it down, or I'll stick you inside a tree until spring comes. Do I make myself clear?'

We both nodded like naughty children caught misbehaving by their parents. Julia strode back into the room and slammed the door shut. I turned to Devon and gave him a grin. 'Roel is going to be in for it later.'

Devon chortled. 'Should we find popcorn?'

'How very God-like of you, entertaining yourself by watching the puny humans be punished. Just because you're a big powerful son of a God – no wait, two Gods. '

Devon grinned. 'Yes, fetch me my grapes and a gold-leaf fan, puny human.'

I heard the bell from the reception hall ring. I let out a groan of frustration. 'What is it now?'

'How about you check it out while I put this in your room?' Devon motioned to the chest. I nodded and took a deep breath. Was it too much to ask for a moment of silence? Or a quick nap? Just a small one.

I left the chest with Devon and made my way downstairs, stopping between the second and first floor to see who was expecting me. I blinked in surprise. Waiting by my desk was none other than Sentinel Elaine Hughes, wearing a white blouse and long floral pattern skirt, an outfit completely at odds with the stoic woman I had met last night. Well, at least she was alone this time. I furrowed my eyebrows, wondering what the hell had I done now to warrant law enforcement, mortal or otherwise, coming to my inn.

Well, there was only one way to find out.

# 9

'Sentinel, what a lovely surprise! It's a pleasure to meet you without any normie pretenses between us.' I put on my best welcoming smile, trying to mask how tired I was, and stepped onto the landing. 'Are you here to rent a room? We have a few vacancies at the moment, and since you're a friend of Alice's, I'll even give you a discount. Four gold pieces a night.'

Elaine smirked. 'Given that your usual rate is five, that's not much of a discount. How about a free stay instead?' She gave the inn a cursory look, 'I've always heard great things about this place, especially the food.' Even when she was dressed casually, she emanated that same badass, kick-your-teeth-in aura I had sensed before.

I shook my head. 'Sentinel Hughes, I still have to make a living. How about three a night for the first two weeks in our best room, warm pillows and sheets every night, and I'll personally deliver your breakfast. That's my best offer.'

'Please, call me Elaine. Alice was right; you *are* a charmer.' She stepped towards me and a waft of fruit and warm honey slid through the air. 'But I have too much work. Taking a vacation right now seems like an unreachable dream.' She moved her short brown hair away from her face, and her dark eyes peered into mine with laser focus, like a tiger sighting prey. 'Now, would you mind telling me why I have several reports of a battle royale with two magical creatures in Lone Fir Cemetery? And in full view of the public, no less.'

So she was here on official business then. 'I'm certain I have no idea what you mean.'

'The descriptions I was given match you and Devon perfectly, even down to your flannel shirt. Did you really tell that civvy you were shooting a movie? Like that was going to stop people asking questions when you're battling a monster in broad daylight.'

Ah shit. 'It wasn't in full view of the public. We put up a fog wall to keep the normies out.'

'So, it *was* you.' Elaine scowled. 'You know I can have you both arrested for openly displaying magical abilities to mortals, right?'

I snorted. 'The Assembly only governs over mages, and I'm not a mage. Neither is Devon or Leann, so your laws don't apply to us. But maybe you're right. Next time, I'll let the giant chimera snake eat the bystanders. I'm sure they won't notice that.'

'Elaine? What are you doing here?' I jumped and we both turned as Devon made his way down the stairs.

'This is just a friendly visit that has *nothing* to do with the large magical battle that the two of you were involved in earlier today.'

Devon shot me a quick glance like I'd confessed or something. Except, I guess I sort of had. 'Oh, and you should probably know that Alice was very pleased to hear about the life-threatening danger the father of her children had put himself in.' Elaine smiled, stepping around me to give a suddenly pale-faced Devon a peck on the cheek.

'Shit. You're going to have to take one for the team, Nathan. Alice will believe me if I said you made me do it.' Devon winced and looked at Elaine before pointing at me and mumbling, 'Don't tell my wife any different. Besides, it's true! Weird shit happens when he's around. I'm just an innocent bystander.' He pulled out his phone. 'If you'll excuse me, I have to call my wife.' He walked toward the living room grim-faced, and I snorted.

'Someone should definitely get the license plate of that bus he just threw me under.' I sighed and gestured to the dining room. 'Why don't you have a seat? This seems like it's going to be a long conversation, and if I don't get some food in me, I'll fall asleep within a minute. Can I get you anything?'

Elaine smirked at me as she took a seat. 'Well, who could pass up an invitation like that?'

I rolled my eyes at her and made my way towards the kitchen, returning a few minutes later carrying a tray filled with freshly baked honey-sweet bread, sliced ham and turkey, as well as cheese, pickled onions, lettuce, tomatoes, and a pitcher of iced tea.

I sat down next to Devon, who had apparently managed to survive his call with Alice.

'So, have you thought about what school you're going to transfer Margie to once she has her magic?' Elaine asked, reaching for some bread the moment I set the tray down.

Devon shook his head. 'I'm not sure at the moment. First, we have to see what talents she develops. We don't know who she'll take after. You know how some schools feel about necromancers, especially powerful ones like me.'

'What do you mean by that?' I said as I helped myself to a sandwich and shot a quick glance at Elaine. I knew surprisingly little about necromancers and how the magical community treated them. It wasn't a common gift in Faerie, and Devon was the only necromancer I knew.

My friend shook his head and served himself a glass of iced tea. 'My powers are more concentrated than usual for a necromancer. While most have to kill a chicken to raise one zombie, I can do it with just a drop of my blood.'

'That's it? I don't see why they would treat you any differently just because of that.' And if any idiot made my niece cry, they would have something coming their way worse than any zombie.

'My power also extends to any kind of undead.' He shrugged. 'Ghouls, vampires, ghosts. Anything that has a touch of death, I can command. The community at large doesn't like me and my family because of that. If Margie inherits my powers...' He took a deep breath before continuing. 'A baby necromancer can usually only channel enough power to raise a hamster or a squirrel. When I was Margie's age, I could raise a human adult. She's going to need special training that standard magical schools can't provide.' He framed his face with both hands. 'I just don't want my baby to feel different or excluded.'

Elaine frowned and shook her head. 'I get why you're worried given the public view on necromancy, but just because you're unusually strong for a necromancer doesn't mean that Margie will be the same. Don't stress unnecessarily; just wait and see what happens.'

Devon put his iced tea down, flicking a quick warning glance at me. 'It's because I come from a long line of necromancers that I worry. My gifts run pretty strong in my family, and I don't want my little girl to be bullied because she doesn't have pretty magic like throwing fireballs or summoning creatures from the arcane realm. You know how cruel kids can be.'

Elaine hummed noncommittally, seeming to buy his story as she chewed on some honey bread. Her eyes widened, and she quickly reached for another slice, making herself a sandwich. I didn't hide my small smile. Julia's cooking skills were somewhat legendary, and she would love to hear about another happy customer. It was clear Elaine had no clue about Devon's scion heritage. Good to know I wasn't the only one who had been kept out of the loop.

Elaine brushed away crumbs as Devon and I tucked in. She pulled out a piece of folded paper with a drawing of the mark we had seen on both Maria and the chimera and placed it on the table. 'Like Alice told you, we don't have much on a flying gorilla-pig-boar creature. As for the second beast you battled, well, the closest thing I can think of is a chimera.' She turned to Devon. 'But you said it was ... wrong?'

Devon nodded as he swallowed his food. 'The parts were all in the wrong places. Also, as far as I know, a chimera can't reassemble itself as a different creature.'

Elaine nodded. 'So far, the only thing we have is this symbol.' She tapped the paper. 'That's where it gets complicated. There are too many references to mouths in mythologies. The Slavs have Baba Yaga, who eats children with her iron teeth. Japanese folklore talks about Futakuchi-onna, a woman with a mouth on the back of her head. The Irish had the Buganne, a nasty cousin to the trolls with boar-like tusks. Then there's every vampire myth under the sun.' She shook her head. 'There were also some mentions of giant sea demons in an Irish story, but not a lot of writings survived, so I can't dive deeper into that one.'

'Fomorians. They're not sea demons but giants that were driven into the ocean by the Tuatha Dé Danann. They're mostly extinct, though. No one has heard from them in millennia.' I filled them in on what little I knew about the sea demons from my time in Faerie.

Elaine raised an eyebrow at me. 'I'm pretty sure we would've spotted a twenty-plus-foot-tall creature rampaging through Portland but thanks for the input,' she said sardonically.

I rolled my eyes at her. 'Anything for you, Sentinel.' I took another bite of my sandwich and a heavy feeling washed over me. 'So we got bupkis on the monsters and too much on the mouth.' I looked at the drawing again. 'The mark was on both Maria and the creatures. That creature was happy to kill us but spared Maria, marking her but leaving her alive. I just don't understand why. Then we find the chimera attacking Leann? It seems like a lot of coincidences. When Leann wakes up, I'll ask her if she knows anything we don't.'

'Speaking of...' Devon stood up and started clearing the table. 'I'm going to check on Leann and then take off. Alice is probably waiting for me.'

'Thanks, bud. I'll be up in a sec.' I nodded as he picked up the tray and headed toward the kitchen.

I turned back to Elaine. Her eyes focused on the drawing as she hummed thoughtfully. 'You might be onto something with the witch angle, but we just don't know enough yet. Just let me know what Leann says when she wakes up.' She tapped the table decisively. 'I'll see what the Vault Keeper has to say about the mark and the witches. We couldn't dig up much on the creatures themselves, but maybe looking at all three elements will turn something up.'

I knew the Portland Vault Keeper. His name was Selenic, a powerful mage who also happened to be a merman and the owner of The Pearl of Wisdom, a bookstore catering to the supernatural. He was with us when we battled the Fae last September. He suffered greatly while helping us, losing not only his hand but also his wife. We killed the creature who murdered her, but the damage was done.

'How is Selenic doing?' I asked Elaine. 'I tried to get in touch with him, but he ignored my calls, and there was no answer when I went round to check on him.'

Elaine's features turned downcast, and she shook her head. 'Not good. Losing Malia was … he's been drinking – a lot. Hope granted him some time to mourn, and nobody fought her decision. He has been our Vault Keeper for the past thirty years; nobody likes seeing him like this.' She leaned back in her chair and rubbed her face, suddenly looking very tired. 'I went to visit him a couple of times with the pretense that I needed his expertise, and it became clear to me that his pain is over-whelming him. His kids are with him, but it's like a part of him died with Malia.'

Gods, poor Selenic. Mermen mated for life. I couldn't imagine what he was going through. Granted, my love life was a mess. A swirl of emotions rocked my heart; love, yearning, wariness and trepidation. I rubbed the back of my head. Spending a decade longing for the woman who you thought sentenced you to death wasn't exactly what you call healthy. My heart pounded in my chest like a caged beast, sweat covered my hands, and I let out a breath. Meeting her again several years later and finding out that she didn't want to kill you – before she disappeared yet again. It definitely put a damper on a relationship. But at least Silera was alive.

'Is there anything I can do to help?' I asked finally, pushing the memories away. Remembering led to heartache, and I really didn't need that right now.

Elaine folded the drawing and stood up. 'Not really, but I'll take this to him and see what he can find.' We got up, and I escorted her to the door. She turned around and gave me a peck on the cheek. 'Thanks for the food, give Julia my compliments. Tell Devon bye from me.'

I watched her walk to her car with a wave and then made my way back up to the third floor, where Julia stood talking to Devon. She looked paler than usual. Whatever magic she used had sapped all her strength.

'How's Leann?' I asked, letting my gaze assess Julia's wan face with concern.

Julia frowned and clicked her nails against each other. My worry grew. She only did that when she was upset. This day needed to be over; I couldn't take any more bad news. 'As I was just telling Devon, I managed to expel the poison, but the damage it did was significant. Whatever that creature was, it wasn't natural.'

I nodded. 'Yeah, when we were fighting the chimera it felt wrong – it seemed *made*.' I shrugged. It was the best way I could explain the bizarre creature.

'Well, that explains a few things,' Julia murmured before continuing. 'Snake venom is a tricky thing. Usually it's neurotoxic, hemotoxic or cytotoxic – whatever bit Leann was all three. I've never seen anything like it.' She looked back to the room, weariness washing over her face. 'I put her under a sleeping spell and will do another healing session on her when I'm rested. For now, she's stable. That fox is keeping an eye on her, and Sabine is keeping an eye on the fox.'

I smiled at that. 'I don't think the fox is a threat to us, but Sabine will definitely keep it in line. Go and rest up. I'll take care of the inn.' She must've been even more tired than I thought because she didn't even protest. She pointed a finger at me. 'Stay away from my kitchen.' She started walking down the hall. 'And where the hell is Roel? I have a bone to pick with him about touching my cooking utensils.'

I said a silent prayer for Roel, may the gods have mercy on his soul. I turned to Devon and gave him a small smile. 'Listen, I know we were going to go to the hospital today to check on Maria and the baby, but—'

Devon shook his head and clasped my shoulder. 'Don't worry about it. You've got your plate full here as it is, and if those beasts come back for Leann, she's going to need you here. I can swing by before going home and see how Maria is doing.'

I nodded. He was right, but it still felt wrong to bail on him. 'Thanks, brother. I'll walk you out.'

I walked with Devon outside and mentally checked the wards. With monsters on the loose, we couldn't skimp on protection. There had been two attacks on witches in the last twenty-four hours, my kitchen boy almost got killed by my dragon, and I'd welcomed a new, mysterious guest. It wasn't even noon yet.

Who said running an inn for the supernatural was a boring job?

# 10

I was frustrated. The last few days had been a whole lot of waiting idly: waiting for Leann to wake up, waiting for Elaine to come back to me with more info from Selenic. The need to be productive and actually *do* something was overwhelming. So, I pulled on my thick gardening gloves, opened the back of my truck and decided to tackle the overlooked saplings. I had finally managed to set aside enough time to plant the little guys.

Julia had been going in and out of Leann's room, treating her every twelve hours before almost collapsing out of sheer magical exhaustion. Meanwhile, I had spent the remainder of the week making sure my guests were settled and checking out a lovely shark shifter couple that had stayed with us for a week. Since my cooking skills, well, sucked, and Julia had threatened to cut my bits off if I stepped into the kitchen, it fell on Roel to cook for the guests, with Julia directing him via video chat. The results were less than satisfactory.

Julia's lack of time in the kitchen had made her grouchy as hell, so I'd decided being outside lessened my chances of catching her on the warpath. I walked the inn grounds and renewed the wards outside, squeezing every drop of magic I had into them each day. They were now charged with so much power that even Godzilla couldn't break through my defences.

I had also taken the chance to fully inspect the gift Kathour had sent me via rainbow. I had carved out a set of runes for my equipment, shrinking them down to a handy-dandy size that wouldn't make the normies faint while I carried them around. The hammer now lay in a silver bracelet on my left hand in its charmed form, and the pendant around my neck concealed my armor. I was a little concerned about the runes working as I hadn't attempted anything like this before, but a quick test had alleviated my worries.

Devon had called me from the hospital yesterday to say that there were no changes to Maria's condition. As soon as something happened, they would notify him, and he would call me. I sent up an errant prayer to whichever God that might've been listening for a miraculous recovery and set to researching the symbol and creatures myself, but the internet yielded nothing useful.

The other thing that had been playing on my mind was my dream. I was hoping that having my hands in the dirt, distracting my mind while I planted the saplings, might grant some sort of epiphany. The last time I had dreams as vivid as that, they had been prophetic. I hadn't worked things out in time then, but I could try now. There was something familiar about the vision, like I had met the bearded man before or seen his staff, but the more I thought about it, the harder it was to grasp whatever was floating around in the back of my mind.

I took the saplings to the back of the inn, where a thirty-foot tall obsidian spire pierced the air, reflecting the sunlight like a polished mirror. I had summoned it to defeat the rampaging fae that had messed up my backyard. However, just like a maniacal djinn who escaped from its lamp, no matter what I did, the spire refused to go away.

I tried using Talamh, the same rune from before, but the spire did not budge. Hacking at it didn't work. I had broken two hammers and a saw just trying. Hell, even Xaris went full dragon on it, swiping at it with his claws, and the thing only shook a little. In the end, we gave up and decided to decorate it with red and green lights, our own improvised Christmas tree. If you can't beat it, make it part of the family.

I walked around the spire and started planting the saplings one by one, feeding them a little bit of magic and connecting them to the forest around us. 'You know, I might not have Julia's green thumb, but I think you're going to like it here,' I told them while digging into the cold earth and transplanting them from their pots. 'It gets a little chilly here in the winter, but Julia and I will help take care of you.'

'I see you've taken up my habit of talking to the plants.' I turned around to see a pale-faced Julia standing behind me, wearing a purple winter coat over a loose yellow shirt and sweat-pants. Portland usually enjoyed a mild winter compared to other states, but lately, the temperature had been in the low twenties, each day colder than the last. The normies were getting worried, but I wasn't concerned – they hadn't witnessed what a true fae winter was like, especially when Queen Mab was on a murder spree.

I smiled at Julia and went back to planting. 'Well, my usual conversation partner has been babysitting a puddle fox, so I made-do with what I had.'

Julia knelt next to me and caressed the sapling's leaf like a caring mother. A green glow emanated from her hand, seeping into the earth beneath us. Each of the saplings I had planted shone with that vibrant emerald light. I closed my eyes and basked in the sensation. It felt like taking that first deep breath as you meet the sun for the first time in the morning. When I opened them again, the seedlings had all grown a foot taller.

Yeah, it was good to be a dryad.

I turned to see Julia swaying. Her breathing was shallow, and she could barely keep her eyes open. I swore as I scooped her off her feet and began my trek back to the inn.

'Nathan, let go of me. I'm not a little girl; I can walk by myself,' she said, but her eyes stayed shut. She sounded like she wanted to fight me, but her words came out as a tired whisper.

'Julia, you can barely string two sentences together, let alone climb a flight of stairs, so shut up and let me carry you.' I pushed the door open with my foot and walked right in. 'Besides, it's not every day our all-powerful dryad swoons in my arms like a bride on her wedding night,' I said with a grin.

Julia's eyes opened suddenly and flashed crimson. She grabbed the front of my shirt with surprising strength. 'I may have overdone it a bit back there, but that doesn't mean I'm some delicate flower that needs coddling. Now put me down, or I'll break your arm.'

Her voice might have sounded confident, but I could feel her shaking in my arms. I pulled closer to my chest. 'Nope, you're going to let me put you to bed, and that's final. Boss' orders.'

She snorted and released my shirt. I didn't berate her for overtaxing herself with the plants. Taking care of them was an uncontrollable compulsion for her kind. She sighed and rested her head against my shoulder. 'I came down to tell you that Leann is finally awake. She's weak, but you can talk to her.'

I paused mid-step between the second and third floor, relief flooding through me. 'That's great. Maybe we can get some idea of what the hell is going on.' I continued up the stairs. 'Did she say anything?'

Julia shook her head. 'Just asked where she was and how she got here. When I told her, she started cursing.' I stopped in front of Julia's door and gently put her down. She held onto the door frame and looked at me with a concerned gaze. 'I know you feel responsible for what happened to Matilda, but it wasn't your fault. Don't let her make you the villain.'

I frowned at her. 'If I don't take responsibility, then who will? At the end of the day, her mother died because I was too weak to save her.' Bitter regret stung inside. I clenched my fist and looked away.

Julia cupped my face and forced me to meet her eyes. 'You were injured, battling impossible odds.' She gave me a small smile and kissed me on the cheek. 'You're a good man, Nathaniel. Don't let her grief drown you, okay?'

I nodded, and she went into her room. I made my way to the second floor and sighed when I saw Roel standing in front of Patrizzia's room, the two of them talking. Or, more accurately, Roel was talking and gesturing while Patrizzia looked like she wanted to disappear. I walked close enough to hear a part of their conversation.

'...you recognized the hex, so that means you know how to break it. All I'm asking is for you to help,' Roel pleaded.

Patrizzia arched her eyebrow. 'I've told you time and time again that I don't want to get involved in whatever mess you're in. You can ask, plead or beg, but I still won't do it.'

Roel frowned. 'You know this type of magic is beyond my kind. Name your price, and I'll pay you triple.'

'Listen well, little mágissa.' Patrizzia's voice vibrated with magic. 'There's nothing you can offer that will make me conduct a ritual of such magic for you.' She slammed the door in his face, and Roel swore, looking up and jumping when he saw me standing there watching.

'What's going on?' I asked, nodding my head towards the closed door.

The kid hesitated before answering, 'Nothing, boss. Don't worry about it.'

I grabbed his arm gently as he tried to pass me. 'If you're having some sort of trouble, you know you can come to me.'

Roel looked at the wrist I was gripping, and I let him go. 'You're a great boss, Nathan, and a powerful magic user, but you don't know anything about witchcraft. This is a witch problem – there's nothing you can do.'

He walked off abruptly, leaving me staring after him in concern. 'That went well,' I mumbled to myself as I stopped by Leann's door and braced myself. I knocked and waited a few seconds before entering. Leann was lying on the bed with the sheets pulled up to her chest. The arm where she had been bitten was wrapped in a familiar green bandage that still glowed a faint emerald. Sabine was lying on her stomach on the red lounge chair at the foot of the bed, keeping an eye on the water fox floating in mid-air. As soon as I entered the room, both canines looked at me for a second before going back to their staring contest.

Leann turned her head and scoffed when she saw who had entered. Her face was pale, but there was a rosy hint to her cheeks. 'I guess you're expecting a thank you?' Her voice was raspy, probably because she hadn't used it for a couple of days.

I closed the door behind me and shook my head. 'No thanks are needed. You were in trouble, and I was in a position to help.' I nodded towards the herbal cast. 'How are you feeling?'

'Like I got run over by an eighteen-wheeler, and the bastard backed up to finish the job,' she pointed to the cast with her good hand. 'Severe muscle and nerve damage. According to Julia, it will take a month for her magic to heal me completely.'

'You can stay here as long as you need.' I looked at the fox and decided to ask something that had been playing on my mind. 'Normally, I don't see witches summoning their familiars to battle with them. They usually let them remain in the spirit world. But I saw both you and Maria do it. Why?'

Leann looked at the fox, and her face softened a little. 'We only do it when we're weak and can't control our magic well. I was already having a hard time suppressing the venom to effectively cast my spells.'

We stretched into an awkward silence. The tension in the air was palpable. I took a deep breath. 'Listen, Leann, about what happened with Matilda...'

'Don't.' Her voice strained as she turned to look at me. The fox lifted its head and glared at me with glowing eyes. 'Don't you dare say her name!'

'Leann, I'm sorry about what happened. You can hate me all you want—' I started to say, but she cut me off.

'You think I hate you? Please, you're not worth it,' she sneered at me.

I stopped and frowned. 'Then why the animosity towards me? Why pull your business from the inn and cut ties with me?'

She took in a deep breath and let it out slowly. She looked exhausted with big dark rings under her eyes. 'That was the coven's decision, not mine. It was the only thing those vermin could agree on. After mom ... died, those snakes started bidding for the post of Head Priestess. They've been at each other's throats for months.' She glared at me. 'As for you, every time I look at your face, all I can think of is being caught and feeling hopeless while I watched my mother die.' Her eyes shone with tears, but she continued, 'So yeah, I want to stay as far away from you as I possibly can. If it weren't for the constant bickering in the coven, I would've already gone to hunt down the bitch that sold us to the fae.'

What could I say to that? Sorry didn't even begin to cut it. Besides, it was clear she didn't want anything to do with me. 'I just wanted to talk to you about the creature that attacked you. We were coming to see you because the night before another creature, a pig-gorilla thing, attacked a member of your coven – Maria.'

Her eyes widened. 'Maria was attacked?

I put my hands inside my pockets and looked at her. 'One attack might be a coincidence, but two.' I shook my head, 'I feel like something's happening. Can you think of anything that might explain the attacks or the creatures?' I gave her a condensed version of my encounter with the Swinekong, including the death of Angela.

'Angela is dead? Oh dear Hecate, poor Allison. Who will take care of her now?' She shook her head in disbelief. 'They were supposed to be in hiding. I told them from the beginning that we should've just run, I—'

'Leann, what the hell is going on? Is someone attacking the coven?' I crossed my arms over my chest. 'Tell me what you know so I can help.'

I could see the internal struggle in her eyes before she came to a decision and began to speak. 'Two weeks after my mother died, one of our members, Gisela, didn't show up for services. So, some of us went to her place. We found it completely ransacked. Gisela was passed out on the floor with a tattoo like the one Julia mentioned to me.' She took a deep breath and adjusted herself on the bed. 'She was still alive, but we couldn't rouse her. We tried everything, but nothing worked. We looked up the symbol and came up empty. We had nothing. At first, we thought she had tried a spell that was too complicated, and it backfired on her. Gisela was always trying to do magic outside of the power granted by our familiars.'

I frowned at her. 'Is that bad?'

She smoothed the sheets and nodded. 'I don't know how much you know about witches, but we're not all the same. Like shapeshifters, witches come in different flavors. We draw our power from worshiping Hecate, and in return, she grants us the ability to bond with an elemental familiar.' She looked at her fox and smiled. 'We share our thoughts and feelings with them, and they share their magic with us. However, that also limits what we can do. Unlike traditional witches that can cast hexes, curses, and so on, we are limited to the sphere of influence our familiars grant us. Going outside that sphere is always bad news.'

Is that why every ritual Roel tried ended with something blowing up? It would also explain why he was so keen to get Patrizzia's help. If she was able to work outside of the familiar's magic, it could be the key to breaking his hex.

'So, when did you figure out that it wasn't a spell that backfired?' I probed.

'About a week later. We were getting ready for services when we received a distress call from Rafaela saying some beast was attacking her. She had only left to pick up some chips, she should've been back in fifteen minutes at most and—' She shook her head, and her eyes flashed with cerulean light. 'We were too late. Her car had gone off the road, and she lay unconscious on the ground next to it. After that, everyone started being more cautious. We traveled in groups, but it seemed like every week one of us would be attacked. In the end, Maria and I were the only ones left. I told her to hide with the local pride. Her sister Angela was mated to the alpha, and I thought she'd be safe with them. I guess we were both wrong.'

Why did that sound familiar? According to Devon, the Woodland Ripper's victims were being left once a week, sometimes more frequently. What were the chances we had more than one serial killer roaming about? Was the serial killer somehow controlling the creatures? How? And why target the witches? I needed to talk to Devon.

I turned to Leann. 'Why didn't you reach out for help?'

'Who would we reach out to, Nathan? The Assembly? They don't give a damn about us. The shifters? Unless you grow fangs and fur, you're a stranger to them. This was a witch problem, and we had to handle it ourselves.' Suddenly, something flashed in her eyes.

She tried to get up, but I moved to stop her. 'Easy, you need to rest.'

She slapped my hand away, eyes gleaming with panic. 'No, you don't understand. I completely forgot about Makayla! She's been out of town for the last two months taking care of her father, but she was supposed to come back today.' She looked at me, desperation clear in her eyes, 'If she goes to the coven headquarters and gets attacked...'

I nodded in understanding. 'Don't worry, now that I know when this all began, I might be able to focus my research a bit more. I'll make a trip down there today and see if she's there.'

She regarded me skeptically. 'Why would you do this for us?'

I looked at her solemnly, clenched and unclenched my jaw. 'I owe you.'

There was a long pause before she finally nodded and let herself relax on the bed. I looked at Sabine. 'Come on, girl, we have work to do.'

Sabine got up from the lounge chair, shook herself and ran outside, phasing through the door. I shook my head and opened the door the normal way. She was waiting for me on the other side. I gave her a peeved look. 'Most of us can't walk through walls, you know.'

She whined and scratched the back of her head before running towards the stairs. If I was being honest with myself, there was another reason why I wanted to help Leann so bad. I couldn't shake my thoughts of the little girl we had rescued; she was so small and had already lost her mother. She would never know her embrace, the tone of her voice or the warmth of her smile. Someone had robbed her of the one person who would love her unconditionally, and they weren't going to get away with it. It reminded me of Leann, who would also never again embrace her mother.

I bumped into Roel downstairs, walking towards the kitchen with a determined expression on his face. 'Kid, Sabine and I are going out for a while. Can you keep an eye on things around here? Julia is resting, so you just have to make the meals for the guests.'

Roel nodded. I noticed that he was twisting his ring around his finger and seemed to be struggling with something. He looked towards the stairs and back to me. 'Hey boss, can I ask you a favor?'

I followed his line of sight. 'Does it have anything to do with asking Patrizzia for help?'

He pursed his lips thin in frustration and nodded. 'Please. I know we got a lot going on, but I've tried every spell, ritual and prayer to Hecate, and nothing's working.' His hands clenched into fists. 'I know my familiar is alive, I can feel that ... but that bitch Valentina has me blocked, and without my familiar, I can't take her on.'

I knew exactly what he wasn't saying. Without access to his magic, he couldn't avenge his parents, who were murdered by his psycho aunt. I looked him in the eyes and nodded. 'Okay, I'll ask her when I come back. But you need to dial it down a bit with the begging.' I placed my hand on his shoulder. 'I know you're desperate to get justice for your parents, but Patrizzia is a guest. And, from what I've seen, she came here to get away from her own problems. I'm sure the last thing she needs is a kid pestering her about magic, okay?'

Relief and hope sparked in his eyes. 'Sure thing, boss. You can count on me.'

I watched him go into the kitchen. Sabine growled beside me. I turned to her and smiled. 'Yes, I'll get you some steak while we're out.'

She sneezed, then turned around and headed for the door. I sighed. 'Yeah, I know he cooks better than me. No need to rub it in.'

I grabbed my jacket from the coat rack and followed Sabine outside. A gust of cold wind blew through the parking lot, and I paused with the door open, glancing around. I shielded my eyes from the debris the breeze had stirred, and when the wind subsided, I saw her, standing between a cluster of trees.

Her raven hair that usually perfectly framed her heart-shaped face was flowing wildly in the wind today. Her green shirt looked like it was made out of the softest grass, and her long white skirt made it seem like she was floating a couple of inches above the ground. She looked every inch the Goddess she was. Her medium brown skin glowed in the afternoon sun as she raised her hand slowly towards me, eyes flaring with multicoloured lights as her gaze met mine.

Sabine and I shared a look before starting towards her. When the spirit of the state of Oregon calls on you, you follow.

# 11

The last time I saw Oregon, we were closing a dimensional portal to stop a kraken from drowning the city. After that, she had vanished into thin air, and I hadn't heard from her since. I simply assumed that she had gone back to sleep. It seemed like a bad sign that she was here again, interfering with the mortal world.

Walking next to her, it felt impossible not to notice her power. Bright magic emanated from her like heat from a volcano, washing up against my skin in warm, ceaseless waves. This sort of power ... it was breath-catching. I had only felt something similar in the presence of Mab, the Winter Queen, and her counterparts – the rulers of the Fae courts. That's what Oregon felt like. She was the embodiment of the state and its people.

I smiled at her. 'I didn't think I'd see you again.'

Oregon smiled back, and it felt like watching the sunrise above the horizon. 'It's been so long since I was awake, I needed some time to' – she rolled her hand in the air – 'get my bearings, as the humans say. Would you walk with me?'

I nodded, and we began to stroll through the woods. As we walked, I noticed the trees and the grass became a little greener, reaching out towards Oregon like children welcoming their mother home. 'How long has it been since you last walked the land?'

She tilted her head and frowned. 'Time works differently for my kind. A century is just a blink of an eye, millennia an intake of breath, but I do remember meeting a man from a faraway land who had briefly docked on my shores. I believe his name was Francis, quite the charmer.' If only she knew. 'After he left, I slept until the night we met.' She turned to me and smiled. 'I've been watching the land. It gladdens my heart to see it thrive with magic and possibility.'

Sabine darted between us, wagging her tail in happiness as we continued to walk. The sun was beginning to set, and the moon was rising in the sky. Oregon seemed content, humming a song beneath her breath and caressing the trees as we walked. As pleasant as this walk had been, I didn't really understand *why* she had come looking for me. We came to an old stone building that I didn't recognize, and Oregon paused, her smile dimming.

Sabine screeched to a halt and hacked as if she had something stuck in her throat.

'Sabine?' I rushed towards her, kneeling down by her side. 'What's wrong, girl?'

She didn't answer me but continued to make that dry hacking sound before raising her muzzle and letting out a soul-wrenching howl. Her eyes flashed with ruby light, and I could see her glaring at the ruined building. I followed her gaze.

It looked like a small stone house with a triangular roof. A set of stone stairs protruded from the side as vines and leaves covered the old ruin. A thick, wooden log had fallen next to the graffiti-covered walls. I frowned at the building, the inn was surrounded by five hundred acres of forest, and I had explored every nook and cranny of it. There wasn't a ruin like this anywhere near my land.

Sabine let out a whine as she walked around in a circle, rubbing her nose against the ground.

'Sabine, are you okay?' I rushed to her side and rubbed the side of her neck. I'd never seen her react like that, except in the presence of strong magic. Sabine raised her muzzle, her lips peeled back, and she growled at something ahead.

I turned to Oregon, whose face had grown somber. 'Where are we?'

She looked around, a frown beginning to pull at the corners of her mouth. 'Where we were needed but failed. Follow me.' She led me to a cluster of trees behind the house, and nausea began to grow inside me with each step, rolling in my stomach until I broke out in a sweat.

Pain stabbed me between the eyes like a hot needle. I stopped walking and covered my mouth and nose as I felt my stomach heave. The air was clotted with the stench of rotting wood and stale water. Before I could stop myself, I emptied my stomach onto the grass. Shivers ran down my spine, and my skin itched like crazy.

I looked around and saw blackened, rotting trees, the grass beneath my feet was yellow and sickly. It was unnaturally silent. I was surrounded by death. Next to me, Sabine's growl grew deeper. Her fur shimmered, and she shifted into her wolf form, eyes glowing with crimson light as she walked around me and nudged me with her head. I caressed her soft fur, and her warmth helped to center me.

'What the hell happened here?' I asked Oregon. I had never felt pain like this.

'Death.' Her voice rang with anger. I fumbled my phone out of my pocket. According to maps, I was at the Witch's House on the Wildwood Trail, south of Willamette Heights – a twenty-minute car ride from the inn. We had only walked for what felt like five minutes. I shook my head and put the phone away; there was no use in trying to understand the ways of primordial spirits who decided to take you for a joyride. The graffiti on the walls surrounded an all-seeing eye that seemed to follow me as I walked, raising goosebumps on my skin.

The floor was covered by stones and blood-soaked snow that trailed off into a puddle surrounding the body of a woman. Her long blonde hair covered most of her face, and stray snowflakes had tangled in it without melting. She was unnaturally pale, almost blue, and the redness of her blood was garish, spread out around her. I took a step closer and gagged slightly, my stomach still unsettled.

I didn't know who she was but judging by the gaping holes in her body, I had to be looking at the Woodland Ripper's latest victim. I knelt beside her and brushed the snow-covered hair from her face. Gods, she was just a kid, probably no older than twenty. I clenched my fist, fury pulsing through me. She'd had a whole life ahead of her, hopes and dreams she would now never realize.

I closed her lifeless eyes. *I promise I'll get the one who did this to you.*

I extended my magical senses towards the body and felt another sharp spike of pain. I stood and took a step back, massaging my temples with the tips of my fingers. The feeling of wrongness was emanating from her body, radiating out into the land surrounding it. There was no way to tell if the killer had left any evidence behind, there was nothing obvious like a weapon or footprints, but I had probably contaminated the crime scene by being here. I didn't dare to touch the body more than I already had. I raked my hand through my hair and growled in frustration. I picked up my phone and left a quick message for Elaine. She would know what to do, and if I could avoid further entanglements with Detective Kane, then so much the better.

Oregon watched me in silent curiosity before motioning to the trees around us. 'Someone used foul magic to tap into the land and drain it of life. I don't know what their goal is, but I've found several spots like this.' Her eyes flashed with amber light. 'I tried sensing who and where they are, but the magic they are using is obscuring my vision.' She turned to me, her eyes glowing with power. 'Help me find whoever is responsible for this.'

I let my gaze rest on the lifeless form lying in the middle of the blighted land and nodded, turning to Oregon. 'I will.'

She nodded and walked towards me. Her hands flared with power, turning the night into day for a second. She placed a glowing hand on my chest, and I looked in awe at the faint golden tracery of veins. 'You and I have fought together once before. Now I ask you to fight for me again. You have wielded my power and proven yourself to be trustworthy.' Her eyes glowed with a kaleidoscope of colors as they brightened intensely. 'Nathaniel Mercer, Innkeeper, Winter's Wolf, Scourge of the Fae, Defender of Oregon, would you be my champion and uphold the peace across the earth, sea and sky, keeping my children safe when they are in need?' Magic suffused her voice, and the surrounding desolate area gained a thrum of life. For the first time since I stepped into this place, I felt like I could breathe comfortably.

Sabine whined next to me. She had changed into her wolf form and started rubbing her head against my leg. I stroked her head, quieting her. 'It's okay, girl. Everything is alright.'

I rested my hand on her fur as I considered Oregon's offer. Deals with magical beings were something I always stayed the hell away from. They were the catnip of the Fae who loved using them to sucker poor humans into an eternity of servitude – and those were the lucky ones. I would do anything to put a stop to this senseless evil, but did that mean binding myself to a magical being? Even one as seemingly good as Oregon? She wasn't human, not even close. The brief brush of her power last fall and again today had shown her to be one of the most alien creatures I had ever met.

Yet, I had fought two of these foul-magic creatures, and they had both nearly wiped the floor with me. And that had been with help. I had no idea if I had the power to tackle even one of them unaided, let alone face whoever was controlling them. I needed Oregon if I wanted to stop this bastard. Decision made, I clenched my fist and stared into the ancient eyes that had seen so much. 'I'm willing.'

A smile bloomed on Oregon's face, so pure and delicate it felt like spring had come to breathe life into this dead land. She took a step forward and infused her golden light into a leaf she conjured seemingly from nowhere. 'Now I ask you to be brave and endure, my champion.'

Before I could ask her what she meant, she placed her hand over my heart. The leaf felt hot through my shirt, and then it began to burrow inside me. The heat increased, burning, and I looked down to see golden light streaking my chest. Power always came with a price, but that only felt like getting burned by hot coffee. Uncomfortable but tolerable. 'That wasn't so bad,' I said and received only a slow blink in response as she took a step back. Suddenly, a blast of scorching hot pain flashed from my heart and the golden threads started spiralling outwards, igniting my blood into molten lava. I clawed at the vein-like lines, but they kept moving until they covered me; my entire body glowed like a roman candle and steam permeated the air around me. I gritted my teeth, trying my best not to pass out. The heat continued building inside me as sweat drenched my back and forehead.

A deluge of pure power poured into me, inflating me like a balloon, and my eyes flew wide. My bones popped, and my muscles strained, threatening to tear themselves apart as my resistance crumbled and the scream I had been holding back ripped out of me.

I felt the pulse of the land beneath the inn throb like it was alive. My consciousness stretched outwards, and I could sense every single blade of grass, speck of dirt and all the animals for miles around, straight into the city itself. I clutched my head at the sudden barrage of information pouring into my mind. Millions of beings, both magical and mundane, ignited like candles inside my consciousness.

The strongest presence was Oregon as she was Air, Earth and Water, a maelstrom of power and purity. Her majesty and love for every creature in her domain were palpable. Then I could feel an ancient cold, just shy of Oregon's own power, eternal and unyielding like an iceberg given life. I felt the dragon's white eye turn to me and roar in my head. *What have you done to yourself, Innkeeper?* Xaris' voice echoed, but my senses were firing a million miles an hour. His voice was rapidly drowned by the rush of magic singing like a thunderous clarion song.

I fell to my knees amidst all the chaos. Oregon's voice rang clear in my mind like a silver bell. 'You must endure this challenge, my champion. The strongest sword has to be bathed in the fires of hell before it's ready to slay its enemies.'

I screamed louder as the power in the air threatened to overwhelm me, and tears fell down my face. My fist clenched around the dirt, and I grasped a sharp rock. The jagged edges dug deep into my skin, and I felt myself come back to my body, the sudden sharp pain anchoring me away from the rest. Power thrummed in my veins. I threw my head back and let the power speak through me; ancient words lost to time until I gave them voice. 'As it was in the past, so shall it be in the present and the future, with blood and flesh I give myself to the Spirit of the Land and claim my title as her Champion.' The oath wrung the last vestiges of my strength, my vision blurred, and my chest constricted, making it hard to breathe.

The temperature suddenly plummeted, sending chills across my feverish skin. The wind picked up, gusting through the woods, bringing a blanket of ice and snow with it. The flakes pelted my skin like bee stings. I looked up, and my eyes widened. It took me two attempts to get the words out. 'Rela?'

Princess Silera of the Winter Court of the Fae stood before me. I only had time to note the pinch of concern at the corner of her mouth and the frown pulling at her brow before my eyes closed, refusing to cooperate. Maybe I was dreaming, maybe the pain had finally driven me insane, and I only saw what I wanted to see.

I felt the vibrations of the earth rattling my teeth as Rela walked towards me and took my head between her hands, resting her forehead against mine and began to sing. I couldn't make out the words themselves; they felt old and alien. A language from back when mankind was crawling out of the mud and the elements ruled over the Earth.

Soothing warmth spread through my body, alleviating the pain. Slowly but surely, the power settled down, and my head no longer felt like it was going to split into a thousand pieces. I tried to form the words I longed to say to her. My eyes flew open, and all I could see was her radiant face filling up my vision, haloed by the stars, until everything faded to black.

# 12

I stood upon the wall of a colossal stone castle. The sun was setting, turning the sky afire with orange hues. All around, I could see Fae clad in black armor, looking at something on the horizon.

I followed their gaze and saw nothing but sea. They watched it in trepidation, almost fear, as the calm waters stirred, bubbles rising to the surface at incredible speeds causing foam to blanket the surface. A fae next to me raised an alabaster horn to his lips and let loose a thunderous sound. Everyone in the fortress began to scramble, drawing their weapons. The Fae didn't fear anything, they were the monsters in the dark, the nightmares used to scare children – but there was a clumsiness to their motions now that spoke of an enemy so great that even the monsters cowered.

A crow the size of a horse landed behind me, its talons scraping the stones. It turned to me with blood-colored eyes and opened its beak. A velvety feminine voice came forth. 'The courts were meant to temper you, my sweet. Are you ready for what lies ahead?' It tilted its head to the side and took flight.

I woke to the smell of primrose and winterberries. It was an alluring scent that seduced my senses, slowly bringing me back to consciousness. I opened my eyes and was surprised to see my room. The curtains were pulled back, revealing the starry night sky devoid of clouds. What time was it? The last thing I could remember was accepting Oregon's offer to become her champion, then nothing but pain.

I noticed a warm, soothing sensation spreading all over me, and I looked down to see a soft orange glow covering my naked body from head to toe. Where had that come from? It wasn't Julia's healing magic. The last time I had felt this kind of magic was...

A sound came from my bathroom, and I scrambled to pull the covers over me. The sudden movement sent a small stab of pain through my ribs. I sucked in a breath and managed to pull the covers to my waist when the bathroom door opened and Silera stepped out.

So I hadn't dreamed that part. Tt explained my current orange glow anyway.

She noticed me staring and flicked her gaze down to where I clutched the sheet close to my body, lips curling up in a mischievous smile that made my pulse stutter. 'Have you developed a sense of modesty from your time with the mortals, Rún?'

It took me a second to gather my wits past the lump in my throat. It's not every day you wake up naked in your room while your ex-lover is in the bathroom. 'Rela, what are you doing here?' My heart sped up in my chest; trepidation rolled inside me at what her visit could mean. Then I noticed that she was wearing a blue flannel shirt with the top three buttons undone, showing a hint of milky white skin. 'Is that mine?'

Rela's smile widened. Her long auburn hair was wet and pulled back into a bun, revealing her soft, beautiful features. I didn't know what short-circuited my brain the most, that she was wearing modern clothing, or that she clearly felt comfortable hijacking my clothes and bathroom.

She walked towards me, her hips swaying seductively from side to side. The movement lifted the shirt ever so close to her ... nope, keep it together Nathan. 'You didn't expect me to stay in that dress all night, did you?'

'Honestly, I didn't expect you to be in my room, let alone in my clothes.' I followed her movements as she sat down next to me on the edge of the bed. My pulse sped up like a race car. I wanted to draw her closer to me

'While I'm not used to mortal clothing, I have to say that it's rather comfortable.' She smiled and looked at me. 'You're so adorable, my wolf.'

My ears felt warm all of a sudden. Adorable was not necessarily something you wanted to be called while naked with a beautiful woman perched on your bed. Maybe I was still dreaming. 'Rela, how did you get here? Wait, how did I get here?'

She cupped my cheek and slowly caressed my lower lip with her thumb. Deep-seated need burned inside me at her touch. Like an inferno searing me from the inside out and gods how I wanted to burn. 'The last time we spoke, you said you needed time. Yet it has been almost three months, and I haven't heard a word from you.'

During an intense reunion a couple months ago, she confessed that she had been trying to protect me, not kill me. After that, I wanted nothing more than to have a moment of peace to think about our relationship. Instead, I threw all my thoughts into training with Travis and preparing for the inevitable fae fallout that came with my enemies learning I was still alive. Coming back from the dead was messy, especially when so many people wished I had stayed that way.

'I've been busy training since the Fae discovered I was alive.' I grabbed her hand between mine, the urge to feel more of her overpowering my better judgement and looked into her eyes. 'Though I have to admit you're much prettier than the Fae I'd been preparing myself for.' A small smile appeared on her lips that made my heart do a whole cirque du soleil routine. I squeezed her palm lightly. 'You still haven't answered my question. What happened?'

'I was on my way to you when I found you in the woods. Things have been tense at home, so I thought I'd come to stay at the inn. To stay with you.' Silera's thumb swept across my cheek. Goosebumps rolled across my skin, and I couldn't help but lean into her cool touch. Her skin felt smooth and familiar. I closed my eyes and breathed in her scent. Her touch was like the first ray of sunlight after a storm.

Suddenly, I felt an abrupt sting on my cheek and opened my eyes to find her honey-colored ones glaring at me.

'What the hell was that for?' I asked, touching where she had slapped me. 'Is that how you ask to stay at someone's house?'

'Is there something wrong with your head?' She crossed her arms and tapped her finger on her elbow. 'Why would you get involved with the spirits again? They're dangerous.' I opened my mouth to explain myself, but she cut me off. 'Don't you start with me, Rún. I heard everything from both your cook and the Assembly's Sentinel.' She clenched her fist. 'You're so infuriating. I swear to the eternal darkness that there hasn't been a mortal more vexing than you. Going around the city, battling these creatures – but you were not satisfied with that, so you just had to play hero once again by taking on so much power you almost *died*. So I ask again, is your head broken?'

I opened my mouth to answer, but her words hit me hard. When she put it like that, it sounded pretty stupid. Her hand started to move away from mine, but I grabbed it and looked into her eyes. 'Rela, you know me better than anyone. You know I can't just stand by while innocent people get hurt.' I shook my head. 'I *can't* just stand aside.' The soft glow from my skin illuminated her face, and my breath hitched in my chest.

'If you die because of some foolish crusade you've taken up, I will hunt you down through the halls of Manannán mac Lir and kill you myself.'

'The mighty Winter Princess worried about a lowly mortal such as myself?' I shook my head and smiled at her. 'If the rest of the court finds out...' I let the thought hang between us. We both knew what it would mean, especially for her. Her enemies would target her through me, and while I was good, I wasn't good enough to take on the whole of the Fae. Not only that, but Sidhe, the nobility of the Fae, looked down on humans and anyone who fell for one. I didn't even want to think what Rela's mother Mab, Queen of Air and Darkness, would do. She was the reason humans feared the dark and huddled close to a fire at night.

Silera squeezed my hand and, to my shock, leaned down to kiss me. A small brush of her lips was enough to send electricity through my body. 'So what if the court finds out? Let them,' she whispered, her hot breath gently tickling my lower lip.

'It's a nice sentiment, but we both know it isn't true,' I said almost as quietly as her. She moved her hand to my chest and examined the parting gift of the fae who had almost killed me – the fae who had torn us apart for more than a decade.

'I lost you once before, and it nearly destroyed me. I will not lose you again.' She looked up and met my gaze.

A strand of still-wet hair fell in front of her face, and I moved my hand slowly to tuck it behind her pointed ears. As her honey eyes glowed with faint light, something stirred inside me, like a butterfly flapping its wings, spreading waves of heat through my skin. A drop of moisture rolled down the side of her face towards her neck. Everything around us was so quiet I could feel the thundering of my heart pounding in my chest with the intensity of a landslide.

She caressed my chest with featherlight touches, tracing the scars with the tips of her fingers and sending chills across my body. She knew what her touch did to me. Her hand slowly trailed up my shoulder, then down my arm until our palms connected. A myriad of emotions swirled in her eyes that mirrored my own: sadness, longing, need, hunger, love. They blazed like two golden flames, igniting me from within.

The temperature in the room rose to a scalding degree as she pulled my hand to her lips, eyes like fire, locked with mine, and slowly curled her tongue around the tip of my index finger, sucking gently.

I don't know who moved first as we came together in a flurry of heat, surrendering to the inevitability of our hunger for each other as our lips met. The air felt charged with electricity as the tip of her tongue licked my lips, capturing my mouth. Like a dream, her skin next to mine, her breath on my neck, her body on top of me. Our hearts, beating as one after so long apart. It felt right, like coming home.

A purr of pleasure escaped from her mouth as she straddled me. Her weight was a tantalizing pressure, and I hardened with every caress of her skin. Her scent flooded my senses, all of them zeroing in on the woman in my arms.

My skin was on fire and starving for her touch and the feel of her skin on mine. My hands found the buttons of her shirt, and I fumbled them before grabbing both ends of the shirt and ripped it open with a curse. Buttons flew all over the room, and Rela shrugged the shirt off with a small laugh. She took my hands, placed them on her breasts and rocked her hips. I groaned and focused my gaze on her face.

Her eyes flared like golden torchlights and like a moth seduced by the allure of the flames, I let them burn me. I captured her lips with mine, drowning in her taste, the press of her breasts against my skin, our hearts beating in cadence. I moved my head towards her neck and kissed it, feeling her pulse race beneath my lips as I took it between my teeth, soothing the pinch with a kiss. A moan escaped Rela's lips, echoing in my head, and I kissed my way down to her breasts, wanting to hear that sound again. I could hear her breath quicken as the tip of my tongue lightly grazed her nipple. She grabbed my hair and whispered my name under her breath. Her moans acted like a catalyst, pulling me closer, making me suck harder. I savored her taste as it fuelled the inferno inside me. She was mine, and I needed her to know it. She responded with equal passion, rocking her hips against me, letting loose the fire that burned beneath the ice.

The door suddenly flew open. 'Hey, if you're done treating Nathan, we have an issue with—'

The sudden intrusion was like a bucket of ice-cold water. I scrambled like a drunken madman from under Rela, trying to grab a blanket to cover us, but the damn thing was on the floor, so I ended up looking like an idiot. I turned to see Julia standing there with wide eyes. She grinned and turned to Rela.

'So *this* is what you meant when you said you could 'get him back on his feet'. Got it.'

I felt my cheeks burn and moved to cover myself with a pillow. I looked back at Silera, who had propped herself on her elbows, her hair tousled to the sides. Her lips crept up into a satisfied smile. 'What can I say? I know my man.'

# 13

J ulia was visibly biting her cheeks in an attempt to conceal her laughter. 'When you get yourselves squared away, come to the dining room. Elaine is waiting for you.' With that parting comment, she left, shutting the door behind her.

It closed with a soft click, but all I heard was a deafening boom rocking my insides. The burning desire that coursed through me just a minute ago had been doused, leaving me cold and bereft. And then the realisation came – I wasn't ready to do this with Silera. Not yet, not after so long apart. Especially with the distance still between us and the past filled with deception and hate.

I looked at the wooden door then let out a deep breath. 'We shouldn't have done that.'

Rela shifted her position and looked at me curiously. 'What do you mean, my love?'

I turned to her, motioning to the space between us. 'This ... us, kissing. We shouldn't have done it. It was a mistake.'

She furrowed her eyebrows. 'Are you saying you did not enjoy it?' She gave a pointed look to my mid-section. 'Because I seem to recall feeling something very different from you just a second ago.'

A hollow smile visited my lips. I wanted to joke around with her, I knew that's what she expected of me. Instead, I shook my head. 'We can't do this, Silera. Not again. Not now.'

Her expression grew cold as she heard the seriousness in my voice. She sat up fully. 'Are you saying this because of what occurred *that* day?' She shook her head and quickly stood up, her arms crossed, her eyes focused on me. 'I told you that I had nothing to do with that. I did not order your death, Nathaniel. You know I can't lie. Do you want me to trice affirm it? Would that make you believe me?'

'This isn't about believing you or not, Silera.' I shuffled off the bed and walked towards her. This wasn't a conversation I wanted to have naked, but so be it. 'I believed you ordered my death for ten years,' I told her. 'I'm not fae. I don't measure my lifetime in centuries or millennia. I have to live every day to the fullest, and for the last decade, I believed you saw me as nothing. I believed that I meant so little to you that you didn't even do me the honour of sinking the blade in yourself.' I crossed my arms. The fury I had carried ever since I left the Fae bubbled inside me as if it was just waiting for the right time to explode.

'But you kissed me when we were fighting Muirín and her entourage.' She pointed at me, her tone glacial. 'You. Did. That. Not me.'

'I thought we were going to die and your confession rocked my world, so forgive me for being a little emotional at the time.' I sighed. 'We spent a day together and then you disappeared for months without a word.'

'You said you needed time!' She threw her arms up in the air. As her voice rose, her eyes grew colder. Magic pulsed from her, coating the entire room in a sheet of ice. A shiver ran down my spine, and I clenched my teeth to keep them from chattering. 'While you were licking your wounds in the safety of your home, *I* had to deal with my mother. She demanded answers I did not have because that whore Muirín didn't leave any evidence behind. The nobles she associated with were all 'surprised' by her actions and denied all knowledge of her plans. Months of investigation and threats provided me with nothing!' She crossed her arms again, and I could see the ice glistening on her skin.

'I meant what I said.' She let out an empty sigh, and I spread my hands to the side. This was getting us nowhere. 'I'm not the man I used to be, Silera. I told you that last time, I'm no longer your knight.'

'And yet, here you are, surrounding yourself with powerful players and running about from battle to battle. Very little seems to have changed to me,' she countered, arching a frost-covered eyebrow at me.

'You've seen me twice in the last ten years!' I ground out through clenched teeth. 'You have no idea what things are like when I'm not running for my life. I've built a different life for myself in Portland.' I motioned to the room. 'I'm an innkeeper; it gives me purpose and I like who I am now. I can't just go back to being your shadow.'

'If you've moved on as much as you think, you wouldn't be rushing in to save the day again.' She pointed at me. 'You wouldn't be hunting a serial killer right now; you'd be tucked up enjoying a quiet life inside your inn. You,' she said, moving closer until her pointed finger hit my chest, 'are too cowardly to admit that you miss it. You miss being my shadow, miss the importance it gave you and the challenges it set. You're living here, Rún, but you're not thriving. Not like you could be with me.' She took a step back and clenched her fist. Her eyes hardened as frost coated her arms, spreading through her entire body. 'But if you truly feel that I am nothing but a shadow in your life, then I'll darken your precious inn no longer.' Her face held all the warmth of a Winter storm as she glared at me. 'The fae had it right all along – Winter's Wolf is dead.' She stepped around me and went for the door.

'Silera, wait!' I grabbed her arm. Her skin was cold enough to burn. 'I'm sorry, but we both know that we can't go back to how things were. Everything's changed and we're different people. We need to learn who we are after all this time apart before we fall back into old patterns. You can't just show up in my life again and expect us to pick up where we left off.'

Rela took her hand back and cradled it to her chest. Her gaze was focused on the floor, her tone remote. 'What do you suggest then?'

A strand of hair had fallen in front of her face, and I raised a hand to brush it aside, promptly lowering it when she took a step back. 'I'm not saying I don't love you, Silera. You were the greatest joy of my life, and all my best memories have you in them. But your name is also tied to the worst moments.' She raised her head and opened her mouth, but I continued, 'I know it wasn't you. My head knows that' – I tapped my heart – 'but here, I'm still coming to terms with everything. If we want to have any kind of future together, we need to take it one day at a time.'

She said nothing for a moment, and then her face, normally so unguarded around me, shut down. Her eyes were steady and unaffected when they met mine. 'I better leave you to get ready then. We wouldn't want the Sentinel to wait any longer.' She opened the door without looking back at me, wholly silent. The soft click of the door shutting shattered the stillness of the room.

I felt sick as I stared at the closed door. What I'd said had been the truth. Despite the pain it caused, I wouldn't lie to Silera. Or myself. That thought, however, did little to ease the twisting of my stomach as I made my way to the shower. The hot water was heavenly on my skin, and I felt my battered body loosen and muscles relax.

I tried to escape Silera's words, focusing instead on what had happened with Oregon and the possibility of Elaine uncovering new information, but every time my mind found its way back to Silera. Her accusations were drilled deep into my mind, playing on repeat, telling me that I'm a coward. That I had never really left my life with the Fae behind. That I missed it. It wasn't true, was it? No, my life no longer revolved around going from danger to danger. I had changed. I had turned away from the violence, hadn't I? I slammed my fist against the shower wall. *Damn it.*

I quickly finished showering, hoping the negative thoughts would swirl down the drain with the water. I toweled off before throwing on a dark green flannel shirt and jeans, tugging on my boots and rushing downstairs.

Elaine was pacing the length of the dining room. She held a yellow manila folder in her hand. Sabine lay on her side, keeping an eye on the Sentinel. I stopped mid-step, noting the large Maine Coon cat who was sitting next to my dog.

'Tundra?' I mumbled. The cat took her time, finishing licking her paw, her white fur dusted with silver, before looking at me. Her icy blue eyes gave me a once over before she went back to grooming herself.

I scowled at her. Apparently, she was as pissed at me as her Princess was. I turned to Elaine and smiled at her before I was reminded of the reason she was here. My smile faded as quickly as it appeared. 'Did you get my message about the body?'

Elaine stepped forward and offered me a grim smile in return.'Yeah, thanks for the heads up.' She placed the folder on the table and took a seat as I settled across from her. 'I came here as soon as Devon got to the scene. I told Kane that I was going to check on a lead with one of my twitchy C.I.'s.'

I crossed my arms and stared at her. 'Yes, well, twitchy is my middle name. Though 'informant' is a new one – didn't anyone tell you that snitches get stitches? I can't offer you a bed again if you keep bringing trouble around here.'

Elaine grinned. 'I promise the only trouble I know of is Detective Kane, and he keeps strictly out of my bedroom.'

Suddenly, the temperature in the room plummeted, and I could see my breath condense in front of me. The slow staccato of heels on my wooden floor felt like hammers pounding in my chest. I looked over my shoulder to see that Rela had changed to a one-shoulder dark blue gown that split from mid-thigh downwards. A pair of silver earrings dangled from her ears. Her lips were painted a crimson shade of red, and her hair fell softly around her shoulders. She glided towards us with the liquid grace of the Fae. She arched an imperious eyebrow at me, and then bent down to scoop up Tundra before taking a seat next to me.

She turned her eyes towards Elaine and inclined her head. 'Sentinel Hughes.'

I cleared my throat nervously as I searched Rela's face for any hint of her emotions. 'Elaine, this is...'

'Princess Silera of the Winter Court.' She nodded towards Silera then turned to me. 'We've met actually; no need for introductions.' She gave me a wink, and I felt frost coating the left side of my body. 'As I was saying before, Devon will be performing the autopsy, but the preliminary cause of death is massive blood loss,' Elaine continued. 'From what he could determine at the scene, the victim had her heart and womb removed just like all the others. The cuts were made with surgical precision, and Devon is positive that the same person is responsible.'

My thoughts drifted to the girl we found. If she was like the others, then according to what Devon told me, she was still alive while they removed her organs. I shuddered. 'Can you tell me if the other locations where the bodies were found had patches of dead land around them?'

Elaine frowned. 'Dead land? What do you mean? It's the middle of winter, Nathan, all the trees look dead.'

'Winter doesn't kill the land, Sentinel,' Silera said as she slowly caressed the top of Tundra's head. 'Winter comes to give the land a reprieve to gather its strength after a good harvest. It might look dead to you, but life is gathering and vibrating beneath the surface.'

Elaine blinked slowly before inclining her head. 'My apologies.' She turned to me. 'What exactly are you talking about, Nathan?'

'The forest around the body was completely devoid of life and magic. It just felt *wrong,* as if someone had drained the vitality out of it while they were killing the victim.'

Elaine opened the manila folder and pulled out a map with several places marked in red. 'These are all the areas where a body has been found. We still don't know if the Woodland Ripper kills them there or just uses the locations as a dumpsite.'

She went over several sheets of paper until she found the one she was looking for. 'After we discovered we had a serial killer operating in our area, we contacted the local shifters, and they sent one of their people to the latest crime scene.' Her eyes darted over the page. 'He stated that he couldn't get a scent and left after a few minutes. Apparently, he couldn't bear being there any longer.'

'Shifters are creatures of the earth. Their nature is so closely linked to the land that they feel its spirit in their bones,' I said automatically. 'If something was wrong with it, they would have a deeper reaction than anyone else.' I blinked, not really knowing where that information had come from. Rela gave me a curious look before turning her attention back to the map.

Circled in red were Powell Butte Nature Park, Council Crest, Washington Park, Tryon Creek Park, and finally, the old Witch House, which, contrary to its name, was not supernatural in the least. I pointed to the map. 'I bet you anything that there's patches of dead land around these areas.'

Silera turned to me. 'Why don't you just check?'

'I don't have time to drive around to all of these places—'

"No,' Silera said, patiently while staring at me as if I were an idiot. 'You are the land's champion now, are you not?' Her tone was frigid. Yeah, she was still furious with me. 'As her chosen, you can tap into your connection with the Spirit.' She pointed a finger at me. 'Reach within you. If the land has been blighted as you say, the wrongness will call to you, grating through your bones and blood.'

Well, that sounded extremely pleasant and not at all painful. I sighed and closed my eyes, attempting to dive into the core of my power. It took several attempts – I really needed proper rest and food to recharge.

I let my mind quiet as I reached out with senses I wasn't used to having, feeling the hum of the trees and grass surrounding the inn. The saplings I had planted were brimming with life thanks to Julia, and I smiled slightly as I reached further out towards Council Crest. My smile faded as nausea rolled through me, the land there felt thick, poisoned, leaking corruption into the earth surrounding it. I moved to the next site, Tryon Creek Park, and felt the same thing. I checked each murder scene and felt sweat break out above my lip as I fought to observe the darkness only, not wanting any of it to reach me. 'I was right,' I panted, relinquishing my hold on Oregon's magic. 'There's a patch of dead land around every single one of them, exactly like the one around the Witch's House.'

Elaine studied the map a little closer. 'Those are leynodes,' she said, her tone giving nothing away. 'A number of ley lines make their way through this city which explains the overabundance of supernatural creatures here.' She traced a line on the map connecting the different areas. 'When several lines intersect with one another, it creates a node which can be used for many things. For example, you can draw magic from the pulse of the planet itself to cast powerful spells.'

'You can also use it to create a gate and bring through large numbers of creatures from Faerie, the spirit world, or any number of places at minimum cost to yourself,' Silera supplied as she continued to pet her cat. 'From what the innkeeper has described, it seems to me like this Ripper has completely drained the nodes of power. For what purpose, I don't know. But they haven't succeeded yet.'

So I was just 'the innkeeper' now? Gods, could this day get any worse?

Elaine looked at Silera intently. 'What makes you say that?'

'Because, Sentinel,' she said with a smile, 'if they had succeeded in draining all of the ley nodes dry, it would have sent a ripple through the very fabric of reality. They're not finished yet.'

'So, we have a killer who is working some world-ending spell and seems to have a grudge against mortals and witches.' I looked at Elaine. 'Did you get anything useful from Selenic when you went to visit him?'

She nodded and pulled out a picture of the symbol. I took it from her and examined it again as she filled me in. 'The only thing he had connecting it with witches is a brief mention in one of the grimoires about a witch from a thousand years ago named Arianwen of the Silver hair.' She pointed to the symbol. 'Selenic was ... indisposed when I went to visit him. But he did say that she was bad news, as in Sauron level bad news – his slurred words, not mine. He was going to do some research and get back to me.' My heart went out to the merman. I knew what it was like to drown in your own fear and trauma, but the inn had brought me back from that lonely place. I only hoped Selenic could do the same.

'Did you just say Arianwen of the Silver hair?' A voice asked behind us. 'Are you absolutely sure that's the right name?'

I turned around to see Patrizzia at the foot of the stairs. She had covered the fading bruises on her face with a touch of makeup, but I could still see her turn a shade paler beneath the powder. I motioned for her to join us. If my latest guest had any knowledge of these events, I needed to know.

'I've never heard of Selenic making a mistake.' Even if he was struggling at the moment, Selenic's knowledge was awe-inspiring. 'I don't know how long you were in town before you came to the inn, but there's been a series of killings for the last couple of months.'

Patrizzia snorted. 'You'd have to be dumb, deaf and blind not to know about the Woodland Ripper. Besides, I'd never go somewhere without researching it first.'

Patrizzia took a seat next to Elaine and looked at the symbol. 'The proper name for the creature that bears that symbol is Grisharu or Grishari if we're talking about more than one. It's an ancient and dreadful spell that dates back to when witchkind was at each other's throats.' She tapped the symbol with her nail. 'It was created by a black witch who wanted to exterminate the mágissa. This was her symbol.' She shook her head. 'If this is her, and she is picking up where she left off, then there's going to be a lot more bodies.'

Elaine looked at Patrizzia with renewed interest and a slight wariness tightened her mouth even as she kept her gaze fixed on the other woman. 'I have never heard of such a spell. It's not even in our records, and they're extensive. How do you know about it?' Elaine's tone was neutral, but I saw a hint of suspicion in her question. I shot her a look. The last thing I needed was her offending my guest.

'This is my history. Shared from mother to daughter through the ages,' Patrizzia said sharply and then shook her head. 'You wouldn't have heard about it because there are no records. It was deemed knowledge too dangerous to write down. Only the warning was passed on, generation to generation.' She took a deep breath, and when she spoke, her cadence took on a different tone as if she was trying to mimic someone. Maybe her mother? 'It was millennia ago, back when the blood of heroes still roamed the earth. The witch had a beautiful daughter, gifted in magic, but unlike her mother, whose magic was as black as a raven's feather, the child was pure of heart and soul. She used her powers for good and healed all those that came to her.'

Why did I have the feeling that this wouldn't be a 'they lived happily ever after' type story.

'Arianwen, as that was the mother's name, was proud of her child and let her run unrestrained. She could do no harm, and everyone in the village adored her.' Patrizzia shrugged. 'But, as the old saying goes, the sons pay for the sins of the father or, in this case, mother. One day, one of her enemies discovered the existence of her daughter and travelled to the village under the guise of an old man.' Elaine opened her mouth to interrupt, but a look from Patrizzia stopped her. 'The girl had lived a happy life thus far and had never known cruelty or deception, so she took the old man to her house. When the door closed, the mágissa sent his familiar to attack the girl. It tore her apart.

'Once Arianwen had learned of her beautiful daughter's fate, she was distraught with grief. It was said that her anger and pain was so great that the whole forest around her turned the color of coal, and the sky bled red,' Patrizzia continued. 'She tracked down the mágissa and tortured him for thirteen days and thirteen nights.'

I frowned. If someone had done such a thing to my child, I might've reacted in the same way. The sudden thought scared me. I forced my mind away and focused on the story.

'Arianwen inflicted so much pain that, by the end, the mágissa's mind lay broken. No one knows how she did it, but during those days, she managed to steal the mágissa's familiar and corrupted it to her will. Everyone thought the cruelty would end there. They were wrong.' She shook her head slowly. 'Her fury and pain could not be sated, and so she declared war on all mágissa. She would attack entire covens, rob them of their familiars and create her horde of Grishari. It's the reason why witchkind has been split into two camps for the last millennia. '

I cleared my throat. 'How did they stop her?'

'After years of terror, the mágissa came together for one last effort against the grieving witch. Some say their leader was a Scion of Hecate. Others say he was a mágissa who had broken through the restrictions of his kind and learned magic that was not granted by his familiar. No one knows for sure.' Oh, if they did, it would be too easy, wouldn't it? 'All that is known is that he led a bloody campaign against Arianwen, but she was too powerful and couldn't be killed. So, in a last-ditch effort, he sealed her away in a book while she was attempting a ritual to bring back her daughter.' Patrizzia turned her gaze towards me, and a feeling of foreboding slowly crept up over me, as if someone was reaching into my chest to squeeze my heart. 'It was during the fight with the witch that the mágissa realised when you killed a Grisharu, you would also kill the witch whose familiar had become corrupted. It was Arianwen's final revenge. They could rid the world of the Grishari and its corruption, but doing so would kill their clansmen.'

I stood up abruptly. My chair fell backwards with an audible thump that echoed through my chest.

The chimera.

The witches.

I had killed the witches.

# 14

'I'm sorry, what?' My voice came out harsher than I wanted, but the anger thrumming through my veins slipped past my filter.

Patrizzia looked at me, her eyes hard. 'This is a spell born out of grief, heartbreak and hate – the richest source for black magic. Once a familiar is stolen by this spell, the only thing left to do is kill the Grisharu before the dark magic can infect the mágissa too.'

'No.' I began pacing the length of the room. It was less of a denial than a plea. I didn't want to be responsible for the deaths of the coven members. There had to be another way to stop those creatures without killing the witches. There had to be.

'Magic is a balancing force,' Silera said with an approving nod in Patrizzia's direction. 'To take, one must give and vice versa. For example, ice is the absence of fire. I can create a spear of ice by pulling the heat out of the surrounding area.' Her frozen eyes thawed slightly as they took in my clear distress.

Elaine folded her hands in her lap. 'Merlin's first law states that every spell has a weakness, a chink in the armor that can be exploited.' She looked at Patrizzia. 'Just because in the past they couldn't figure it out doesn't mean we can't now.'

Patrizzia clenched her jaw, shaking her head at us. 'This isn't a simple hex like the one cast against your mágissa. I could break that with only a moderate amount of effort.' She slid her head into her hands, fingers curled tightly against her skin as she thought aloud, 'This is a curse born out of the pain of losing something more important to you than your life. Trust me, a spell born out of that can't be reversed or broken.' I shook my head, but she trained eyes filled with what looked like pity on me. 'There's nothing you can do for them but kill the Grishari and end their misery before they become as corrupted as their familiars.' She gathered her arms around herself. 'Hovering on the edge, being drained to fuel something terrible ... that's a fate worse than death. You know them better than me, what do you think they would want?'

I knew the answer, but that didn't mean I had to like it.

Patrizzia looked around at all of us and then, apparently having shared all she was able to, rose from the table and headed upstairs. I wondered if I was the only one who caught the look she gave Elaine before leaving the room.

The silence she left behind was strained. I turned to Elaine. 'We need to make sure that Patrizzia is right.'

'She is,' Silera said with no small amount of irritation. 'Whoever this witch is, she is trifling with the balance of life and death with no fear of the repercussions, Nathan. That is not something to take lightly. Nature *will* take its balance, one way or another.'

I pointedly ignored her. She didn't want me to get involved, especially now the stakes were higher than ever. But I was Oregon's champion. Nature was already disrupted, and I knew I had to do something before restoring balance became impossible. 'Leann said the witches were in their apartments, I just – I need to check, okay?'

Elaine stood up. 'This is an official investigation. You need to sit this one out.'

'Like hell I will.' I looked at her in disbelief. 'You might be part of the Assembly, but Oregon picked *me*.' I crossed my arms, impatience thrumming in my blood. I needed to get out of here and confirm what Patrizzia had said, one way or another. 'I'm going, and it's not up for negotiation. Things would've been a lot worse with the other

Grishari if I hadn't been there, so either get on board or get out of my way.'

Elaine assessed my hard eyes and tight jaw before she sighed and pulled a pair of car keys from her pocket. 'I'm driving.'

I turned to Silera, and she gave me an arched look. 'Julia has been running herself haggard trying to heal Leann, if you could...'

'I'll see what I can do, Innkeeper.' She stood up, carrying Tundra with her. 'Consider it payment for my stay.' She walked upstairs in silence.

I grimaced before turning back to Elaine. 'Ready to go?'

E laine drove us around the apartment block several times before parking at the back of the building. I tapped my foot quickly, slowly getting impatient as my eyes darted between the buildings, and the street lights began to light up. I needed to be out there already – reconnaissance was not my style.

'We don't know if the Grishari are here,' she had said sternly when I complained.

'As if safety is ever my top priority,' I mumbled to myself, but Elaine heard me.

'Maybe it should be.' I caught a hint of annoyance in her voice.

My magic prickled under my skin, I felt uneasy, like I was living history in the making. Ancient witches set free, terrifying creatures on the prowl. Not to mention the disaster I'd made of things between me and Silera. Then there were my dreams about the staff and crow; I hadn't been able to make heads or tails of them. I'd had prophetic dreams before – I just had to hope I could work out what they meant before it was too late. I rubbed my shoulders to ease the ache in them. Silera's healing magic was good, but it wasn't a miracle cure. I pushed thoughts of the princess away as Elaine finally stopped the truck and gave me the nod to get out.

If Patrizzia was right, I doubted the thousand-something-year-old witch was leaving the coven members unprotected, seeing as they were powering her creatures. If the blighted land around the mortal bodies was any indication, this witch was ruthless and would stop at nothing to get what she wanted.

'Are you coming?' Elaine called, jolting me out of my deep thoughts. I hurried to catch up with her, peering around cautiously.

Everything around us seemed normal, as if the huge battle a couple of days ago had never happened. 'Did you have something to do with this?' I motioned to the clean streets. The quietness felt unnatural, like the world was holding its breath, waiting for something to happen. It made the hairs on the back of my neck stand to attention.

'Apparently, the company producing the movie came by and tidied up the place.' She gave me a sardonic look. 'We need to work on your cover stories.'

'Well, it worked, didn't it?' I walked towards the front door of the building. The witches took the top floors for themselves while the bottom floors housed normie tenants.

I looked back to see Elaine, holding a golden staff in her hand. I arched an eyebrow at her and she shrugged. 'Sentinel-issue staff. Mortals can't see it.'

Handy. I would have to see about putting a charm like that on some of my weapons. I gathered my magic on the tip of my finger and drew a keyhole-shaped rune on the doorway. 'Oscaíl,' I whispered. The rune glowed with faint silver light before the soft click let me know that the door had unlocked.

I opened it and motioned for Elaine to enter first.

'My, what a gentleman.'

'I just figured you would give me a heads-up if something tries to eat you.'

She rolled her eyes, and I smirked as I walked inside, glancing at the elevators before shaking my head and heading for the stairs. 'The last thing we need is to get trapped in a metal box,' I explained to Elaine. Given my luck the last couple of days, the cables might snap for no reason and kill us. 'Besides, a little cardio never killed anyone.'

Elaine gave me a once over. 'Try to keep up.'

I made it to the top floor slightly winded and wiped the sweat off my forehead. Elaine snorted in my direction but didn't say anything. My knees were burning, but at least the stairs had been relatively risk-free. I stepped into the hallway and noticed that someone had boarded up the huge hole the chimera had made.

Who knew what state the witches would be in once we got inside the rooms? That is, if they were still— 'The production company, I take it?' I pointed to the board, trying to distract myself from my thoughts.

'Sorry, what was that?' Elaine cupped her ear with her free hand. 'I couldn't hear you over your labored breathing.'

I rolled my eyes at her. 'Leann told me that the chimera had broken through their defensive wards. Depending on the kind they used, they could still be down since no one had come to redraw them.' Or perhaps they were like mine, and once breached, drew the magic from the surrounding area to slowly regenerate. 'Give me a moment. I have a way to tell which are still warded without frying my brains.' Years ago, I had carved a pair of runes into my eyes that allowed me to see through illusions. I channeled my magic into the runes and whispered, 'Féach.'

The veil that hid supernatural from the mortals slipped away, and suddenly, I saw vibrant colours and eddying swirls of energy in the air. I shook my head and took a deep breath before letting it out slowly. It always took me a few seconds to get my bearings and adjust to the new reality after activating my eye runes.

Elaine gasped. 'Holy shit, your eyes are glowing silver.'

'It's just a little side effect.'

Elaine's gaze didn't leave my face, and I felt oddly naked as she dissected me. 'I've never seen it before.'

'So?'

'I've seen a lot, Nathan.'

I snorted. She might've seen a lot, but no mortal mage, even one of her caliber, could hope to decipher what even the greatest Sidhe nobles failed at – my magic too strange and unique even for them.

After a quick look around the hallway, I focused on the warded doors before me and noticed that all but four of them were protected. Black paw marks on the floor led to one of the unwarded apartments. I gave it a closer look and noticed that the doorframe was splintered in several places.

I frowned. Wards were simple yet versatile applications of magic, and you could set one up in an infinite number of ways. Most set up their ward to prevent a certain race, for example, a fae or a shifter, from entering a place. I was vaguer while setting up wards around the inn, creating ones that prevented anyone with hostile intent from crossing them.

Once in place, you needed to keep them charged like a battery, otherwise, they would weaken and eventually fade away. Unlike the unprotected doors, the wards around the other apartments were glowing with bright blue light. The magic moved and shifted like a flowing river. The coven was strong, their wards should have easily lasted over a week, yet some of the wards had already faded.

I pointed out the unprotected doors to Elaine. 'You take half, and I'll take the other?'

'You should be a cop,' she said and rolled her eyes before entering one of the apartments.

I walked toward the first unwarded door and stepped inside. My eyes immediately landed on one of the bright pictures hanging on the wall, and I felt a sharp stab of guilt sear through my chest as I recognised Leann. She was being hugged by her mother, Matilda. They were both smiling as if they hadn't a care in the world. Leann had lived with her mother, and it seemed like she hadn't changed anything since she died. Everything spoke of Matilda's taste, from the expensive furniture, through the grandiose velvet window curtains, to the collection of her photos in every corner of the room. It was like the apartment was a shrine to her.

'I'm sorry,' I said, pulling my eyes away from the picture. I focused my attention on the rest of the apartment and noticed a blinking red light. I frowned at the old but well-kept answering machine. It must be another item from Matilda that Leann hadn't or couldn't throw away.

I hit the button on the answering machine, and a woman's voice sounded loudly through the speaker. 'Would it kill you to have your phone charged, Leann? I've been calling your cell for the past hour so you could pick me up at the airport.' The voice paused, letting out an exasperated breath. 'Listen, I'm tired and don't want to wait anymore, so I'll be taking a cab home. You better make it up to me with a new hand-bag. I saw this cute one at the mall last time we were there, and you're totally buying it for me. See you in a bit.' The message clicked as it ended, I checked the caller ID.

'Well hello, Makayla.' I looked at the time stamp, it had only been ten minutes ago that she'd left the message.

Depending on the cab and traffic, she could be home in the next half hour. Good, the sooner I could get her to the inn, the better. Maybe I could save at least one witch while we figured out what was going on here.

There was nothing more to find in Leann's apartment and still time to check the other rooms before Makayla showed up, so I opened the second unwarded door without any issues and stepped inside a cozy looking apartment. A set of folded clothes sat on one of the couches, and a glass table by the kitchen had two cups sitting on top of it, like whoever lived here had stepped away for just a moment but hadn't returned. The whole place felt like someone had hit pause. I shook my head and sighed.

I made my way deeper into the apartment and turned to the first door on the right. Beyond was an altar with a statue of a three-headed woman holding a torch. It was clearly carved by someone with an exquisite eye for detail. I touched it, and the flames flickered, lighting up the room. Hecate, goddess of magic, crossroads and matron of witches. Not that her protection had made any difference, considering the current state of the coven.

Aside from the altar, there was nothing else in the room, so I moved on, only to find a bathroom. I opened the cabinet and saw a prescription bottle for one Gisela Watkins.

'So this is Gisela's place.' The creatures' first victim.

I closed the cabinet door and caught sight of my reflection. My eyes were glowing like molten silver. The runes I had carved into them while living with the Fae had permanently turned my blue irises gray. Activating them was like turning on a pair of headlights. My pale face seemed ghostly and hollowed, lifeless enough to belong in this apartment. The thought made me whip my eyes away from the mirror; I still had more rooms to search. My mind kept drifting back to my hollowed cheeks as I left the bathroom. I had really let myself go. For the last decade, I had always kept my hair short because long hair was the fashion of the Fae, and despite what the princess claimed, I was done with that part of my life. I cursed softly. It seemed that no matter how many distractions I found, I just couldn't stop thinking about my fight with Silera.

I went into another room, a bedroom decorated in earthy tones. A large canopy bed occupied most of the space, and lying atop it, like Sleeping Beauty, was a woman. I didn't recognise her, but it was possible this was Gisela. She looked to be in her early forties with shoulder-length black hair that framed a sophisticated face. A soft blue glow surrounded her body and cast an eerie light on her pair of red and blue pajamas. I couldn't detect the purpose of the magic, but it didn't *seem* harmful. The witch's breathing remained deep and slow like she was just sleeping.

I walked slowly towards her, half expecting her to spring up and yell at me to get out of her room. But she didn't. She looked peaceful in her sleep, but the stillness of the room, more precisely the lack of magical energy that should have been in a witch's house, was absent, except for the glow around her. Comatose patients usually needed several machines to keep their body alive, but the blue light surrounding her seemed to be taking care of all that as she looked clean and relatively cared for, like the spell was keeping her in some sort of stasis. This place wasn't a home anymore – it had become a tomb.

Gods. Patrizzia had been right. I focused on Gisela, trapped in eternal sleep, being used as a battery to power the Grisharu. Looking at her, no one would ever think that there was something wrong with her. Maybe that was the most hateful aspect of this spell. Unless you knew what was going on, you wouldn't think the victim needed help. I quickly looked over the room and made my way to Gisela's night table, where a book sat face-down like she was going to pick it up again at any moment.

I picked it up and opened it. Inside was a small dedication written in a feminine cursive letter. *To my wild Gisela. With love, Anastasia.* I flipped through the book, but it was in Greek. Of course it was. I looked at Gisela. 'Couldn't you make it easy for me? I'm trying to help.'

The witch continued her uninterrupted rest. I closed the book and put it back. Unlike the Fae who had the gift of tongues allowing them to speak and read any language perfectly, I had to do it the old fashioned way. I made it a priority to learn as many languages as possible since I had guests from all over the world, but my Greek was rusty at best. I also didn't think Arianwen would leave her diabolical plan just lying about.

I moved to the foot of the bed, where an old wooden chest stood on top of the cream colored carpet. It had a heavy iron lock but no magical protection. It was as if the moment Gisela went into her coma, she took all of her magic with her. It was consistent with what Patrizzia had told us about the spell draining her magic, though it wasn't the best news to know that an ancient witch was supercharged with the power of a coven. There had to be a physical mark for that link. Power like that needed focus – like my runes or Elaine's staff. Maria had been fine until the Swinekong had hit her with that tattoo.

'Sorry about this, but it's important,' I said to the witch as I strode back to her side. I raised both the arms and legs of her pajamas to inspect her for any marks. Nothing. I was debating whether to completely search her when something caught my eye. I raised her shirt over her belly button and swore. Just above her hip was a tattoo of a crooked mouth with two spears crossing below it.

I examined the mark carefully and tested it with my magic, but all I got was the same sense of wrongness that I felt from the forest. How could I save them without killing them? I prayed to every God I could name that the other witches would be different.

I left Gisela's apartment and entered the third unwarded room. There I found a woman with curly brown hair that had started to gray at the temples. After a quick search I found the same mark as Gisela and Maria. The next apartment was empty, so I ripped a few hairs from a brush in the bathroom and pushed them into a nearby plastic bag. Hopefully, Sabine or Elaine could help me track whomever they belonged to.

'Elaine!' I called out. She needed to know what I'd found, and I wanted to ask if she could trace the owner of the hairbrush. I walked into the hallway outside and found a middle-aged woman at the other end of the corridor.

Her silver hair was tied up in an elaborate bun, and her familiar dark eyes regarded me with equal parts curiosity and disdain as if I was a new insect that she had stumbled upon. She wore a flowing long-sleeved black blouse and jeans with six-inch stilettos. Had she walked up the stairs in those things? The only thing more impressive than that was the magic emanating from her; it was like nothing I had ever felt or seen before. Instead of a uniform color or a blend of two, her magic was a dark gray-purple miasma that radiated from her skin like heat off a scorching pavement. My eyes caught on the golden necklace draped around her neck, sporting a familiar design – a crooked mouth with two crossing spears beneath it.

'Elaine?' I called out again, certain that trouble was incoming.

'I've seen your actions through the eyes of my children,' the woman spoke with a crisp Welsh accent. 'You even succeeded in destroying one – though, of course, not unaided.'

'Arianwen, I presume?' I stood in the middle of the hallway, eying the doors. Where the hell was Elaine? 'Why are you attacking the coven?' I asked, stalling. She was a thousand years old at least. There was no way I could match magic like that.

Arianwen tilted her head to the side, ignoring my questions. 'Are you their protector?' She shook her head as if dismissing herself. 'No, you would've come to their defense much sooner.' She gave a warped smile. 'I have no desire to waste my power on you. This is not your battle. I will give you this one chance: walk away.'

I arched an eyebrow at her. 'I owe a debt to their leader. So, I'll ask again, what is your business with the coven? Why send those creatures after them?' Another thought occurred to me. 'Are you attacking and ravaging those mortal women too? They had no affiliation with the coven. What purpose are they serving?'

Her face took on an eager expression. Where the *fuck* was Elaine? 'You're a fool to ignore my warning. I can see Nature's spirit burning within you, making you bold. Do you think you can best me?' She chuckled to herself. 'I see men haven't changed; you're as arrogant as that king who took everything from me. I had thought to save the bloodshed for later, but I'll make an exception for you. However, since you have proven yourself useful to me, I will grant you the courtesy of a quick death.' She smiled delicately, but I couldn't help but notice the razor edge of cruelty to it. 'After all these years, I finally have everything I need to see my daughter's face again. Thanks to you, Nathaniel Mercer.' My blood chilled. I definitely didn't like that she knew my name. Names had a lot of power in the supernatural community. If she knew that, what else did she know about me?

She waved her hand in the air, and a stag shimmered into existence between us. It looked similar to Maria's familiar, but it looked just as corrupted as the other Grisharu. Its eyes flashed dark to match Arianwen's, and I glanced about quickly for an escape route. Instead of being the embodiment of nature, it looked just like the other monsters I had seen; a crown of razor-sharp antlers oozed black sludge onto the floor, and its whole body was covered in spiky quills. Dark gray mist seeped from the Grisharu's mouth. I stared, horrified, as its muzzle split like a Venus Fly Trap and from inside its cavernous mouth, a pair of tentacles shot forth lined with jagged teeth.

I felt my mouth go dry looking at the horrific monstrosity. '*Elaine!*'

# 15

The Grisharu let loose a terrifying screech as its tentacles charged at me. Arianwen gave me a cruel smile before walking away. I wanted to stop her, but the rampaging beast had other plans. Seeing this Grisharu through my runic vision was a completely different experience. Revulsion rolled through me as I watched its aura leaking out of it like a poison infecting the air. This was an abomination of nature. I had to take it out. I channeled my magic towards my pendant. 'Armúr ar!' It grew hot around my neck as the runes ignited, and my armor spread over my body, wrapping itself around me.

The black material was flexible, which came in useful as I dodged a tentacle swiping out at me. The silver dwarvish script engraved on it glinted in the faint light seeping around the edges of the boarded-up window, and I swore as a tooth caught me on the shoulder before sliding smoothly away. It was similar to the combat armor used by SWAT and, thankfully, was resilient, the tooth having left not so much as a tear.

The magic in the armor responded to my will, conjuring a two-foot-wide blue shield, sizzling with energy. The Grisharu reared its tentacles back and slammed them against my shield; sparks flew upon contact. I didn't have time to fully admire the shield before the creature charged.

The Grisharu hit me like a bullet train and knocked me backwards several feet, the breath leaving my chest in a *whoosh*. My head slammed into the floor, and stars bloomed across my vision. There was a faint metallic taste in my mouth, and I groaned when something had wrapped itself around my ankle.

Vivid colours swirled before my eyes, and the hallway began to spin like crazy as the Grisharu whipped me up and around, slamming me against the ceiling with one dark mottled tentacle covered in a slimy, viscous ooze. I scrambled to raise my shield between me and the incoming monster as it threw me back down and then up, trying my best not to spew my breakfast everywhere. My forearms groaned as the Grisharu pressed me harder against the ceiling, and for a moment, I feared they might break. The pressure stopped as suddenly as it started, but the feeling of relief didn't last long as the monster yanked me sideways and *through* one of the warded doors into an apartment. My ears rang as I hit the warded door, the world deafened to only the piercing ringing sound of the wards complaining before all the sound came rushing back, making my temples throb.

The ward flashed with violent aquamarine light that sent a stab of nausea through me. Suddenly a torrent of water gushed from the wards as they activated, quickly filling the space as if the gates of a dam had been blown wide open. The salty water entered my mouth and nose. Anger rose in my chest as my lungs filled. *No! I wasn't going to die here.* The tentacle around my ankle vanished, and a hum crackled in the air behind me as I realised belatedly what the Grisharu must have already sensed: the other wards were awake, and they were ready to fight. The apartment began to quickly fill with water, and I struggled to rise as a wave swept towards me and pinned me to the ground.

I pushed up on wobbly feet, slipping several times before pushing into the hall while the water quickly rose above my thighs. The surge from the wards raged on as my heart pounded in my ears. The only plus-side was that the Girsharu was in the same tough spot as me. The water had battered the corrupted familiar, drenching its quilled hide and pressing it against a wall of the corridor. Black blood flowed from its maw as it retracted its tentacles inside.

I channeled my magic towards Fjall's charm on my wrist. 'Ag Fas!' The hammer grew in size, and I exhaled deeply at the comforting weight of a weapon in my hand. I turned towards the Grisharu, brandishing Fjall at it. Pain wracked my sides, but I pushed through it and grinned. 'That's right, you tentacled freak, come and get some!'

The beast's eyes flashed darkly before it turned around and rammed its huge body through the wooden window-covering that its brother had leapt through the previous day, jumping outside. Broken pieces of wood splashed into the water as it began to flow through the hole. My grip on Fjall slipped as the liquid swept me off my feet. I tried to hang on to the door frame, but my muscles groaned from the strain. The current was simply too strong. From one of the unwarded rooms, Elaine was washed out and towards the opening – *shit*. All of the wards must have tripped each other if she was being flooded out. I let go of the door frame, and the water forced me towards her.

'Nathan, what the hell?' she spat out some water as I wrapped my arm around her waist. The opening loomed towards us as we gained speed.

'No time, hang on!'

The water shot us out into the air. For a moment, I sympathized with Wile E. Coyote and how he must have felt right before he fell off that cliff for the thousandth time. Then gravity kicked in, and my heart sped up as we plummeted to the ground. I pulled Elaine closer to me with one hand and drew a rune in the air as quickly as I could with the other – a triangle with two lines crossing it at the top. 'Gaoth!'

I closed my eyes and sent a silent prayer to the Morrigan, begging to be left at least battle-worthy after the fall. I couldn't let that beast run around my city freely. A column of wind shot from my hand, crashing into the ground below, the force of it slowed our descent, but we were still falling too quickly. I pushed Elaine on top of me, taking the brunt of the hit as we crashed into the sidewalk with a thud. Pain racked my body in waves, and I could taste blood.

I looked at Elaine to see how hurt she was. She groaned in pain and pulled away from me. 'That's the last time I follow your lead.'

'We're alive, aren't we?' I struggled to my feet as pain lanced through my body in one continuous wave.

The corrupted familiar was on its feet, gray blood mixed with the black ooze dripping from its antlers. The beast looked only slightly worse for wear as if jumping out of a three-story building was child's play. Fjall laid on the ground between us, out of reach. A rattling sound caught my attention as the quills covering the creature's fur rustled for a moment before a hail of them shot towards us. Damn it all to hell! Of course he could shoot the bloody things.

I raised my wobbly arm, using magic to shape it into a tower shield big enough to protect the both of us. The spikes struck with such force it felt like getting hit with a baseball pitched by an angry dragon. The shield sparked with energy but held against the barrage. Elaine wiped some blood from the corner of her mouth, and I eyed her with concern.

'Keep that thing up a little longer, I'm going to get us some help,' Elaine said as more sparks flew from my shield. Its edges began to fade, and sweat poured down my face as I forced energy I didn't have into reinforcing it.

'Easy for you to say. Hurry it up!' I growled.

She took several steps back and slammed her staff on the concrete. 'Armis simiae!' Magic swirled around her in a navy-colored typhoon, cracks appearing on the sidewalk to form a circle of arcane glyphs. Above the Grisharu a hole in the dimensions appeared with a grating tearing sound. A large shadow flew through the air, slamming its four arms downwards into the unsuspecting monster's head. The beast howled and spun, searching for its attacker. I rushed forward and grabbed Fjall. With my hammer safe in hand, I looked up and gaped.

Elaine's Summon reminded me of an orangutan, if orangutans were eight feet tall, covered in orange hexagon-shaped scales and had four long arms that were currently pummeling the Grisharu's head. The Summons's wide oval face roared in rage as it unleashed itself on the corrupt familiar with unrelenting fury. A piece of its antlers broke, falling to the ground.

The Grisharu let out a sound of pure hate. It slammed its head into the Summon's stomach, pushing it towards the other side of the street, crashing into a street sign that bent under its weight. I sprang forward, using the Summon as a distraction. Thunder rang through the night, and I could feel bones crushing underneath my hammer as it connected with the beast's shoulders.

The orangutan was back on its feet and jumped into the air, grabbing the Grisharu by its flanks and hurling it straight into a silver Mercedes parked several feet away from Elaine. Glass exploded from the windows as the creature landed on the roof, metal crumpling around it. The beast struggled to get up, causing even more damage to the car. I winced in sympathy for the owner.

Elaine tapped her staff on the ground once again, and the circle beneath her lit up with a midnight glow.

'Velamen Sphera.' Her voice vibrated with power. Above her the air cracked in a spiderweb pattern before a navy ball of light shot out. The light dimmed as the crack vanished, revealing a puffy ball of fur with triangular ears and a long fluffy tail. The whole thing was about the size of a tennis ball. The ball floated towards Elaine and rubbed itself against her face. She smiled, petting it back. 'I need some cover; think you can do that, Velka?'

The puff-ball let out an excited chirp and expanded to the size of a bowling ball. My eyes widened as Velka opened its mouth, and a stream of mist snaked out of it, covering the street and isolating us from the rest of the world.

I shook my head. 'And look at me without my pokedex. I knew I shouldn't have left it at home.'

Elaine gave me a scalding look. 'I will not have you compare a Class 3 Concealment Globe and Class 1 Armor Simian to a children's cartoon show.'

'How about we discuss that after we take care of this thing, okay?' I pointed Fjall in the direction of the Grisharu.

The orangutan regarded me with mild interest before focusing back on the Grisharu, who apparently had given up on pulling itself out of the car. A black mist covered the entire length of the vehicle, spreading out from the beast, and continued to expand. It felt the same as the wrongness Arianwen and the bodies had reeked of, raising the hair on my arms. I didn't know what the creature was doing, but it sent shivers down my spine. I ran towards it, knowing the darkness could mean nothing good. The orangutan sailed through the air beside me, towards the cloud of darkness that crackled with purple lightning that repelled the Summon back with unrelenting force.

Light pierced through the Grisharu's hideout and tore apart the black cloud. The Mercedez was just a piece of scrap metal at the beast's feet. It had grown to ten feet tall, twice as muscular, and with no sign of the injuries it had sustained. Somehow Arianwen must have fed her creature more power, healing it and making it stronger. She wanted us dead. Badly.

'Come on! Really?!' I turned towards Elaine. 'We need to take that thing out as fast as possible and find Arianwen. She must still be close by if she's able to channel that much power into this thing.'

I spun as a rumbling noise pierced the air and saw only an orange blur as Elaine's Summon moved in front of me, deflecting the piece of Mercedes the Grisharu had launched. Elaine practically vibrated with power as she tapped her staff to the ground and commanded, 'Kill it.'

The orangutan pounded its chest with its four arms and hurled itself at the corrupted familiar. I swore under my breath and raced to follow it. The creature's tentacles, now doubled in quantity, launched themselves at the Summon and wrapped themselves around it. The beast's teeth tried to dig deep into the orangutan's flesh, but its scaly hide was more than adequate protection. The orangutan let out a guttural noise and ripped the tentacles apart, freeing itself. I swung Fjall with all my strength while the Grisharu was distracted, aiming for one of the beast's legs. If only we could get it down, killing it would be easy.

Its hooves came down on me, quills quivering even as the Summon pummeled its head. I instinctively raised my shield, and the monster slammed into me. Sparks of magic crackled from the shield and through my body. I bit back a scream as I felt my arm break. Pain flashed bright and hot inside me, and my arm hung useless at my side. I tried to run now that I could no longer hold up my shield, but the creature was too quick, slamming its head against me.

Time flowed like molasses, and I knew if it hit me again, I was dead. My blurry eyes found Elaine and watched seemingly in slow motion as her mouth opened, shouting my name in alarm. I tried to rally my magic into another shield and almost puked with effort as my armor flashed with indigo light, and an orb of energy coalesced around my entire body. The Grisharu's head connected with it, and I felt myself becoming almost weightless as I flew through the wall of fog, crashing into the metal railings of the cemetery on the other side of the street.

Black spots danced across my vision. I tried to catch my breath, but a heaviness settled on my chest as if an elephant had stepped on me. Gods, it hurt like hell. The blue glimmer of the shield sparked and fluttered away, its energy spent. No matter what Kathour wanted in the future, he was going to get it. This armour had just saved my life. I slowly got up, cradling my broken arm to my chest. I looked down and saw my forearm was bent at an unnatural angle, warm blood coursing down the length of it. I stumbled my way back through the fog, trying to run, but my battered body was screaming at me that it was time to lay down and rest. I told it to shut up.

I passed through the fog and saw the Grisharu lower its head and charge at the Summon. It was on the ground, black sludge from the Grisharu's tentacles in its eyes. I drew upon my dwindling reserves of magic, using Fjall as a stylus, and carved a pair of intersecting lightning bolts in the air. I poured the remainder of my power into it, but it seemed to be barely enough to fuel a lightbulb. The rune was pale, too weak to inflict any serious damage.

*Fuck.*

Out of the corner of my eye, I saw Elaine standing in the circle of her magic, pouring more power into the orangutan. Her hands held her staff in a white knuckle grip, the ape for his part moaning weakly as it tried to stand up to get out of the way before it fell back to the ground.

Oregon's voice whispered in my ear. *Take heart, my champion, for we are one always and forever.* A deluge of power poured into me, filling me up to the brim. *What's mine is yours and what's yours is mine.* I gripped Fjall harder and channeled everything Oregon gifted me into the rune.

The rune flared with fluorescent silver light. Magic drenched the air around me as the blue night sky darkened, turning the area pitch black. Thunder rolled across the sky as if an angry God had awakened from its slumber. Streaks of light penetrated the darkness, and I could feel my blood sing in cadence with the magic. Suddenly, the lightning bolt rune began to shift and twist into itself, darkening from pure silver color to a dark burgundy. Sweat began to pour down my body, evaporating instantly as the temperature around me continued to rise.

The lines of the rune twisted and broke apart again, this time taking the shape of a crow wreathed in flames with bright crimson eyes, just like the one from my dreams. It pulsed like a heartbeat, and for a second, I thought it was alive.

A perfect circle of asphalt beneath it melted, bubbling like black bean soup. I looked down at my armor and almost cried out. The black metal was glowing cherry red. I braced myself for the pain of burning flesh, but it never came. Whatever was happening with my rune wasn't hurting me, or maybe the armor was just that good. Fjall had also begun shining like a red poker, the heat it exuded licking uncomfortably at my skin. What the hell was going on?

The smell of burnt rubber clogged my throat and nostrils, making it difficult to breathe. Magic swelled inside me, growing, expanding, demanding to be released. My body groaned with the strain of the increasing pressure. I wanted to pass out, to escape from it, but my senses were going into overdrive, and I couldn't focus.

I could see everything around me with crystal clarity. The crow was not just made of magic; it was formed from countless miniature balls of flames that blended together into a beautiful yet powerful force, waiting to be unleashed. The steady drumming of my heart blasted in my ears like the footsteps of a giant, and the rush of blood flowing through my body sounded like a maelstrom. There was a sweet taste in my mouth, an interesting mix of blackberries and apples. Strange yet comforting.

The Grisharu had stopped its charge and turned towards me. Eyes wide with fear as they landed on the rune, the irises glowing the same dark coffee color as Arianwen's once more. The Grisharu pawed at the asphalt with its hoof, and black ooze began to flow from its antlers in

139

large quantities, covering its entire body. Letting out a loud shriek, the monster took a running charge towards me.

The crow saw the incoming attack, spread its fiery wings, and opened its beak. A roar like a forest fire emanated from it. The pressure inside me continued building, threatening to blow me to pieces if I didn't release it. From the crow's song, I heard a single word loud and clear. I fought with everything I had to simply open my mouth.

'Lasair!'

The word exploded out of me, leaving a coppery aftertaste behind. Time slowed to a crawl, and the dark sky suddenly lit up as a pillar of white flames descended onto the crow, bathing it in searing heat. I fell to the ground like a sack of bricks. I wanted to look away but couldn't; my body was devoid of strength.

The crow took flight towards the Grisharu. The entities clashed, foul crooked magic against this ancient-feeling creature of light. The Grisharu tried ramming the crow with its antlers, but the living rune let out another cry, and its flamed body ignited like a forest fire, pushing it back. Tongues of flames fell upon the Grisharu like a meteor shower, burning away the ooze that was protecting its hide. The creature shrieked, trying to replenish it, but the crow was burning it faster than it could be produced.

'My god, Nathan, what did you do?' I heard Elaine say as she ran towards me and helped me sit up. 'Oh shit, your arm.'

The Grisharu tried to wrap its tentacles around the crow's body. The second they came into contact the flames flared once more, burning the appendages to ash. The crow flapped its wings and sank inside the beast.

The Grisharu staggered forward a couple of steps before it burst into a pillar of white flames that reached into the sky. An inhumane sound came from the creature as the flames bathed its body. It was unlike anything I'd ever heard before. Amidst the roar of the flames and terrible moans, I could distinctly hear the cry of a woman. I frowned, trying to make sense of what was going on, but my vision was growing blurry, and I could feel myself falling into unconsciousness.

The pillar of light vanished. The only thing that remained of the

Grisharu was a charcoal statue, a gentle breeze blew from nowhere, and the monster crumbled to ash. As darkness crept up on me, I could've sworn I saw three distinctive figures appear in the sky: a floral stag, a porcupine made of precious gems, and a translucent octopus. Just as I was wondering if I had stepped into some kind of Looney Toons episode, Elaine shoved something into my mouth.

It felt like getting a shot of double espresso. 'Come on, tough guy, you can't pass out now.'

I blinked a couple of times. 'What did you give me?'

'Just an emergency pick-me-up, it will give you a boost of adrenaline and numb your pain receptors,' she explained as she helped me stand. 'Sentinels use it as a last resort, now shut up and let my Summon carry you to the car.'

# 16

The roads were dark and empty as we drove back towards the inn. Now that the adrenaline of the fight had left my body, everything hurt. I had retracted my armor back into its pendant form, and with Elaine's help, had ripped my shirt and turned it into a makeshift sling. The armor had definitely saved my life, but I had overestimated its energy reserves.

Elaine put in another call to the Sentinel HQ requesting a clean up at the apartment building while I tried not to pass out from the pain. My vision blurred, and I closed my eyes as the headlights of oncoming cars started to make my head throb. It wasn't the first time I'd dealt with pain like this. It undoubtedly wouldn't be the last.

My thoughts wandered back to the Fae. I had lived most of my life with them. Hell, I didn't even know how old I was. My earliest memory was cowering in fear in some dark corner of the palace kitchens, hiding from the chefs that used human children as tasters for their latest concoctions. Fae food played havoc with the human body as we aren't equipped to digest magic-rich fruits and meats. More often than not, one of the children would take a single bite before falling dead on the floor – if they were lucky. If they survived without sprouting a third arm or growing scales all over their body, then they would face the same ordeal again and again.

The kitchen wasn't the worst that could've happened to human servants. Some were tortured for seemingly no reason. Others were used in magical experiments or turned into all manner of creatures for the amusement of the Sidhe. For some reason, I was one of the lucky ones that didn't sprout wings or die on the spot. Once my magic awakened, I became an oddity among the servants, like a dog who had learned to do a summersault. So unique, a noble took an interest and groomed me to be his hidden weapon.

In all my life, there had only been two fae that I could genuinely say I cared for. Basant, my brother in arms with a life possibly as bad as mine ... and Silera. She had taken an interest in me after a bloody massacre in Winter and requested my services as her personal guard. One thing led to another, and before I knew it, I had fallen head over heels for the Princess. Even crazier, she reciprocated my feelings. We began a forbidden relationship up until the moment one of my men betrayed me and left me for dead in a place worse than hell.

At the time, I was happy with my lot in life because I didn't know any better. There I was, human vermin sharing laughter and forbidden meetings with the Princess of two fae courts. Silera's heritage from the Autumn court gave her a set of magical abilities that no winter fae would ever dream of having, but it also raised her status to unobtainable heights.

At first, I had thought she was just amused with her latest human slave because that's exactly what I was. One with a particular set of skills that made the Fae wary around me, but a slave nonetheless. Humans were not allowed to eat with the Fae, look them in the eye or speak unless spoken to. And those were just the useful ones.

I didn't realise how unhealthy the power imbalance in my relationship with Rela was until I moved in with Cassius and Ava after escaping the fae court. They took me in and taught me how to live as a human for the first time in my existence. And, after spending years interacting with Devon and Alice, it dawned on me that a couple had to be equals for a relationship to work.

That's why I couldn't just go back to being with Rela. Why I had said those things to her and would say them again if I had to. Even though she had never treated me as someone beneath her during the time we were together, we couldn't escape the reality of our statuses. She even had to brand me, claim me as her property, to keep the rest of the Fae away from me. I shifted in my seat. Now that I had my own place away from the eyes of her people, it would be so easy to pick up where we left off, regardless of what anyone else thought. But then we would be doing the same thing as before, hiding. I didn't want that. I would never bow my head to fae, any fae, ever again.

And then, of course, there was the biggest issue with our relationship: the attempt on my life. Even though I knew now that she didn't have anything to do with it, it was impossible to automatically continue loving someone after spending a decade trying to hate them. Since learning the truth, I'd been wondering who could've told Galesh, the knight who left me for dead, about my relationship with the princess and what they had stood to gain by taking me out of the picture. As far as anyone knew, I was just the captain of her guard. Silera was a force to be reckoned with, trained by her mother to one day take the throne. If they were trying to attack the princess by removing me, they would have failed.

The only conclusion was that someone wanted to emotionally weaken her or retaliate for some slight by taking me out of the picture. The only clue I had was that it was a princess who gave the order. Sadly, that didn't narrow things down since there were dozens of those in Faerie.

'Nathan, we're here.' Elaine's voice pulled me away from my thoughts, and I looked up to see the familiar building. I was home.

With Elaine's help, I managed to get up the front steps without collapsing. The door opened, and Roel stared at us with wide eyes.

'Shit, boss, what the hell happened to you?' He looked behind him, 'Julia! Nathan is hurt!' He grabbed my other side and let me lean my weight on him.

'Careful with his arm, kid,' Elaine said as we slowly walked inside.

'Sure thing, I got it.' He settled me down on the couch. 'Damn, boss, you look like someone dropped a building on you.' I looked down at myself. My wet clothes had dried a little on the way over, but I was still covered with blood and some of the Grisharu's black ooze.

I leaned my head back and tried to smile but even that hurt. 'Not the *whole* building...'

Hurried steps caught my attention, and I turned to see Julia and Silera walking towards us. Sabine darted between them and jumped on the couch. She started sniffing me all over before letting out a bark.

I snorted. 'You're probably right. If I had taken you with me I wouldn't be in this mess.'

'What in Hades' name did you do to yourself now, Nathan?' Julia asked as she started prodding my chest with her fingertips. I winced and tried to move away from her.

'Ouch, careful.' I jumped as she felt my ribs. 'I'm a little tender in places.'

Rela turned to Elaine with a scowl. 'What happened? I thought you were going to check a residential place?'

Elaine took a seat in one of the chairs. 'We were, but then we were attacked by one of the Grishari and Arianwen herself, according to Nate.' She saw Rela opening her mouth so she raised her hand and cut her off. 'I didn't see her myself. I was exploring one of the apartments when the whole place flooded, and next thing I knew, we were flying out of a window.'

I snorted. 'I'm shocked you didn't hear the Grisharu beating me into a pancake.'

Elaine frowned in deep thought. 'Yeah, me too. I wouldn't be surprised if the apartment I was in had a silence spell on it.'

Rela arched an eyebrow at me but otherwise remained coolly silent.

Sabine barked at me again. I turned to her and let out an exasperated breath. 'Hey, not all of us can phase through solid matter. And yes, I will take you with me next time so you can be responsible for my health. There – happy?'

'You got all of that from one bark?' Roel asked.

'He coincidentally left out the part where she called him an idiot for

145

going out when he was low on magic with only a single mage for back-up,' Silera said, her tone cold.

Elaine glared at her, magic swirling around her. 'If you have something to say, Princess, say it. Don't use the dog as an excuse.'

Rela shrugged lightly. 'I was merely translating what the Guardian said.'

'Wait, wait, wait.' Roel raised his hand. 'Are you saying that Sabine can actually talk and that you two can understand her?' His eyes jumped between me and Silera. 'I always thought that was just Nathan being his weird-ass self.' He then looked at me with an apologetic smile. 'No offense, boss.'

'Would all of you shut up. I'm trying to heal the idiot here,' Julia snapped. She opened my shirt and placed her hands on my chest. A soft, warm glow emanated from them, spreading through my whole body. She shook her head. 'You have a broken arm, at least three cracked ribs, torn muscles, several cuts, and that's just from a cursory search. Not to mention your magic is practically non-existent.' She moved her hands away. 'Dryadic magic is good for stimulating the body's own healing process but knowing you, you probably want to be up and mobile as soon as possible, and I can't do that.' She turned to Silera expectantly.

Rela crossed her arms and looked me straight in the eyes. 'Are you regretting your choice to help them?'

I gritted my teeth against the pain. 'You know the answer to that.' Her glacial eyes softened a faction. 'I owed it to Matilda to make sure her daughter lives. I owed it to Leann because I couldn't save her mother, and now I owe it to the witches I killed.' Her eyes narrowed. I held her gaze and continued, 'So no regrets, even if it kills me.'

Rela shook her head. 'Stubborn fool.' She brushed her fingers over my chest, her skin frigid to the touch. 'This will hurt.' Her palm ignited with orange flames.

'I gave him something to numb his pain receptors so he shouldn't feel anything, but given the extent of his injuries, it will only help so much,' Elaine said.

At first, all I could feel was my heart hammering in my chest at having Rela so close to me. Then warmth started spreading through my battered frame. The feeling grew hotter, rawer, as if I had taken a dip in a bath of menthol. Numbed my pain receptors, my ass. My skin felt raw and exposed, and I clenched my fist as Silera poured more magic into me. My bones felt like they were being immersed in molten metal, and my blood boiled inside me. Sabine patted my thigh with her paw.

'You're going to be the death of me,' I said through clenched teeth as another pulse of searing heat flared through me. I groaned. 'You did that on purpose.'

'I'm trying to repair the substantial damage you administered to your body. Perhaps, if you had a little more care, I would not constantly have to patch you up.' She placed her other hand on my shoulder. 'Now, be silent.'

As if I could talk with her torturing me. Damn it. She was going to finish what Arianwen started. 'I thought healing magic was supposed to feel good.'

Julia turned to Roel. 'Did you finish gathering the ingredients?'

Roel shook his head. 'I was about to head out when Nathan arrived.'

'Then you should get going. You only have a couple of hours.' Julia pointed to the door. 'Take Nathan's truck, the back should have enough space for everything you need.'

Roel nodded and gave me a thumbs-up before leaving. I tried to turn to Julia, but Rela's hands held me in place. 'Take Nathan's truck where? What's going on?' Suddenly, it felt as if lava pulsed through my chest. 'Ouch! What the hell Silera?! Are you *trying* to boil me alive?'

'I said be silent.' Her tone held so much steel, I instantly quieted.

'How come it didn't hurt this bad when you healed me before?' I grumbled a moment later.

She regarded me with a stoic expression while sending another wave of heat that concentrated around my ribs. I felt myself jump on the couch. 'The more you move and speak, the longer it takes.'

'Nathan, just let Silera heal you.' Julia picked up Sabine and scratched her behind the ears. My dog gave me a happy doggy grin, not the least bit worried that her owner was getting barbecued in front of her. 'After you left, she went to Leann and helped her considerably. The damage from the venom was extensive, but we are optimistic she will make a full recovery in a couple of days. Though, I have to say, Leann didn't make as much fuss as you.'

I opened my mouth to say something, but I felt Rela's grip tighten, her eyes focused on me. I clenched my jaw and remained quiet.

'Also, I had a chat with Patrizzia, and she agreed to lift the hex on Roel,' Julia continued. 'She had some conditions, and I said you would be okay with them.'

I wanted to ask what the conditions were, but instead, I shrugged with a wince. It didn't really matter. We were going to need all the fighters we could get, regardless of Patrizzia's price. Plus, I trusted Julia. She wouldn't have promised something I couldn't give.

Silera's hands flickered with light for a second longer before she removed them. The heat from her magic lingered on my skin then slowly ebbed away. 'I managed to heal your physical state to the best of my abilities. Your magical reserves, however, are a different matter.' She stepped away to stand by Julia, who had finished tending to Elaine. 'You will need proper rest and food to regain your strength. I advise you not to move for the next hour to let your body recuperate from the healing.'

I let out a deep breath, trying to get my heartbeat under control. 'Your efforts are appreciated,' I said. It was the closest you could come to thanking one of the Fae. Silera nodded slightly, her eyes never leaving my face.

I sat up and looked at the women in the room. 'Well, I can definitely confirm that the thousand-year-old witch is up and about.' I recounted the events of my conversation with Arianwen to them. 'She's furious and has an axe to grind with the whole world.' I turned to Rela. 'You were right. She isn't done, and whatever her end goal is, she didn't want to waste any of her power killing me.'

Elaine frowned. 'If she caused all this death and destruction while saving power, how much worse will she be when she no longer limits herself?'

# 17

The room seemed tense, charged with dread as Elaine's words hung in the air. I shuddered at the thought of what Arianwen might be capable of when fully unleashed.

'Elaine, can you contact Hope and see if she can call for a general mobilization of the Assembly?' I asked, knowing that as the head of the Oregon branch, she had that ability. 'I'm sure with the full force of the Assembly, we can take her, although we still don't know how many Grishari Arianwen controls. We already killed two that were each made up of three familiars, and given that a conventional coven is made up of thirteen witches and that we know Leann is alive, that must leave three potential Grisharu.'

'Is Leann awake? Maybe she can fill us in,' I asked Julia, then paused when something occurred to me. 'Elaine, can you send some Sentinels to check if Makayla arrived at her house? She was on the way right before the witch sucker punched us.'

Elaine nodded and pulled out her phone, texting someone, and Julia shook her head at me in answer. 'Not right now. The healing session really took its toll on her. I doubt anything short of an explosion would wake her up.'

'I can call an emergency meeting, but the general mobilization has to be approved by the High Circle,' Elaine said, tapping her fingers on her staff. 'Some in the Circle would view the evidence we have and rule that Arianwen hasn't targeted any mages, so it's out of their jurisdiction.'

'I wouldn't bother with them if I were you,' a voice said, and we all turned around to see Patrizzia standing in the hallway, a glass of water in her hand. 'Mages only care about policing their own. Why else would they take so long to act when the mágissa were being attacked?'

Elaine frowned. 'That's not true, not for all of us. Hope cares about all of the supernatural community, and many follow her example, myself included.'

Patrizzia walked into the living room, her gaze trained on the sentinel. 'Yet to move on an actual threat to the supernatural community, you need to call an emergency meeting, explain the situation and then have a vote.' She shook her head. 'And even then, it would probably result in nothing.' The witch turned from Elaine dismissively and gave me a once over. 'So you saw Arianwen?'

Elaine opened her mouth to argue when a buzzing sound interrupted her. She pulled out her phone. 'Give me a moment. This is important.' She left the room.

I nodded. 'We had a small chat before she set one of her beasties on me.' The pain from the fight and the healing had dulled to a simmering ache, and my eyelids felt like they were made of lead. 'She said she was saving herself for something and that she had finally found what she was looking for because of me. Do you have any idea what she's after?'

'Not really.' Patrizzia frowned. 'All I know about her is what I already told you. She must be recreating the ritual to resurrect her daughter.' She took a sip of her water.

Elaine reentered the room, her face grim. 'You told me that Maria's familiar was a stag, right? Like the one we just killed?' I nodded. She pointed at her phone. 'That was the hospital. Maria Collins was pronounced dead an hour ago. Preliminary cause of death is multiple organ failure.'

The room fell silent, digesting the news. I looked down at my hands and found them shaking. 'I killed her,' I mumbled, my voice hollow. I let out a brittle laugh. 'I fought so hard to save her, but I was the one who ultimately killed her.'

Someone stepped in front of me and lifted my chin with their fingers. I looked into Julia's orange eyes and felt a stinging pain across my cheek. 'What the hell was that for?'

'For being a monumental idiot.' Julia crossed her arms over her chest. 'We don't have time for you to feel sorry for yourself about something that isn't your fault.' She placed her hand on my shoulder. 'What we need is for you to rest and recover your strength so we can kill the bitch.'

I saw Patrizzia shake her head. 'I told you, the fates of those women were sealed the moment the mark was placed upon them. The sooner you come to accept that, the greater chance you stand against Arianwen. Otherwise, she will only use this weakness against you.' She turned to Julia. 'Let me know when the mágissa gets back.'

Elaine watched Patrizzia as she left the room, her face determined. 'I'm going to call an emergency meeting.' She looked at her phone. 'If I go now, I should have an answer by morning at the latest.' She began walking towards the door.

I stood up and began to follow. 'I'll go with you. Having an eyewitness will strengthen your case.'

'Nathaniel, wait,' Rela called after me.

I paused mid-step, caught between escaping this inevitable confrontation and knowing this chat had to happen.

'We, as the mortals say, need to talk.' Silera gestured towards the couch.

'I'll let you two figure this out,' Elaine said as she opened the door and walked out.

Julia picked up Sabine, who was busy scratching her ear. 'I'll go and check on Leann before heading to bed. Try not to freeze my living room.' She hesitated. 'And I suppose be careful with Nathan as well. You've only just healed him.'

'I'll do my best,' Silera said. Julia nodded and walked out with Sabine, who was wagging her tail as if nothing was wrong.

I opened my mouth to say something when Silera silenced me with a look.

'Sit,' she said.

The seriousness in her voice made me pause. There was something different about this situation, starting with the glacial distance she had adopted since our talk. I fought a shiver and sat on the couch.

'I'm furious, Nathaniel. Do you know why?' I opened my mouth to answer, but she gave me another quelling look. She wrapped her hands around herself, her honey eyes blazing like liquid fire. 'I'm furious at myself. I'm furious for being so foolish as to fall in love with someone who values himself so little that he would throw away his life for a bunch of nobodies. And I'm doubly furious at the misguided sense of guilt you're choosing to prioritise rather than being with someone you claim to love.'

'That isn't fair Silera—'

Her eyes flashed with indigo light. The temperature in the room dropped, and I quieted, concerned about the vaguely murderous look on her face.

'You want to talk fair? Fine, let's talk fair.' She placed her hand on her hips. 'I'm old, Nathaniel. I watched kingdoms rise and fall. Entire civilizations died out while I remained unchanged. But then I met you, and for the first time in millennia, I began to shift. To feel and experience new things. But that's not enough for you.' Her voice thawed, giving a glimpse of the raw emotion she had been repressing all this time, and I wanted to kick myself for causing it. 'After what happened to my parents, I vowed never to fall in love, but you slipped past my defenses and made yourself at home in my heart. Evernight take you for that.'

She shook her head slightly and looked somewhere behind me. 'You talked about the terror of living with the Fae.' She clenched her fists, her voice taking a darker edge. 'Do you know what it's like growing up as the heir to the Queen of Air and Darkness and the daughter of the King of Harvest and Bonfires? As a sister to the King of Wind and Life, who hates our dear mother and would love nothing more than to conquer our court?' Her eyes swirled with a myriad of hues from blues to reds, and I realised that no, I had never wondered about any of that. I had been too consumed by my own hardships to ever even think about Silera's. 'My life was full of Fae expecting me to fail, pushing at my bottom line just to see what I would do, attempting to murder anyone I got close to as part of petty court politics. My mother and father were testing me at every step because weakness means death. The Fae value ruthlessness and strength. There will always be a dagger waiting to stab you behind every smile.'

My stomach knitted itself into a Gordian Knot. I knew she hadn't had an easy life – no daughter of Mab would ever enjoy one. But having it thrown like that in my face... 'Silera, the last thing I wanted to do was to cause you pain.'

'But you did!' Sapphire flames ignited in her hands. 'You damnable bastard. You died, Nathaniel!' The flames rose a foot into the air. 'You were there one day, and the next you were gone, and for ten years, all I could think about was getting revenge for you.' The fire caressed her skin like an obedient pet. Heat scalded my body as the living room was bathed in a blue glow. 'I plotted, threatened, tortured and murdered to find out what happened to you, but all I got was the same response. Then you miraculously rose from the grave, told me you still love me, and then pushed me away like I was nothing. Did you ever stop to think that what happened to you was just as hard on me? Just as confusing? Just as deadly?'

The flames circled her head like a crown, and it made her look both ethereal and lethal. 'You can't tell me you love me and then abandon me. You can't just expect me to sit still until you get your feelings sorted like I'm a dog waiting to be summoned.' Her voice held a deadly edge that raised the hairs on the back of my neck. 'You stated your demands, here are mine.' Frost slithered across her skin while the blue flames continued to dance around her head. 'All or nothing, Nathaniel. Either you fight for us as hard as you're fighting for these strangers, or this is the last we'll see of each other.'

I opened my mouth but she raised her hand. 'I love you, and I don't care what the rest of the world thinks. I only ever cared about what *you* thought.' She withdrew her power inside her and then walked towards the double doors that connected the living room with the garden. She paused at the door and looked over her shoulder. 'I'll give you time to come to a decision. You have 'til morning. I hope it won't be our last.'

She opened the door and walked out. I stood there for a second, completely frozen and bereft of emotion. I didn't know what to say. Was I being completely selfish and unfair to her? To us? Was she right, and I was being a coward? The thought of never seeing her again hit me like a battering ram. I ran outside only to see a fresh patch of snow on the grass. A gust of wind swept over the grounds sending a lonely chill down my spine.

I looked up to the cloud-covered moon and felt hollow inside. 'Damn it!' I wasn't a coward. I just wanted some time until this whole mess was sorted out to make sense of everything. I rubbed my hand through my hair as frustration gnawed at me.

I glared at the patch of snow. 'The hell this is over.'

I stomped back into the living room and laid down on the couch. I was too keyed up to go back to my room, where the sheets still smelled of her. I closed my eyes and forced myself to relax. It wasn't working; my head spun with Silera's words. I sighed and rolled onto my side, wincing at the lingering soreness and forced my mind onto something else.

The other thing that weighed on me were the dreams I'd been having lately. How did they fit in with everything that had been happening? The rune-crow from the apartment building seemed like it could be the same one from my vision, but if it was, what did it mean? I tossed and turned, my brain running in circles before I finally drifted to sleep.

*I was standing in the middle of a circle of trees covered in dense blood-red snow. I looked up to see a crimson moon glaring down at me like a demonic mistress. A cracking sound caught my attention, and I turned around as the oldest tree in the grove split down the middle, and a familiar-looking staff appeared inside it. The weapon let out a pulse of magic that cleared the ruby snow from the forest, revealing a patch of blighted land beneath.*

*Bile rose in my throat, and I fought not to gag as I covered my mouth to keep the stench of rotting wood away from me. A disembodied hand reached out of the surrounding darkness and snatched the staff. It emitted a pulse of red light that made my breath freeze in my chest as the blight on the ground spread. I turned to run, my movements sluggish as unknown power pressed down on me. I glanced back just once as the hand raised the staff. Darkness erupted.*

# 18

I was awoken by Sabine licking my face, her tail wagging enthusiastically.

'Morning girl, what's up?' I groaned as I raised myself from the pillows. My body felt like it had been through several rounds with a troll.

Sabine *woofed* at me then pointed to the kitchen with her nose. I smiled at her and gave her a kiss between the eyes. 'I get what you're saying. Any advice?'

She thumbed the floor with her paw.

I snorted. 'Grovelling or bacon huh? So you're on board with her 'all or nothing' mentality?'

Sabine let her tongue loll out as she gave a yip of affirmation.

I sighed. 'You're right. I do love her and I want to be with her, so I guess I should tell her that. How can you be so much smarter than me, girl?'

Sabine huffed a breath and walked out of the living room. I rolled my eyes at her. 'Hey! No need for name calling,' I called.

I stood up and stretched, taking inventory of my body. I was still a little stiff but it was nothing the hot water couldn't cure, I thought as I jogged up the stairs. I would be in fighting form in no time. Damn,

Silera was good. At least my magic had partially regenerated overnight, so I wasn't completely defenseless.

Silera was sitting at the dining table when I emerged, feeling clean and fresh. Wearing an off-the-shoulder emerald dress, her auburn hair fell in waves down her back. The table was set with a mix of different dishes, from meats to desserts, not the usual breakfast melee. Julia finished serving a plate of ribs to Sabine when she noticed me at the door.

'Afternoon Nathan, I told Sabine to let you sleep as much as possible.' She pointed to a chair. 'Sit down. I'll get you a plate.'

I shook my head. 'That's okay, I got it.' I grabbed a plate and served myself two pieces of steak, baked potatoes and a plate of fruit. I was starving, my body had been through too many battles without a proper meal and rest. The food tasted good, but I was only half interested in it. All my senses were honed on Rela.

She was focused on feeding Tundra, but her shoulders were tense. I thought about what I should say to her. She had told me I had until morning, and I had technically slept through that deadline. Would she take that as my answer? I hoped not. I wasn't sure what I wanted to say, but I knew we needed to talk before the gulf between us widened further.

Julia stood up and went into the kitchen. It was now or never. I cleared my throat, and Silera turned her head towards me. Her face was devoid of expression, focused. It felt like I was looking at a frozen lake.

'I thought about what you said last night.'

She raised an eyebrow. 'And?'

'It's not going to be easy – it's going to possibly be a hundred times harder than before.' I put my fork down. 'You're right. I wasn't being fair to you; neither of us has had it easy.' I took a deep breath and let the words out. 'What I'm trying to say is that I'm a paranoid, angry asshole with a chip on my shoulder the size of Jupiter. I don't really know *why* you want to be with me. But the thought of not seeing you again, not being with you, is unacceptable. I can't stand it. I won't.'

'Nathaniel, you're rambling, speak clearly or don't speak at all.' She leaned back on her chair and regarded me with an icy look.

'You're not making this easy on me, you know?'

'I don't know what you mean.'

I got up and knelt next to her chair. I took her hand in mine, feeling comfortable with the familiar coldness of her skin. 'I'm in.' Her hand tensed. 'As soon as this mess is cleared up, we'll go somewhere quiet. Just the two of us.' I smiled at her. 'And if any of the Fae decide to stick their nose where it doesn't belong, I'll be more than happy to smash it for them. What do you say?'

Her shoulders visibly relaxed, and she touched my cheek with the other palm. 'Whoever said that romance was dead? For someone a thousand years old, I'd have hoped you would be better with women.'

*Ouch.* I got up, frowning as her words hit me. 'A thousand years old?'

She looked at me, amusement sparking in her honey eyes. 'After we saw each other in September, I became curious. I had thought it impossible to survive the trip from Faerie to the mortal world, so I tried to find out more about you and when you came to the court.'

While mortals could grow up in Faerie, we stopped ageing around twenty-five. After that, time stood still to balance our life spans with the near-immortal fae. Yet, as always, when it comes to the Fae, there was a catch. As soon as we stepped into the mortal world, we would become little more than dust on the wind as our years caught up with us all at once.

I hadn't planned on ever leaving the Fae, but I had been left with no options, trapped in that hellish forest, bleeding out like a stuck pig. I decided to risk losing my life in the mortal lands rather than wait in the forest for a fate worse than death. Yet, somehow, I didn't die. It had always bugged me. For a time, I thought I must have misremembered my own age since time does move oddly in Faerie, but it just made no sense. The only thing I could think of was that my rare rune magic had somehow protected me.

'So what makes you think I'm a thousand years old?' Gods, if that were true I was older than dirt. No wonder I ached after being thrown about a building – I was literally too old for this shit.

'More like fifteen hundred years old, if you want to be precise. From the information I gathered, you were there as a child when Saint

Patrick roamed Ireland, and that's as far back as anyone can remember seeing you. The Fae don't pay much attention to mortal servants.'

The number stunned me for a moment. 'Fifteen hundred years?' I murmured underneath my breath. Damn, I really was older than dirt. I looked at her smooth skin and wondered how old she was.

She must've known what I was thinking and smiled. 'A lady never reveals her age, but let's just say I'm quite a bit older than that.'

Julia chose that moment to re-enter the room, slightly out of breath as if she'd been running, with a newspaper in her hand. I let out a sigh, but given Julia's heightened hearing, she knew what we were talking about and wouldn't have interrupted us if it wasn't important.

'Patrizzia was right. There were more bodies this morning – look at this.' She passed me the paper. The cover read: *Ripper strikes again, blood soaks Mt Tabor.*

I scanned the article quickly. 'Fourteen bodies were found in Mt Tabor Park during the early hours of the morning by a jogger.' I grimaced. 'This escalation is far worse than Patrizzia expected. Something changed, something rattled her. She went from two bodies to fourteen in a single night. Arianwen must have killed them after she attacked us. She told me I had helped her find something she needed. That has to be why she upped her game.' I thought uneasily about the hand snatching the staff in my dream and the horrible darkness that had spread as a result.

Julia shook her head worriedly. ' Also, Elaine called. They found Makayla's suitcase at the coven building, but she wasn't there.'

I rubbed my face with both hands. 'Hopefully, she saw the mess we left and had enough sense to run away,' I said, even though deep down I knew that the most likely scenario was that she was gone. Arianwen might've gotten to her just like the rest of the coven. Julia's phone rang, and she left the room as I turned to Rela. 'We have to find out where Arianwen is hiding. Makayla might still be alive and—' I stopped when my cell started buzzing.

A picture of Devon and Margie flashed on the screen. I swiped to answer. 'Hey, bud. I was about to call you.'

A low wheezing sound came through the line. I frowned and

glanced at the screen again before putting it back against my ear. 'Devon? Is that you? Are you ok?'

The sound of labored breath answered me, followed by a low moan of pain. 'Nathan.'

Fear spiked through me as I strained to make out Devon's voice. Rela stood up with a frown on her face and my worry grew. 'Devon, bud, where are you? What's going on?'

Another moan, this one fainter, then Devon's voice came through, sounding incredibly broken and weak. 'Nathan, she took them. She took the girls. I tried to stop her but she was too strong. Help, please, get them back.'

*Alice and Margie ... taken?* 'Devon, tell me where you are, and I'll come right now,' I asked urgently, dread pooling in my stomach as I listened anxiously for his answer.

'Home,' Devon's barely audible whisper answered. I tried talking to him a couple more times, but the only thing I could hear was his rattled breathing.

I cursed and flipped through my contacts until I got to Elaine. She answered on the second ring. 'Nathan, I can't talk right now. The meeting—

'Devon's been attacked and the girls were taken.'

'What! When?'

I gritted my teeth to curb my impatience. She needed to get the Assembly's resources and search for the girls. We didn't have much time. 'I don't know. He just called me. Tell those old bastards at the Assembly that one of their own is in danger; maybe they'll finally deign to do something.'

I put my phone away and made for the door.

'Nathan, wait! Lucas just called, he needs to talk to you. It's something important!' Julia called after me.

Urgency bit at me like a rabid dog. I hadn't spoken to Lucas in months. Every time I called, his phone would go to voicemail, or his parents would tell me that he was busy. I wanted to speak to the kid and see how he was doing, but Devon needed my help right now. I turned back. 'I'll call him later. Do me a favor and ask Leann to make a list of all the coven's familiars, text me when you have it and tell Roel to meet me as soon as he is done with Patrizzia.'

I didn't wait for her to respond as I bolted through the door, jumped the porch stairs and ran for my truck. I tried to open the door only to remember that I had left my keys inside. I looked back to see Rela and Julia both standing on the porch. Julia was holding my car keys in her hands.

'You'll need these.' Julia threw me the keys and I caught them with my free hand. A look of worry flashed through her eyes. Rela must have filled her in. 'Nathan, bring them back safely. And for the sake of the Gods, don't get killed. I'd hate to break in a new boss.'

I smiled. 'I'll get them back to you. As for the not dying part' – I looked at Rela and smiled – 'I'll do my best.' Julia glared at me, but her expression softened when she turned to Silera.

Rela nodded and strode down the stairs. She motioned impatiently at the passenger door. 'Open this damn contraption. I'd rather not get burned.'

My truck was an older car primarily made of metal. To the Fae there wasn't anything more lethal than iron. 'Rela, you can't come with me.' Being surrounded by that much metal would be torturous, and I didn't have time to argue with her about it.

'I can bear it for a little while if you hurry.' I was about to tell her no again when Julia interrupted me with a huff.

'Athena, grant me patience,' Julia growled as she walked down the steps and faced the back of the inn. Her skin glowed with faint emerald light, and a wave of magic pulsed from her. The sweet fragrance of fresh olives tinged the cold December air.

The sounds of hooves rushing through the grounds and a horse's neigh could be heard in the distance until two horses appeared from around the corner.

Epona and Hades. My two Morgans. I frowned at the horses. Both of them were saddled and ready to go on a journey. I turned to Julia. 'How did you—'

She cut me off. ' You'd better get going.'

The horses came to a halt in front of us as Julia made her way inside. Epona nudged my hand for a pat on the head, her chestnut coat casting a deep contrast to Hades' raven black hair. 'Hey there, girl, thanks for coming. We're going to need to go fast. Is that okay with you?'

Epona neighed happily. While I took them out for exercise once a day to stretch their legs, during the winter months, those walks were shorter than usual. Hades pawed at the ground impatiently with his muscular hoove as Rela patted his side, his body brimming with energy.

'You always had a fine taste in horses, Rún. He is magnificent.' She leapt onto the saddle in one smooth practiced movement. Her dark green dress shimmered in the morning light and shifted into a white shirt, a pair of black riding trousers that molded to her figure, and black boots, all in the time it took her to center herself on the saddle.

She looked at me and frowned. 'You can't ride like that.' I groaned at the itchy feeling coursing through my skin as my clothes rearranged themselves, forming an outfit similar to hers. A gray shirt, black trousers and boots. I shook myself and snapped Epona's reins.

*Hang on, Devon. We're coming.*

## 19

If you're riding into battle at full gallop across a city like Portland, the chances are that you'll spook the normies and get pulled over by cops asking very uncomfortable questions. I don't know what illusion Rela used to conceal us, but drivers were doing everything possible to get out of our way without realising we were there.

It took us about half an hour to get to Devon's house. As we drew near, I could see the flashing lights of several cars. My heart stalled in my chest as I recognized the shape of an ambulance and I urged Epona on.

The police had barricaded the whole street, and there was a crowd of bystanders pressed up against the cordon. I turned to Rela, and she nodded, letting go of the illusion a couple of feet away from the crowds. I jumped off Epona and threw the reins to Rela before running towards the police tape.

Two officers were keeping the gawking neighbors away. I extended my magical senses towards them, but they came back as vanilla, mortal. Shit. I approached one of them, a young cop who couldn't have been more than twenty years old, probably fresh out of the academy.

'Officer, I'm a friend of the family that lives here. Can you let me through? I need to see if they're okay,' I asked with polite urgency, ducking beneath the yellow tape before they could respond.

The cop stepped in front of me and pushed me back. 'Sir, please stand behind the line. The police are handling this matter.'

I stood my ground, and magic boiled inside my skin in response to my desperation. If he didn't move, I was going to move him. 'Listen, I'm sure you're trying to do your job, but my friend is in there and I'm going inside, whether you like it or not. So, unless you want to arrest me for assaulting an officer after you wake up, you're going to let me through.'

The officer's face turned pale, and he took a step back before he stopped himself and squared his shoulders. 'Sir, I'm going to ask you again to stand behind the police line. If you continue to be uncooperative, I will have to arrest you.' The officer's hand moved towards his belt slowly.

Fuck this. I clenched my fist when Rela stepped in front of me and the officer froze. The Fae were ethereal in their beauty, and usually when they walked amongst mortals, they glamoured themselves to appear a bit more normal, but Silera had blasted the kid with her true face. She was considered stunning even among the Fae. The poor guy didn't stand a chance.

'Oh, Officer, my boyfriend does have a temper, but you have to understand how upsetting it can be when you can't help someone you care for.' She dazzled him with a smile that made the cop blush to the tips of his ears. She straightened the officer's collar even though there was nothing wrong with it. 'I would appreciate it dearly if we could speak to whoever is in charge.'

The cop stumbled over his words before nodding his head and rushing towards the house. I gave Rela a sidelong look. 'You just ruined that poor kid for life.'

Rela chuckled and took my hand in hers. 'Then he knows how to appreciate true beauty. Besides, if you had gone through with your plan of punching poor Officer Ryan, then you would have to also fight all these mortal enforcers. It would have been a waste of time that your friends don't have.'

I took in a deep breath, trying to calm the anxiety that was coursing through me, and squeezed her hand. 'Thank you, but could you please tone it down a little? We don't want the boss turned into a bumbling fool.'

'Jealous, my wolf?' She let out a small laugh, and I could feel a tiny pulse of magic radiate from her. She hadn't done anything major, just a few small details here and there. Her hair looked less glossy and thick, her honey-colored eyes a bit paler, more hazel. The delicate lines of her face lost some of their sharpness. She still looked beautiful, like a supermodel, but it wasn't an earth-shattering beauty.

'Not jealous, just practical. Can you see if there's an illusion cast over the property?' I asked, assessing the house. Judging by the exterior alone, everything seemed the same. Over the phone, Devon had sounded really hurt, but I couldn't see any signs of a battle.

She shook her head. 'No, everything looks normal.' She was about to say something else when Officer Ryan returned with my least favorite detective in tow. I killed an urge to scream.

Lady Luck enjoyed messing with me. It was official.

Detective Kane stopped in front of us and sent Officer Ryan away before looking at me with a stoic face. 'Mr Mercer, we just keep bumping into each other, it seems.' He gave Rela a once over, taking her measure. 'Who is your friend?'

'It would appear so, Detective. This is Arelis Winters, she's also a friend of Devon.' I used the alias she had given me once before and forced a polite smile. 'Could you please tell me what's going on?'

'I know of your close relationship with Dr Othonos, Mr Mercer. That's why I will tell you he is alive and being tended by the paramedics.' I opened my mouth, but the detective shook his head. 'I'm sorry, Mr Mercer, Ms Winters, but I can't say anything else. This is still an active crime scene.'

I tried to keep myself calm and not blow up in Detective Kane's face. He sure would love any opportunity to take me in. The man was as normal as they came, but he knew something wasn't right about me and was determined to find out what it was. 'Detective, please, just let me through so I can speak to him. He called me to tell me that something was wrong. I have to get in there.' I pulled out my phone and showed him the call. 'I just want to make sure he and his family are ok.'

The detective opened his mouth when a familiar pair of paramedics came out of the house, carrying Devon on a stretcher. I pushed past Kane, who didn't even raise a finger to stop me, and rushed towards them. 'Devon, oh my gods, what the hell happened?'

Devon's face was covered in blood from a nasty cut above his left eyebrow, and his arm was wrapped up with a splint. His clothes were torn to shreds, and what little remained was splattered with gray Grishari blood and covered with some kind of dust on his ribs. He smelled like mint and rot. His breathing was labored despite an oxygen mask. Rage boiled inside me, and I fought hard to control myself as my magic coursed through my veins, eager to lend me its strength. I clenched my fists, closed my eyes, and made a vow that Arianwen's death would be slow.

Devon was clearly struggling so Lane spoke instead. 'Nathan, he's in pretty bad shape. We need to take him to Ohsu Hospital. Now.'

I nodded absentmindedly. 'I'm going with you.' I turned to Rela, but she was already walking in the direction of the lamppost where the horses waited.

I watched Lane and Hernandez put Devon inside the ambulance. Hernandez remained in the back with Devon while her partner went around and started the engine. I got in as well and turned to close the door, but Detective Kane stopped me.

'This is the second unusual crime scene you have landed yourself in, Mr Mercer,' Kane said, eyeing me suspiciously. 'First the car accident a couple of weeks ago, then last night you found that girl's body, and now you're here. Trouble seems to follow you everywhere, or maybe it's the other way around?'

I was about to set him straight when Hernandez cut me off. She spoke with a sharp tone. 'Detective, we need to get Dr Othonos to the hospital immediately. Close the door so we can leave.'

Without waiting for a response, I jerked the door back and closed it. The engine started as Hernandez pulled out some gauze, needle and thread. 'Lane, keep it steady. I'm about to stitch the wound.'

'You don't tell me how to drive, and I won't tell you how to sew,' Lane said from the front.

Hernandez grumbled something underneath her breath while the gauze floated in the air, and she began to clean Devon's face. A telekinetic, great. A skilled one at that. 'Now we can finally talk without Detective Douche breathing down our necks. I don't know what his problem is with you, but you have to be careful.' Another pair of gauzes floated towards Devon. 'You're lucky we were close when the call came in.' She looked back at Devon. 'He's not as hurt as we made it out to be. A couple of cracked ribs and that cut above his eye. He's mostly just tired from magical overuse.'

I leaned back on the seat and let out a breath of relief. The knot in my stomach loosened an inch. I thought about Alice and how worried she must be for the babies. In her condition, anything could go wrong. Margie must be terrified, facing the darker side of life for the first time. Even with her grandfather being the God of the Underworld, Margie had been raised with love and care.

I wanted to help give her the best childhood possible, the one I didn't have, but in the end, she had been hurt because of my meddling. It was my fucking fault they were dragged into this mess.

Hernandez took out a bottle of water and drained half of it in one gulp before turning back to me. 'We got there just before the cops, so he managed to tell us that his wife and daughter had been kidnapped by some creatures and a witch. He tried to stop them, but they overwhelmed him. By the time we arrived, he was face down in the backyard, surrounded by a mountain of corpses. He used the last bit of his strength to turn them into dust before he fell unconscious.'

Creatures? Dread filled me at the only possibility I could think of. The Grishari, obviously, but how did they know where Devon lived? And why would they attack him? The floating gauzes were replaced by the needle and thread that were now closing the wound. 'Thank you so much for your help. I got here as soon as I could after he called me.' I clenched my fists together to keep them from shaking and looked at Hernandez. 'Did he have any idea where they had taken his family?'

She shook her head. 'He just said they were taken, dusted the corpses, and passed out. The house looked like a warzone, so I couldn't say for sure if there were clues amongst the broken furniture.' The needle and thread had finished stitching up the cut and went back into the bag. 'We'll have to wait for him to wake up, but I don't know how long he'll be out.'

'Umm, guys,' Lane said from the front, amusement ringing in his voice. 'You know when they say 'Keep Portland Weird'? Do you think they foresaw an ambulance being chased by a beautiful woman on horseback?'

Hernandez frowned and stared at Lane. 'Are you high?'

I looked through the back windows and saw Rela on Hades with Epona at her side, catching up with the ambulance. I had to admit that it wasn't something you saw every day, even in Portland. None of the other drivers noticed anything weird. 'Lane, pull over.'

'What why? You know that lady?' Lane asked. I felt Hernandez move towards the window and let out a low whistle before nodding appreciatively. 'She's cute.'

'That's my girlfriend. Pull over,' I said. I heard Lane chuckle as he maneuvered the ambulance to the side of the road.

As soon as Lane killed the engine, we all jumped out. 'Were you able to get a location?' Rela asked as she neared the ambulance, getting off Hades.

I shook my head. 'Devon's still passed out. The paramedics say that while he isn't injured too badly, he overused his magic during the fight. Can you help him?'

Hernandez pulled her hair into a ponytail and went to stand by Lane. 'Hey, I didn't just say that to get away from Kane. Dr Othonos still needs hospital attention, even if it's not as urgent as we made it out to be.'

Rela shook her head. 'We don't have time to wait. As I understand it, a pregnant woman and her child's life are in danger.' She motioned with her hand towards the ambulance. 'Get him out of that metal contraption so I can heal him.'

The partners shared a look before they took the gurney out of the ambulance. Rela approached the still form of Devon and placed her hand over his chest. Her palm began to glow with an orange light that enveloped my friend. Unlike when she had healed me after my last battle, Devon didn't seem to be in any more pain. Good. I looked around to see if anyone was reacting to our little light show, but the pedestrians were too busy rushing towards the coffee shops and breathing hot air into their palms to protect themselves from the cold December air.

Even Lane and Hernandez had their hands stuck inside their jackets, and I could see their breath condense in front of their noses. I rubbed my own hands together. I had forgotten my jacket, and Rela hadn't bothered to give me one when she had magicked my clothes. It probably hadn't occurred to her, as a Winter Fae, she didn't feel the cold.

Rela lifted her hand from Devon's body, and his eyes flew open. He took in a deep breath and immediately went into a coughing fit. She stepped back and let the paramedics check on him. Devon blinked several times, then turned towards Rela. 'Than—'

I was about to cut him off as thanking a fae was a sure fire way to be indebted to them for life, but Rela beat me to it. 'That's unnecessary. I only healed your physical wounds. Your magic will return in time, and you will need to rest to get rid of your exhaustion. You can do that as soon as you tell us what happened, so we can go and rescue your family.'

The paramedics helped him to his feet. He turned to me, and I could see the anguish in his blue eyes. 'Nathan, they took my girls. That bastard Swinekong flew from the sky while we were having a picnic in the backyard. He was bigger than before by at least two feet and a hundred pounds heavier.'

The thought of an eleven foot tall, thousand pound flying pig-gorilla made me shudder involuntarily – that thing was the stuff of nightmares. Devon clenched his fists, and I could hear his knuckles popping. 'I tried to fight it off while Alice and Margie ran, but something came out of the lake and knocked me into the side of the house. I didn't see the witch until it was too late. I must've blacked out for a moment because, by the time I came to, they were gone.' His eyes were flickering with ominous green light.

I stepped forward and clasped him on the shoulder. 'It's okay Devon, take a deep breath. We'll find them and make her pay.' I gave him a quick rundown of what was going on. 'Do you have any way of finding them?'

He closed his eyes and took a deep breath. His body was shaking beneath my hand, and for a moment, I thought he was going to pass out again. Suddenly, he opened his eyes, and I took a step back. His left eye had gone completely black, a shade so dark the iris was almost invisible. It felt like staring into a deep abyss and having it stare back at you. The other one turned a pale jade green with flecks of gold. I had never seen him do anything like this, not even when he was summoning a horde of undead.

He walked towards a small patch of grass and waved his hand in a semicircle above his head. For a second, his hand turned translucent. He made a grabbing motion and pulled his black kukri blade out of thin air. The colors around him became opaque as he stepped into a curtain of shadows. With one swift motion, he ran the end of the blade across his forearm, letting the crimson blood flow from the wound and spill to the ground below.

'Ma to aema tis parthenou odigise me stin ikogenia mou.' His voice echoed with power as he let the earth drink.

For a second, I didn't understand what he was saying, then the words translated effortlessly in my mind. *By the Maiden's Blood, guide me to my family.* 'How did I understand what he just said? Did you guys mentally translate that too?'

Rela looked at me and smiled. 'You're Oregon's champion now, Nathaniel – bound to the land. How could you protect it effectively if you cannot understand what its denizens are saying?'

And here I had spent all that time learning new languages.

I turned back to watch Devon and saw that the grass beneath his feet was quivering as a single black and golden rose in full bloom sprouted from the ground. Devon knelt reverently, plucked it, and then walked towards us. His complexion had gone paler than a vampire – if that was even possible – but thankfully his eyes were back to their usual color.

'This will lead us to the girls,' he said between labored breaths.

I shook my head. 'No, you're not going anywhere. You'll stay here, and I will go get the girls back.'

Devon glared at me, and his hand tightened around the blade's handle. 'Nathaniel, this is my family. There's no way in Tartarus that I'm going to sit back and wait with my thumbs up my ass while you risk your life to save them.'

'For Gods' sake, you can barely stand.' I pointed to the rose. 'Give it to me, I promise that we will get them back.'

He lifted his chin defiantly, and I saw that no amount of words would convince him to stay behind. I growled in frustration. 'Morrigan, take my soul!' I poked his chest, 'Fine, you stubborn asshole, you can come but you stay out of the action. I don't need to be saving your skinny ass too.'

Devon's eyes hardened, his face grim and determined. 'Get on a horse, we're leaving.'

Lane took a step forward. 'We're coming with you. If any of you get hurt, we can provide immediate medical care.'

I seized them up and down before nodding slowly. 'We'll take all the help we can get.'

I could only hope it would be enough.

# 20

Even as Epona's legs ate up the miles, I felt like we were getting nowhere. I clenched the reins tighter, wishing with all my might that I could just teleport to the girls' side.

I urged Epona ahead as we rode back south towards Lake Oswego and got onto the I-5. What if we didn't make it in time? The image of Alice's broken body, her heart ripped out and her womb splayed open, flashed through my mind, and I gritted my teeth. I swore I could hear Margie's voice crying out for help as the cold wind slapped my face.

'Faster Epona! Faster!' I yelled. She was already at her limit, but it didn't feel quick enough.

The skies began to darken as the sun set on the horizon. Time was slipping between my fingers like melting snow. I shook my head and tried to focus on the signs along the highway. We were entering the city of Salem, and before the night was over, I was going to make sure it had its first witch trial. We continued south, down Enchanted Way, following the slowing ambulance into a deserted parking lot as the last of the light faded.

Where the hell had that bitch taken the girls? A nasty thought crossed my mind, and I delved into my connection with Oregon. I almost fell off Epona as pure, adulterated power coursed through me.

Silera looked back at me. 'What is it?'

'You told me certain places are best suited for working complex spells because of the power the site gives off,' I reminded her. 'Because of the leynodes, correct?'

'Yes,' Silera said, raising an eyebrow in question as we dismounted from our horses in one fluid movement.

'Well, if what I'm feeling through my connection to Oregon is any indication, we're standing on the mother of all nodes. It's nothing like I've ever felt before. The other murder sites were drained of power but this feels ... suffocating.'

We tied the horses to the railings of the entrance ramp, leaving them huffing before joining Devon and the paramedics. The ramp led to a tall metal fence painted green so that it blended into the large wooded area it guarded and served as entrance to the park. The moon peeked behind the cover of the clouds, illuminating a trio of snow covered buildings in a natural spotlight to the right and another on the left. My magic tingled beneath my fingers as I looked over the buildings. Something about this place was calling to me; it was a hum in my blood, like a siren singing to a sailor.

The rose in Devon's hand had wilted, its magic spent. Lane stood nervously twirling a dark wooden wand in his hands under Hernandez's watchful gaze; her own hand tightened on the strap of the medical bag slung across her shoulders. Her long, white staff remained firmly on the ground while she peered anxiously up at the entrance gates. Cassius had once told me that mages who used wands for combat preferred them because they amplified their magic while staffs allowed them to better control their power. I was glad that they were on my side.

I shivered in the parking lot as I stared past the green gate to the multistory house on my right. It was similar in design to a medieval cottage, with brown shingles on the roof and cream coloured walls. It reminded me of the architecture prevalent in some of the villages in Faerie. Tension crept up my neck as the prickle of magic stung my skin. Something about this place was off. I blinked several times, suddenly realising that I shouldn't be able to see the house this clearly in the low light – but I wasn't imagining it. *Another nifty benefit to being Oregon's champion?*

A stillness had descended. I was breathing too loudly, hyper-aware of every scuff of my shoes as we moved warily closer to the entrance. I strained to listen for any movement beyond the gates, but everything was quiet. The place felt like a tomb. I hoped it wasn't a sign of things to come.

The central building, much like the first, was constructed to resemble an old stone house with a faded yellow brick roof in the shape of a smurf's hat. Cold wind crept in from the east, carrying the scents of pine and musk, and I rubbed my arms, eyeing the buildings shrewdly. Even in a place as big as this, a thousand-pound gorilla-monster had to make some noise, no? I licked my dried lips. The thick magic felt like ants crawling over my skin. The power washing over me was second only to standing in the presence of the Sidhe.

I turned to Silera and quietly murmured, 'Is there a gate nearby?'

She shook her head. 'No. The node is too strong for a gate to be stable.'

A gate to Faerie might not be here, but the fae's influence was all over the area. This had to be a place where the veil between worlds was razor thin.

I made a quick check of my pendant and hammer charm. The weapon would be my only means of defense against the witch and her creatures. My magic was still depleted, so our heaviest hitter was Silera until Roel could get here. Devon still looked pale, and we would need Hernandez and Lane as our medical back-up. Though, from the way they held their staffs, I was betting they had seen their fair share of combat too.

My phone chimed, and I glanced at it to see a text from Julia. Worry spiked through me as I skimmed over her message.

*The next time you decide to let a guest perform a hex-breaking spell in my woods, I will nail your testicles to a wall.*

I winced.

*Leann's fox put out the fires. She wanted to help you guys, but she could barely stand. I managed to convince her to stay in the inn. According to her, the coven's familiars are: her fox, then a gorilla, pig, bat, cobra, goat, lion, stag, porcupine, octopus, crocodile, scorpion and a penguin. Roel is on his way, so don't do anything stupid. He said he will know where to find you.*

I relayed the information to everyone while Devon tapped his foot impatiently on the ground, the sound setting me on edge. 'So, the Swinekong that Devon and I fought was made of the gorilla, pig and bat.'

*Tap, tap, tap.* Devon crossed and uncrossed his arms before running a hand through his hair, stilling his foot momentarily. 'We took out the chimera that was made of the cobra, goat and lion, and you killed the one that was made of the stag, octopus and porcupine.'

'Which means that we'll be dealing with the Swinekong and a monster made from the crocodile, scorpion and penguin,' I finished. 'We can rule Leann's fox out. We can only hope that Arianwen didn't manage to get Makayla's familiar yet, but we should be prepared for anything.' I turned to Devon. 'Do you remember what the other creature that attacked you looked like?'

Devon shook his head. 'I was busy fighting the damn ape with my back to the lake, so I didn't see the second creature. I barely even got a glimpse of the witch.'

'How far along is your wife?' Lane asked as Hernandez began passing flashlights out to all of us.

'She just entered her twenty-eighth week yesterday.' Devon's hands went for his weapon and tightened around its handle.

Lane nodded. 'We'll be on hand to provide medical support.'

Devon's jaw tightened in response as he abruptly turned and began walking up the ramp towards the entrance without slowing for us to catch-up. It led to a metal archway with a sign that read 'Enchanted Forest' in bright red letters. Behind it sat a squat little structure with a brown roof stood apart from the others.

The forest behind them spanned as far as I could see, and I stopped a shiver before it could form. Gazing up at it felt like walking towards the edge of a precipice, and looking down, aware that one wrong move could send you to your death. My palms sparked with silver and red light as my emotions got the best of me.

I just couldn't shake the feeling that not all of us would be walking out of here. Just what kind of shit would we be walking into? Only the Gods knew. My heart continued to pound. A forest could hide many dark and nasty surprises.

I made to follow Devon when Rela stopped me with a careful hand on my arm. 'Nathaniel, there's a real possibility that they could be already dead. We still don't know why she took the hearts and wombs of those girls or how long she kept them alive. You have to be prepared for the worst.'

I took a deep breath and shook my head. Darkness crept up the edges of vision as if an angel of death was resting his hand on my shoulder. The wind picked up once more, sweeping snow and dead leaves into the air. The rustle of the breeze rattled like bones. 'I can't think like that because that's just not an option. Everyone will get out of this unharmed, and Margie will get to be a big sister to her brothers.' Heat surged through me at the thought of something happening to the girls and not being able to save them. I clenched my fist tightly and felt my knuckles pop.

'The ability of you mortals to challenge the odds is something that has always intrigued me,' she said, looking towards Devon and the mages.

I nodded. 'We have to take each day as if it were our last and fight for a small shred of happiness. Even if it means laying down our lives for it.'

We caught up to Devon as he reached the top of the ramp and the entrance gates. They were closed, a rusty chain dusted with snow wrapped around them. If I had the magic to spare, I could have used 'Oscail' to open it. But since we didn't know what we would be up against, every drop of magic had to be rationed.

Before I could make the suggestion, Devon raised his kukri in the air and sliced the chains off as if they were made of putty and rushed inside. I gave the blade a wary look and once again wondered what the hell it was made of. Knowing that Devon was the son of not one, but two Greek deities, the possibilities were endless.

We trailed Devon through the gates. An odd feeling coasted over my skin as we passed the threshold and the smaller building. I shot it another longer look. Now that we were closer, it looked like a ticket booth, but there was no telling what might be lurking in this park. Devon hurried past it, and the only thing we could do was follow at a brisk pace. I winced as several branches snapped beneath our feet, their sound ringing out like a gunshot in the silence. Snow and dead leaves sloshed, and my eyes scanned the brush around us constantly, watching, waiting. I nearly collided with Devon as he suddenly stopped.

'What the hell is this place?' I asked as we came to a fork in the road and eyed what lay ahead.

'It's a theme park built in the late sixties,' Hernandez whispered. 'They have all sorts of attractions based on different fairytales as well as a haunted house, roller coasters, a theatre and stuff. I bring my niece every year. Right now, it's the off-season.'

Before us was a cluster of trees with a small wooden sign planted in front of it that read: 'Start at Castle and follow trail' with a big red arrow pointing to the left. It directed us to an inclined cement path that turned into a cobblestone road, leading to an orange brick castle with purple stone archways. I flicked a glance up at the sky and winced at the sight of dark clouds rolling in, reducing our visibility even more.

'This place is giving me the creeps. Why would anyone bring their kids here?' Lane asked, his breath condensing in front of him. He kept his wand ready at his side in a white-knuckled grip; his eyes darting around the surrounding gloom. 'The magic is so thick I can barely breathe.'

Lane wasn't wrong. Magic swept across my skin in increasingly uncomfortable waves. The temperature inside the park was colder than the parking lot by several degrees, and I wished I had gloves. At this rate I wouldn't be able to grip Fjall.

'Let me try something. Maybe I can give us some direction instead of us just following the trail.' I closed my eyes and tried to use my connection to Oregon to pinpoint where Arianwen's foul magic was originating from. I swore softly. It felt like hitting a thick wall made of cotton; my magic caught and unable to push through. 'The magic of this place is interfering. There's just too much magic in the air for me to differentiate it.'

'We'll just have to follow the trail then. The best way to access the rest of the park is by going through the castle,' Hernandez said, teeth chattering lightly.

I looked to Devon, and he nodded, ready. Without a backward glance, we started towards the castle.

I wasn't amused by the fairy-tale themed park, given how ninety-nine percent of those tales were deathly real. I gave Rela a sideways look, and the corner of her mouth twitched as we continued along the trail toward the castle. A rustle of leaves came from somewhere to my right, and my body was moving before my mind caught up, magic flowing to my bracelet, warming it against my skin.

'Ag Fas!' I yelled.

The double-faced hammer charm grew to its regular size, and everyone around me aimed their weapons at the trees. My heart roared a battle cry in my chest, but after a few seconds, nothing came to attack us. I walked towards the trees with Devon at my back but couldn't see anything lurking in the dark. I shook my head and we went back to the others, the surge of adrenaline making my hands tremble.

The castle had looked huge from the outside, yet the interior consisted of a single corridor that led deeper into the park and forest. Snow crunched underneath our feet as we passed through the faux stone archway, and I was scared to even blink for fear of missing some secret trap or ambush. The wind rustled outside, moaning like the dead rising to reap the living. The smell of stale dirt and wet earth burned my nostrils, but I ignored my new Oregon-heightened senses and kept my eyes on Devon. His breath was coming in short bursts, and the hands wrapped around his blade were absolutely bloodless from how tightly he gripped it.

As soon as we exited the castle, my body tensed like a coiled spring – we were surrounded by nothing but trees. Ahead of us was the same cobblestone path as before, winding through the trees like a long, narrow snake. On the left side of the path was a wooden railing, and beyond it lay the untamed dark forest. The wind howled louder, twisting between us as we began down the path. A spoiled taste filled my mouth, like curdled milk, as I inhaled the polluted magic. The smell of pine was almost overwhelming, and I struggled to breathe calmly through the thickness of the foul magic surrounding us. Maybe we were getting close.

Something moved in the distance, and Devon bolted ahead as if he had been launched by a cannon. I cursed and rushed after him, my thighs burning from the strain of catching up. He suddenly stopped, looking bemusedly at a colorful statue sitting on top of a multicolored brick wall while I panted behind him. Behind it, the bright red walls of a miniature house were visible through the leaves. I turned my flashlight towards the statue, and the light illuminated its shockingly pasty painted skin. Lane approached it gingerly, his face twisted in disgust. A red bowtie offset the wide-open smile that ended in rosy cheeks. I was just glad it didn't have teeth. Written on the colourful wall was a very familiar rhyme with a slight twist:

*Humpty Dumpty sat on a wall*
*Humpty Dumpty had a great fall*
*All the king's horses and all the king's men*
*Couldn't put Humpty together again, but Roger Tofte did*

Lane stepped forward onto the tiled platform set into the earth, and I swore when it made an audible click. Lane jumped back but it was too late. The statue exploded in a flash of green lightning that blinded me. I stumbled into Rela, grasping pointlessly for Lane as his hazy figure was flown backwards over the railing lining the trees. My ears were ringing, but I could finally see again. Rela mouthed something uselessly at me when I smacked into the shield of ice she had conjured to halt the falling debris. This was a warning. We were on the right track, and now someone knew we were coming.

'Bryan!' Hernandez yelled as she ducked her head and raised her staff in the air, sending pieces of the wall flying back before they could hit her. Devon was on the periphery of the explosion and was only pelted with some plaster and dust.

Before we had a chance to catch our breath, a loud squeal rang through the closed park. It sounded like the world's largest pig had

179

swallowed a megaphone. A massive shadow flew over us and then slammed into the ground between Devon and Hernandez. The cobblestone path cracked and split, dust shifting into the air. I got my first look at the new Swinekong and damn it was huge.

The deformed son of Dr Moreau and King Kong pounded its chest as it eyed Hernandez with its deep-set amber eyes. The thing had to be at least fifteen feet tall and weighed about a thousand pounds of pure muscle. Its large leathery wings fanned the air as it raised its meaty fist to smash the mage. Hernandez stared up at it, her mouth agape, and tried to raise her staff to deflect the hit, but her hand was moving too slowly.

I rushed in front of her as Silera's shield fell, swinging Fjall in an upwards move. The hammer collided with the Swinekong's fist, and a blast of thunder rolled across the park. The kinetic energy stored from my ride on Epona was released in one booming burst. The Swinekong squealed in pain and fell on its back, clutching one of its hands. I would've fallen flat on my ass if Hernandez hadn't caught me with her telekinesis. I felt my bones groan in protest. That had been the largest amount of energy I had released yet, and it managed to only knock the bastard back. This was not good.

I looked back at Hernandez. 'Go check on Lane!' I yelled. The empath had been hit hard by that explosion, and who knew if he was even alive. I saw Hernandez nod out of the corner of my eye and jump over the wooden rail. She rushed into the trees in search of her partner.

'Psofa!' Devon roared as he ran towards the super kong, his kukri held high as he slashed down with all his strength across the creature's abdomen. The blade sunk deep into its flesh. The Grisharu let out a roar of pain and tried to swipe at him. A thick wall of ice condensed between them, and Devon took a couple of steps back as an orb of blue flames streaked through the air and hit the giant monkey in the chest.

The Swinekong writhed in pain as its fur caught fire. It tried to pat the flames out as a stench of burnt fur and flesh clogged my nostrils. I shook my head. That wouldn't be enough to stop him. I had burnt and electrocuted this bastard before, and it had brushed it off almost immediately. Now it was twice as large. This fight was getting us nowhere.

I yelled to Rela and Devon. 'Rela, go with Devon and find the girls. I'll take care of the pigzilla over here. I don't know what caused the statue to explode but be careful, there could be more traps waiting.'

Devon's eyes flashed with green light as indecision crossed his face. He took a step forward before clenching his fist around his blade. I rushed the Swinekong, who was still on its knees and brought down Fjall on its snout. The creature saw me coming and attempted to backhand my hammer away, but the extra force from the swing caught it in a deadlock. I looked to the left to see Devon still standing there.

'Devon, don't be stupid, go!' I roared and ducked underneath a powerful punch. I swung again, hitting the beast on the forearm.

The Swinelong let out a bellow of pain. Its flaming fur made it look demonic. Its leathery wings fanned out from the lump on its back, sending a gust of wind that pushed me back several feet. *Oh no, you don't, you bastard.* I ran forward just as another pair of frozen spears shot above me, piercing its wings and tearing through them. It would be impossible for it to fly with that kind of damage.

A blur of red hair rushed past me while I kept the Swinekong busy, and I saw Rela on the other side of the path, standing next to Devon. The ice and fire magic had been her doing. It was what made her so deadly. Fire from the bonfires of Autumn, and Frost from the coldest regions of Winter. She looked back towards me and mouthed, 'Mo ghrá Thú'.

Warmth spread through my chest, and I found myself grinning like a fool. 'Love you, too. Now go!' I ducked another blow and jumped backwards, keeping my eye on the Swinekong and not their departing figures. The massive form of the Grisharu pounded its meaty fist into the ground and squealed at me. Its six nostrils flared in anger.

'Well, fuck you, you banana-licking-mud-wallowing piece of garbage.' I spun Fjall in my hand and grinned at the beast. 'Have your nuts grown back yet, or are they still burnt to a crisp?'

The Swinekong drew itself to its full height as snowflakes began to fall from the sky. One of its hands looked like raw hamburger meat; the fingers were crushed and bent in an unnatural direction. At the mention of the charred family jewels, its eyes burned crimson, and it charged at me.

I wiped a trickle of blood away from my mouth with a shaking hand. Adrenaline coursed through my body as my smile turned predatory. 'Round three, Asswipe.'

## 21

I rushed forward and rolled between the Swinekong's legs, backhanding Fjall into his calf. Thunder simmered from my hammer as the Swinekong let out a squeal and stumbled forward but managed to send out a vicious back kick. I rolled away just in time for the hoof to only graze my shoulder, but even that was enough force to push me to the ground.

I jumped to my feet as fast as I could, not wanting to be hit with another one of those killer kicks. I ignored the throbbing ache in my shoulder as the Swinekong swiped a piece of Humpty's wall from the ground. I instinctively ducked as the Grisharu launched the piece of debris at me. My shirt had become sticky with blood from where its hoof had cut me.

Magic rolled through my body as I summoned my armor, deflecting another piece of debris with my shield before it fizzled out. Frustrated, the monster lowered its head and charged at me with a roar that made the breath catch in my chest. I threw myself to the ground, rolling over my shoulder to the small patch of grass where the statue had stood undamaged a few minutes ago. Cursing my bad luck, I chucked a piece of Humpty Dumpty back at the beast.

The piece of the statue bounced harmlessly off the monster's fur, but the roll had bought me time. The Swinekong chased me into the woods, swinging its massive fists at me. It missed, smashing into the trunk of a tree and sending thousands of splinters into the air. I swore as one stung my cheek. My foot caught in a root as I tried to widen the distance between us, and I fell forward, rolling over the ground, heart hammering in my chest as the floor disappeared from beneath me.

My back slammed into the ground, and a wave of pain froze me in place as the colossal monster swung its fists downwards. I channelled all the magic left in my armor into a blue dome above me. Cracks appeared on the surface as the beast struck it with all its might. The energy was exhausted almost immediately.

I scrambled to my feet and jumped backwards, dodging another punch and swinging Fjall, hitting the beast on the elbow joint. Energy rippled across the woods as bones cracked underneath my hammer. The Swinekong let out a bellow filled with hate and pain.

It staggered forward, and I managed to put some distance between us. The corrupted familiar ripped a tree from its roots and hurled it at me. I threw myself to the side. With no time to brace, I scraped my cheek on the loose stone. My eyes followed the tree as it sailed past me and crashed into the bright-red house nearby.

The thick trunk smashed through a wall, and planks of plastic wood flew into the sky. The whole house shook, and its front crumbled forward onto a colorful statue of a girl with a lamb. It shattered, sending pieces flying in every direction. The rest of the attraction fell in on itself from the force of the collision.

I freed myself from my daze and ran towards the direction I'd last seen Hernandez and Lane but promptly went flying. My breath left me in a hard *whoosh* as I landed alongside a half-crushed statue of a lamb, surrounded by fragments of a little girl wearing a blue dress. Felled by Little Bo Peep – I'd never live this down.

The Swinekong landed in front of me with a thud that shook my knees as I tried to stand. The monster crashed about as it tried to knock the trees aside to stomp on me. Unsuccessful, it careened into the faux stone castle. I pushed up from the ground and winced as the beast destroyed almost everything it touched. I took a step forward and kicked some stray signage the Swinekong had wrecked, sending it thumping into the beast's back. I spun away to run in the opposite direction before it could charge at me again and shuddered at the sound of heavy, wet snorts getting closer as I tore through the trees. I needed an open area to fight, but the place seemed to be packed with attractions and narrow paths.

I took a peek behind me and saw death gaining on me at breakneck speed. But before me was another attraction: Alice looking up at a giant caterpillar. Behind it was the largest tree I had ever seen.

'Guess we're all crazy here,' I murmured as a shadow of a plan flashed in my mind. I jumped over the light blue picket fence and smashed the bottom of the tree with Fjall as I passed by. The trunk splintered as my hammer cleaved out a huge chunk. A hint of anger came through my connection with Oregon as the tree fell forward, landing directly on top of the beast.

The Swinekong took the hit from the tree right in the face. I had hoped the tree would turn it into a pancake. However, reality proved to be far more disappointing. The thick tree landed with a sickening crunch of bone, knocking the Swinekong down. It bellowed in pain, swaying on its hooven feet but remained standing.

'Why won't you *die*?' I growled and was about to rush forward to finish the job when the giant statues of Alice and a mushroom floated in the air above the beast and smashed into it like a tenderizer. Blood, meat and colorful painted stones flew everywhere. I wiped some liquid off my face with the sleeve of my shirt, shocked by the carnage.

My mouth fell open as I looked up to see Hernandez's eyes glowing with orange light as she pointed her staff towards us while Lane used the magenta railing for support. His face was pale and bloodied, a bandage wrapped around his forehead.

*Note to self: have Julia bake a three-story chocolate cheesecake for the murderous paramedic.*

The mushed up remains of the Grisharu turned gray and melted into goo like all the others. I had to remind myself to close my mouth before walking towards the paramedics.

'I'm never going to the zoo again,' Hernandez panted as she lowered her staff. Her eyes lost their orange light and returned to their natural steel blue.

'Thanks, you just saved my bacon.'

She glared at me.

'Too soon?' I asked sheepishly while I tried to get my heart back under control.

'Little bit,' Lane said as he leaned on the railing.

I looked at him. 'You good?'

Hernandez scoffed and helped Lane sit on the ground. 'He's lucky to be alive. I had to use all the regeneration patches we had to pull him back from the brink. Right now, he should be on his ass, *resting*.' She looked at my arm and frowned. 'Here, let me see that.'

The medical bag floated next to her as she disinfected and dressed my wound. After a minute or two, I thought she was done, but then she stuck a needle in my arm. 'Ouch! What was that for?'

'We don't know if or what kind of diseases those things are carrying, so I'm not taking any chances. That's an immunobooster packed with enough goodies to kill a mutated strain of the black plague if it ever rears its nasty head again.' She then slapped me right where she had poked me.

I groaned at the throbbing ache spreading throughout my arm. 'A little warning next time would be great.' I rubbed the spot, inclined my head towards her and smiled lightly. 'Thanks.'

I looked into the surrounding distance for signs of a battle, but everything was quiet. Snow continued falling from the sky, silently covering the park in a white blanket. I gave Lane a cursory look. 'You should take him to the ambulance,' I told Hernandez. 'Have him lie down and keep an eye on things. Try to contact Elaine Hughes. She's at the Assembly. Ask her what the hell's taking so long.'

Indecision flared in her eyes. I clasped her on the shoulder. 'It's our best play at the moment. We can't have Lane die of hypothermia and risk our only medical aid being wiped out.'

'You do realise I can hear you, right?' Lane's gruff voice sounded from the floor.

Hernandez let out a sigh and nodded. 'Yeah, and if you're not bitching about going and being all stupidly macho, then you know how bad you're hurt.' She took out a radio that she had clipped to her waist and gave it to me. 'When you find them, give me a buzz, and I'll rush over. Even if I have to drive the ambulance through the damn park.'

I took the radio and put it over my shoulder. 'It's not like the park can get much worse at this point.' I nodded towards the path that led back to the entrance. 'Be careful out there, we don't know what other traps are lying in wait for us.'

She shook her head and raised her staff towards the slumped figure. The injured mage began to float a foot off the ground. 'Don't worry about me – go and kick this puta's ass.'

Hernandez turned around and walked back where we came from, towing the floating form of her partner along beside her. I turned back to the path and found myself frowning. If I went back to the cobblestone road, I would be following in Devon and Silera's footsteps, but if there was another trap, I would walk right into it. I couldn't hear or sense any further chaos. Now that the battle was over, the whole park had gone eerily quiet once more. I tried again to use my connection with Oregon to get a sense of where I needed to go but had no luck. If I went off the path, I might evade whatever nasty surprises the witch had conjured up for us, but that would mean taking the risk of missing my friends.

I tightened my hand around Fjall's handle and made my way right towards the woods to avoid triggering any more nasty surprises. I stepped over the crumbled remains of Alice and moved deeper into the forest.

The snowfall had turned the skies dark gray, giving the woods an ominous feel, as if they had come alive and were watching, judging. Having dealt with sentient trees before, I hoped it was just my imagination, but I wouldn't underestimate Arianwen, not with Alice and Margie's lives at stake. The wind picked up, howling through the park like a crying widow reaching fever pitch as it passed the empty, wrecked attractions and danced between the trees.

A shiver skittered up and down my spine that had nothing to do with the cold, and I moved a little faster. I passed several more huge trees and stumbled into worn wooden railings, staring at the house beyond.

It seemed familiar. The colourful fake timber with its jagged lines and concave walls, off-center windows ... it was an uncanny likeness to *his* home. I wanted to walk away, but I couldn't.

I shook my head, blearily blinking the memories away and swearing when my eyes opened, and I found myself next to the house. Alarm swelled as the blood rushed to my head. My gaze focused on a statue standing in front of the house. It was of an old man with a large bulbous nose and bushy white beard. Wearing an impeccable black and blue suit, completed by a top hat askew to the front and a wooden cane.

I took a second to read the sign stuck in the ground in front of him and felt chills roll across my skin as a sweat broke out. I looked back at him, and the statue suddenly had razor sharp teeth and glowing yellow eyes that pierced right through me. My heart pounded in my chest so fast I was surprised it didn't burst. I blinked, and the statue went back to normal. My legs clamped up and nausea churned in my stomach, filling my mouth with saliva as the words became larger and clearer.

*There was a Crooked Man,*

*and he went a crooked mile.*

*He found a crooked sixpence,*

*against a crooked stile;*

*He bought a crooked cat, which*

*caught a crooked mouse,*

*And they all lived together in*

*a little crooked house.*

*I looked around and suddenly found myself no longer in the snowy wooded park but in an ancient forest, sinister and foreboding. My side was bleeding from a stab wound, and I didn't have the strength to move. I knew I needed to get out of here but my body wouldn't respond. My heart ached at the sudden betrayal, not by the man who left me here to die but from the woman who had given him the order.*

I shook my head and took a step back. No – no, I wasn't bleeding. I hadn't been betrayed. I needed to move, to get out of these woods, away from this house.

*The one person in my godsforsaken life I thought loved me had ordered my death without a second thought. As if I were nothing more than an ant beneath her boot. No, I was worse than an ant because she hadn't even bothered to step on me herself. The betrayal hurt more than the injury. She should've at least granted me the small mercy of giving me a quick death instead of leaving me in this hellhole.*

*A soft tapping sound caught my attention as it broke the silence. In this cursed forest, there wasn't a sound to be heard. No animals, no rustling leaves, not even an insect. Nothing at all except for the soft tapping sound that drew ever closer.*

*Tap, tap, tap.* Was that the echo of the memory, or did he approach even now? I turned to the statue. Had it moved? I couldn't tell. My breaths heaved, and my stomach soured as I fought the rising tide of vision and memory.

*I tried to move and hide behind one of the trees, but it was no use. A melodious fatherly voice sounded all around me.*

*'You poor child. Who has left you alone and bleeding in the middle of my forest?' I tried to pinpoint the source of the voice, but it was futile.*

Not real, not real. This was just a wooden house made by a mortal, not *his* citadel of horrors. I needed to get to Alice, to Margie. They needed me, and I needed them.

*I craned my head to the side. Under the silhouette of a tree was a man; half of his body was obscured by the darkness. I could only see a pair of dark trousers and boots, along with a wooden cane that had some sort of silver coin embedded in the handle. A pair of impossibly long pale fingers were wrapped around it. Perfectly manicured nails tapped the coin ever so slightly.*

*Behind the man was a dark shadow that moved on all fours. The musky scent of a big cat flooded my nostrils along with an acrid stench that I couldn't place.*

*I tried to speak, but the words were caught in my throat by an invisible net. 'No my dear, don't try to speak,' the fatherly voice came to me once more. 'You're hurt, and I will take care of you. Anyone who walks into my domain is like my own child, and they deserve nothing but my utmost attention.'*

*No.* I blinked hard and forced myself back to the present, trembling on my hands and knees as I gasped for breath. My forehead felt damp, and I picked up a clump of snow, pressing it to my face, letting the smooth, cool feel of it wash over me.

I tried to take a few deep breaths to calm myself. On the ground next to me was Fjall, covered by a thin layer of snow. I picked it up and felt a little more secure with the weapon in my hand.

Damn it all to hell. I hadn't had a panic attack like that in so long. It somehow felt more than that, though. Almost like a warning. I had forgotten what it felt like to be weak and helpless. Rage exploded inside me, consuming my fear in one big hot wave. I would never let myself feel that way again.

I pushed the memories back to the darkest corner of my mind where they belonged and stood up. I'd spent too much time here already.

I took one more look at the statue of the old man and brought down Fjall in one mighty swing. Thunder rolled across the park as the statue exploded into a thousand pieces. I looked down at the broken scraps. 'Next time I'm coming for you, asshole.'

# 22

A pillar of red light pierced the dark gray skies, startling me as it shot up like a flare. The whole park was bathed in a baleful crimson glow, the trees shivering under the cursed light. The air was charged with an underlying current of something foul. I frowned and tried for the third time to use my connection with the land to find the girls, swearing violently when it yielded nothing but a pounding headache. *Time to do this the old fashioned way,* I thought as I began weaving through the trees, following the source of that beam of power. Arianwen really *had* found a way to keep her actions hidden, even from the spirit of the land, just like Oregon had warned me.

The shadows of the trees grew longer as if they were reaching out to pull me in. The whole place looked like it had been bathed in blood. The air was so thick with magic, it felt like sucking in mouthfuls of lead with every breath as my heart pounded like a war drum. The once pure snow reflected the red light from above, making it look tainted and corrupt. It reminded me of the Frozen Spire and how blood had soaked the ice. The park now seemed more like a hellscape than a winter wonderland. I ran towards the source of the light, jumping over a railing and deeper into the woods. Gods, I hoped I wasn't too late.

As quickly as it had appeared, the pillar vanished. The light was gone, but it had left the night sky tainted with crimson, blotting out the stars. With the light gone, I could feel my connection to Oregon starting to pierce the veil of magic a little. It gave me a small amount of comfort. I wasn't completely alone. Had that beam expelled some of the magic that was clogging the place? Or did Arianwen no longer care if I found her? Darkness closed in around me; the murkiness of the night made tangible.

Ahead of me, there was a break in the trees, and I ran towards it on gentle feet, careful not to make too much noise. I drew closer and stopped behind a tree. Four people stood in a clearing ahead of me, two of them bound to a tree, the others held in place by an invisible force. Standing in the middle of them all was the bitch herself – Arianwen.

The clearing was devoid of trees, and it reminded me of the druid circles back in Faerie. It felt as if nothing dared to grow in there except the ancient oak tree that towered at the centre of the clearing, a forest king. Devon and Silera were facing me, but Arianwen was turned away. I breathed deeply, trying to calm myself, knowing I couldn't rush in half-cocked. The tree hid me well, but I would have to move into the open to be of any help. A spear of aching dread shook me as I noticed a bloody figure lying in the grass in front of the witch.

The moon gleamed above us like a red diamond, and the bite of winter sank its frozen fangs into my skin, making me shudder. My heart thudded even louder in my chest as I slowly peered around the tree once more. A quiet sigh of relief escaped my lips before I could stop it. The body was too big to be Margie, and the hair was the wrong colour for Alice.

I focused on the body from afar and saw blood pooling around her body from two large incisions, one below her ribs and the other one under her navel. I turned slightly and watched the witch grind something inside a stone mortar. My stomach churned. I didn't want to think about what it could be.

Instead, my relief made the scents of the forest seem sharper, more intense. I was sorry for the girl, another soul to add to the list of people that I had failed, but it could have been Alice lying there – or Margie. As my eyes moved over the scene, the scents fed into my vision, my connection with the land fueling me. The musk from the trees, the dampness of the snow. But it was all overridden as I finally spotted the girls, the rich iron stench of blood blending with my panic.

They were tied separately to each side of the ancient withered tree that stood in the clearing. I could just about make out the dried blood smeared on Alice's forehead and a bolt of fear stabbed through my gut. Her head hung to the side, eyes closed but *there*. I breathed a sigh of relief as I saw a puff of breath leave her mouth. Margie's frightened eyes darted around frantically. The sound of her terror was muffled by the branches gagging her, filling my ears until I could hear almost nothing else.

Energy radiated from the tree I clung to, cooling my rage as it bid me to *see*, to *watch*, to *act*. Tears streaked down Margie's face as she struggled to move. The tree holding her called out to me; it felt *wrong*, corrupted. Its branches were straining against thin tendrils of sickly crimson light. They reeked of the rot I had come to recognise as Arianwen's magic. Deep gauges marred the bark and oozed a red sap as if the tree itself was crying bloody tears. The surrounding trees shuddered in the wind like they were waiting for something to arrive. I needed to find a way to get closer without attracting Arianwen's attention.

My eyes found their way back to Devon and Silera, who stood side by side. Thick white roots splotched with fresh blood were wrapped tightly around Devon's body, making it impossible for him to move. His muscles were tensed from straining against his bonds, a vein on his neck throbbed with a steady beat. His kukri blade lay a few feet from him, tantalisingly close. Silera was frozen in place, her form translucent and crimson moonlight passed through her spectral form as she struggled to move. Her hair fanned out in a bronze wave, caught in an otherworldly wind that wasn't of this plane. Her mouth moved, but no sound came out.

This was a fucking disaster. Arianwen had managed to capture and neutralise two of the most powerful beings I knew. How much power was she packing to stop them cold? I saw Silera's hands move in an obvious attempt to cast a spell, but nothing happened.

Arianwen tilted her head back and laughed. Her braided silver-white hair glinted in the bloody moonlight. 'You might as well give up. As powerful as you are, in your current condition, there isn't anything you can do.'

How had the witch incapacitated Devon and Silera so completely? I stretched out my senses slightly and recoiled as I felt the huge amount of foul power Arianwen was channeling. That had to be it – she had corrupted the leynode. She didn't care if I knew where they were because she thought she was unstoppable. She might even be right. Anger burned inside me at the thought of all that stolen life, but I quenched it. Now wasn't the time to lose my temper.

A wave of anger and disgust that was not mine alone rolled through me at the sound of her voice. I pulled my hands from the tree, and the feelings faded, only to strengthen again when I returned my palms to the bark. The tree wanted Arianwen out of the forest as much as I did. It had to be a perk of being Oregon's champion since I had never before been able to communicate with trees, not even the sentient ones I'd found in Faerie.

I wasn't sure what was going on with Silera, but I had to trust she could save herself and instead focused on where I *could* help — getting Devon out. I opened my tether to Oregon and used the tree as a channel to direct the flow of magic. The energy passed through the bark and slithered across the ground to the roots holding Devon. I could feel them slackening as I funneled my power through them.

I delved into the well of power inside me and borrowed as much as I could from Oregon. It felt like tapping into a live wire. Power coursed through me, overflowing in every cell. My bones groaned from the strain of the magic.

Suddenly, a clump of roots shot out from underneath me, wrapping themselves around my waist and making it impossible to raise my arms to defend myself. The radio Hernandez had given was instantly crushed, the sharp plastic cutting into my side. The thick roots pulled me closer towards the tree I had been hiding behind. I glanced down and saw the deep red haze of Arianwen's death-magic coating the vines. I tapped into my connection with Oregon once more and swore. The tree had been corrupted. The longer I held onto Oregon's magic, the tighter the roots grew. They lifted me ten feet into the air above Devon and Silera like a piñata waiting to be smacked.

'It's not polite to spy on people, Nathaniel Mercer.'

The witch turned around to face me, her red mouth curled into a predatory grin. 'Did you really think you could sneak up on me?' She regarded me like a spider about to spin its web around its prey. Her loose white gown seemed to glow and fluttered over the grass as she took a step towards me. I grinned savagely as she came within spitting distance, and I aimed a wad of it at her. Cold anger froze her face, making her look even more inhuman as she raised a hand to her cheek and wiped my spit away.

I had succeeded in loosening Devon's roots a fraction, but it had only given him enough room to struggle in earnest. As Arianwen made her way to Alice and Margie with a slow intent that made the smile fade from my face, Devon's skin began to turn an ugly shade of purple.

She stopped before the tree and spun around to look at us. Cold fear slid through me as the witch showed us who really had the power here. She went back to grinding, letting the sound of a pestle on mortar fray my nerves.

'I can feel your hatred for me; it burns like a bonfire.' She shook her head. 'I suggest,' she said with another threatening step towards Margie, who flinched, 'that you behave.'

Arianwen made her way back to the dead girl near Rela and Devon. I looked away as she reached with her long fingers and started rummaging in one of the wounds. I shuddered at the squelch that followed and looked back just in time to see her add something to the mortar.

'You Champions are all the same.' She nodded towards Silera. 'You kill a few insignificant miscreants, and suddenly, you're a blight on the land.' She walked towards me with steady, graceful steps. 'I must say you have impressed me. You have bested not one but *three* of my creations and have meddled in my affairs time and time again. That takes skill. Or stupidity'

I tried to shrug but being dangled in the air, tied up by a wooden snake, made it a little hard. 'What can I say? I have a talent for screwing things up.' I needed to keep her talking while I figured a way out of this mess before Arianwen murdered everyone I loved.

I shook my head, chasing those thoughts away and turned to Silera. She was still waving her arms, trying to undo whatever spell Arianwen had cast on her. There had to be something I could do.

'Why go after innocent mortal women and mutilate them?' I asked. It was the only thing that didn't make any sense to me.

'This is an interesting age, unlike my own. The mortal and the supernatural dance along the edge of a blade, careful not to step on each other's toes because it will spell mutual destruction.' She stood before Devon and Silera. 'Humans fear what they don't understand. But now they have more advanced weapons than simple swords and shields. So the supernatural evolved. They learned to be comfortable being relegated to myths and legends. They found they could prey on the humans without fearing that people would rise against them. It's a sweet deal, as the mortals now say.' She looked at Silera and smiled knowingly. 'Yet the old powers still exist. The terrible monsters and Gods that once ruled these lands are biding their time for the moment they can claim the world as their own once more.'

'While I love your thesis on modern preternatural society, could you please save it for college and answer the question?'

'Oh, but I just did,' Arianwen said with a smile. 'They were simple prey for an old monster such as myself. You have no idea how much magic lies in the heart and womb. The heart is the body's lifeblood, pumping every single day, providing it with nourishment. The womb is the cradle where the most magical act of them all is formed: life.'

I frowned at her. 'So what, you killed innocent women and ripped out their organs to steal their magic? The women were mortal. They didn't have any.'

She clicked her tongue at me and shook her head, her silver hair fanning across her shoulders. In the red light coating the sky, it seemed imbued with an otherworldly glow. 'How wrong you are. Every person, mortal or not, carries a spark of magic inside them. Some more than others, but even the most insignificant peasant has it.' She stopped grinding her mortar and placed one hand to her stomach. 'Humans all carry within them the potential for life. And, if you know the right spell, one might harvest that spark. Crudely done,' she said, gesturing to the body of the girl on the floor, 'much messier than using the Girsharu to drain the witches, but it was necessary. You have your brother champion to thank for all of this. He left me completely drained of my magic when he sealed me away. '

She turned around and walked towards the unconscious figure of Alice and caressed her extended belly. Devon began to struggle against the roots, and they dug into his flesh, leaving deep gashes. Blood soaked through his shirt, and red droplets sprayed the air as his legs kicked to no avail.

'Devon, stop! I'll get us out.' I pleaded with him even though I was in the same damn situation, but he didn't listen as he struggled harder. If I didn't do something now, he was going to kill himself.

Margie looked at Arianwen with tear-streaked eyes and tried to curl into herself as much as she could, cringing away.

Arianwen paid them no mind. 'If there's one thing more powerful than a spark of creation, it's two.' She turned around and looked at Devon. 'I must thank you Dr Othonos. If you two hadn't killed my creations, I wouldn't have known that your kind still existed.' Her smile turned giddy. 'Scions have so much magic within them, the flame of divinity burns in your blood. Your people are like wildfire.' She smiled. 'Especially the young who have so much life within them. The adults have lived and their flame no longer burns as bright.' She then turned towards Rela and inclined her head. 'I appreciate the role the fae had in my success tonight. If they hadn't attacked that accursed merman and broke the protection wards around that trice damned library, it would've taken me another half a millennia to escape.' She giggled to herself as she kept caressing Alice's belly. Devon screamed through the root gagging him.

Arianwen was too enraptured with Alice to notice. 'How magnificent you are, the perfect meld of the mortal and the divine, life and death both so neatly packed inside. All that brimming power waiting to be released. Claimed.'

She grabbed Alice's maternity gown and ripped it, exposing her belly. Suddenly, a black and green light covered Alice protectively. It felt similar to Devon's scion magic. My eyes widened. But surely not? *The twins?* Arianwen's nail elongated, coated in a crimson sheen, and the scent of iron and rot filled the night air.

Arianwen twisted her finger and jabbed it into Alice's extended stomach, piercing the protective shield like it was made of paper.

'Get away from her, or I swear I will rip you apart with my bare hands!' I let the power of Oregon surge through me and used it to push against the wooden snake's binding. The roots instantly began to tighten, and I screamed, my hold on the magic slipping. The roots lessened their hold, and I took a deep breath.

Arianwen continued, undeterred, carving with slow, precise movements until a familiar symbol began to form on Alice's belly. A crooked mouth with two spears crossed beneath it. A smile crept up her lips as she admired her macabre work. Devon sobbed through the gag in his mouth. Alice's blood began to flow from her belly, mixing with the contents of the mortar. I let out a roar and took hold of the fading magic urging the power to come quicker, spiralling deeper than I ever had before.

The energy flooded into me, too much, too fast, and I screamed as it burned like pure fire. I didn't notice when the roots around me crumbled to ash until I fell to the ground and tried to quell the flow. It was too late. I was the power, and it was me, too entangled in one another to tell where one began, and the other ended.

*Damn it, Nathaniel Mercer, you're not about to let another friend die because you were too weak to stop it!*

A powerful pulse of magic rang through the woods, causing each blade of grass to tremble. It brought me back to myself long enough to cut the connection with Oregon. I grit my teeth, blinked away blood and instinctively looked towards Devon. The pulse felt very similar to when he summoned the undead, but his eyes were wide, scared. He wasn't even looking at me; his gaze focused on the withered tree. I prayed that nothing worse had happened to Alice and turned to look. But it wasn't Alice he was watching. Even Arianwen had stopped her work and stared at the glowing patch of darkness in the sea of red that was Margaret Othonos, Granddaughter of Hades.

# 23

Margie's blue eyes had gone completely black, just two orbs that looked eerily out of place on her pale face. The red glow around her had turned pitch black, so dark that it absorbed and twisted the light as if she were her own miniature black hole. The darkness pulsed from her body, pushing against the crimson light like a tsunami from the depths of hell.

The roots that bound her withered to dust as she rose into the air. The glow around her morphed into a pair of feathery wings of the darkest midnight, carrying her towards her dad and Silera.

'Margie! Run!' I gasped through my lingering pain. She didn't stir. It was as if she couldn't hear me. She turned to look at Arianwen, who appeared perplexed by the sudden development. Margie flapped her wings and slashed her hand through the air in front of her, and the ground below cracked, opening a chasm ten-foot wide that released a dark mist. A cacophony of howls sounded from the chasm, and a black paw raked the earth as it emerged. A muscular frame slowly shouldered its way up, and a chorus of barks sounded from its three heads.

My eyes widened as I took in the enormity of the creature. It was six feet tall at the shoulder and its three heads had powerful jaws, each sporting a forest of white teeth. I took a deep breath, my heart jackhammering in my chest as the beast's gaze moved over and then past me. The beast's necks were thick with loose folds of skin, and its chest was covered in scars that spoke of battle. Margie floated down from the sky, her wings flowing back into her body as she stood next to the beast. It circled around her protectively, its three pairs of eyes were small, but they burned with hellfire. I did not want to be on the receiving end of that gaze again.

Margie's magic had awakened and in the most dramatic way possible. Devon and Alice had mentioned that it could happen at any moment since a child usually awakened between the ages of ten to thirteen. But I never could have predicted *this*. They had jokingly run a bet as to whether Margie was going to be a necromancer like her dad or a telepath like her mom. I had put my money on both. I looked at the massive beast dwarfing her four-foot figure – I guess we were all wrong.

Margie pointed her dainty finger at Arianwen and spoke, her voice thrumming with power, 'Skotóno.'

*Kill,* my mind automatically translated. Cerberus let out a concerto of barks and rushed towards Arianwen like a nightmare brought to life. The witch smirked at the incoming three-headed dog.

'What a lovely puppy.' She turned towards Margie and smiled. 'You are full of surprises aren't you, child? Makes me want your divine blood even more.' Her grin turned predatory as she waved her hand in the air, and from the thicket of trees behind her came a huge monstrosity crashing about until it stood in front of its mistress. It was a massive creature, easily two feet taller than Cerberus. The new beast had the body of a scorpion with deadly looking pincers the size of industrial cranes and spear-like legs. Instead of one tail, this thing had two, the stingers razor-sharp and dripping with a dark liquid that sizzled on contact with the ground below. The two titanic animals crashed into each other. The Grisharu hissed, launching at Cerberus with its two pincers. The hellhound dodged the strikes on nimble feet and bit three of the Grisharu's legs at once.

Arianwen ignored the battle and turned back to Alice, finishing the carving of the grotesque symbol. Once she was done, she threw the contents of the mortar onto the front of the tree with a satisfied smile.

Margie stood watching the fight with unblinking black eyes. Devon tried to call out to her, but she ignored him. Concern gnawed at my stomach. This wasn't the girl who loved to laugh and dance. She was an entirely different person, one I didn't know. I wasn't sure how she might react if I got involved. Would Margie perceive me as a threat?

The liquid paste Arianwen had thrown onto the tree had begun to smoke, and I felt the great tree that had stood for centuries dying. Like dominoes falling one after the other, all around us, trees began to wither and disintegrate. A roar of pain and rage erupted from my throat. Another life had been ripped from this earth by Arianwen, this one older than the city itself. Clumps of snow fell from the branches of the old tree and melted before they hit the ground, like tears. The previously snow-covered grass turned pale yellow before crumbling into dust.

The power inside me bucked like a wild horse as Arianwen further corrupted the Earth, battering at my skin until I was sure I would look down and find blood. Oregon was furious, and I was the vessel of her magic, the conduit for her rage. I panted heavily through the pressure that was trying to suffocate me. With every new death, Oregon's anger grew until it threatened to blow my body to pieces. I struggled to open my mouth as the power surged.

'Amach!' I screamed, at last, the word spilling from me as my magic detonated outwards. Arianwen turned away from Alice, her eyes hardening. A deluge of magic emanated from her as she pushed a wave of death towards me. My bones groaned, and I spat a mouthful of blood as I tried to form the energy to retaliate, my body fracturing under the onslaught of Oregon's magic. Life, the magic of nature, erupted in a wave as Oregon moved through me, heedless of my deteriorating body. I strained to lift my head and gazed in wonder as new leaves and flowers sprouted from the ground.

Oregon was fighting back, and she was pissed.

Death slithered through the air like a rotting snake, and Oregon's fury rose to meet it, raging against my own will. *Give me back control of my body,* I begged her while her magic swirled inside me like a tornado. *You asked for a Champion, not a puppet! Let me be one!*

Death clashed with Life, and Arianwen screamed at the contact with Oregon. A shock wave of pure power exploded from the collision of the two energies, lifting me up from the ground and rolling me onto my back. The roots holding Devon were blown to smithereens, and he fell next to me. The wave hit Silera, and for a moment, her form solidified before vanishing completely. Ice chilled me to the marrow of my bones, and I wanted to scream. Oregon relaxed her hold, and relief flooded through me. Margie's black wings had sprouted again, and the wave passed through her like a harmless breeze.

I turned to Arianwen in time to see her sway on her feet, her skin visibly pale. Fighting Oregon had cost her. She appeared weaker than before and a glimpse of hope surged through me – we might stand a chance at taking the bitch down. A trickle of blood trailed down from her nose as the witch pointed towards me with one bony finger. 'Kill him!'

The Grisharu charged towards me but didn't get very far. Seizing the creature's tail between its jaws, Cerberus pulled the corrupted familiar back. Arianwen hurriedly faced the tree, her hands cupping something between them. 'Mewn enw Chraos-Fhiachlach, lladdwyr y Dagda, Rwy'n hawlio'r staff hyn trwy hawliau concwest.'

*In the name of the Voracious, slayer of the Dagda, I lay claim to her enemy's staff, won by right of conquest.*

Dagda. One of The Tuatha Dé Danann and husband to Morrigan. The name hit me like a punch in the stomach as I realised too late what my dreams had been trying to warn me about. The giant man from my vision had been the Dagda, claiming his famous weapon, Lorg Mór. The staff of wrath. The song of war that had been ringing in my blood since I got to the park exploded in a chorus of drums. It was the staff that had been calling me all this time, but why?

The withered tree Arianwen stood beside shuddered, its branches curling up and rolling back towards the center of the trunk. The scent of putrefaction and blood permeated the air, making me gag. The bark split with a groan and released a sudden wave of magic that raised the hair on my arms. Gods, if the witch got a hold of the Lorg Mór, there really would be no stopping her.

A column of white light pierced the red skies, and an ocean of magic poured from Arianwen into the withered tree. From its center a familiar staff rose, one side pale and smooth at the tip and the other a darker shade with small needles protruding from the end. Lorg Mór.

Ancient, powerful magic radiated from it, and terror coursed through my veins as I thought about it in Arianwen's possession. The thing glowed like a supernova – it wasn't an item made for mortal hands. Odd, that the staff should be discovered again when all the old players were back on the chessboard. I had witnessed firsthand what it could do. It couldn't be a coincidence that Oregon's Champion, a thousand-year-old witch, the Scions of a Greek God, and a fae princess had come together in a battle to the death with the weapon of a slain God at the center of it all. My blood pulsed like a clap of thunder that wouldn't be ignored. Suddenly, an image flowed into my mind: I was in my black fae armor, holding the staff in my hands, battling shadowy figures. It belonged to me, and I belonged to it. I pushed down the strange urge to take it, to claim it as rightfully mine. Right now, all that mattered was Alice and Margie.

Devon walked towards me unsteadily and helped me up onto shaking legs. 'Nathan, what the hell is that?' His voice was hoarse from screaming, and his eyes didn't leave Margie even as he spoke to me.

I started to answer him when Arianwen stepped intently towards the staff and curled her fingers around its middle where the two woods fused, pulling it free from the tree. The light vanished, and the need to *possess,* to *claim,* to *own* crashed through me again. Arianwen stood with her back straight, caressing the staff with loving hands. I stumbled an unwilling step forward and stared. The witch glowed with power, all earlier fragility erased as if the fight had never happened. She turned around. Her eyes flared with magic, silver hair floating around her head as she held the staff aloft.

We could barely stand, and Arianwen looked fresh as a daisy. Where the hell had Silera gone? We needed all the fire-power we could get.

'Finally, after all these years of being trapped in a damn book, revenge is close.' Arianwen turned towards Margie with a hungry look and planted the staff on the ground in front of her. My heart sped up as dread pumped through my veins. Lorg Mór stood up eerily straight, held to a law unto itself, bowing not even for gravity. The witch made a complex motion with her hands and spat out a single word that throbbed with magic, 'Ilygredig!'

The symbol carved into Alice's belly began to glow with a blinding red light. Alice's head snapped upright, her eyes opening in fright, lips trembling before letting out a soul-wrenching scream. Devon echoed her cries, roaring something in Ancient Greek. The gleam from her belly streamed into the staff, turning it the color of charcoal before the light shot towards Margie and pierced her chest.

Adrenaline hit, chasing away the fear and re-energising me. The only way to save Margie and Alice was by defeating Arianwen. Devon and I exchanged a glance and charged at the bitch. I picked up Fjall from where it had fallen and saw Devon scoop up his blade as we ran. Margie crashed to the ground, screaming. I wished she had stayed in that vacant state so as to spare her the pain.

I jumped into the air, swinging my hammer down on Arianwen's head while Devon slashed at her abdomen. We had her. She could dodge one, but not both, strikes.

We had her – until we didn't. Arianwen slammed the staff down sending a shockwave of pure power straight into us. It felt like being hit by a rampaging bull. My back slammed into a tree, and my wrist snapped, crushed beneath me as red hot pain flooded my senses. I could still hear Margie's screams, and from the corner of my eye, I saw her writhe on the ground. I pulled Devon to his feet and cradled my wrist. One of Cerberus' heads turned around to look at Margie as we ran towards her. The momentary distraction cost him as the Grisharu impaled the massive dog in its shoulder using one of its tails. Cerberus clawed at the offending appendage, the wound rapidly turning gray.

A bead of sweat rolled down my face. Was I feverish? No. Devon was looking flushed too, something had made the temperature rise uncomfortably high and my clothes felt sticky. A flash of light came from behind me, followed by a large ball of fire that hurtled through the air, missing me by a hair's breadth. It smashed right into the Grisharu's open mouth before it could bite Cerberus.

I could only look on, gaping, as a figure made of molten rock moved and launched itself through the air to tackle the Grisharu, knocking it down. The rock erupted with burning magma that slowly coalesced into the form of a snarling wolf. *What fresh horror was this?* It reached almost to my shoulder, with bright red and black stony skin. Lava dripped from its massive lupine jaws and burned the ground upon contact. Tongues of flames erupted from his ears and tail. Immense heat radiated from the wolf, the surrounding snow melting into puddles.

Devon rushed back to Margie and tried to comfort her but she continued to scream. He looked at me with desperation on his face as he held Margie in his arms. A rustling of feet caught my attention, and I turned back to see an out of breath Roel sprinting through the woods. He saw me and smiled. 'Hey boss, sorry I'm late. It took longer than I expected to free my boy.'

Roel nodded towards the magma wolf who floated towards him and rubbed its head against his palm affectionately. I stared in stunned silence for a moment. He had given me shit for talking to Sabine when all this time he had a wolf made of *lava?* Roel was unaffected by the heat, stroking the wolf's chin.

I shook my head and picked Fjall up from where it had landed. 'We are going to have words about *this* later,' I said, gesturing towards his familiar. 'Are you back to full strength?'

Roel nodded and then turned towards Arianwen. 'Is that the crazy hag that's been causing so much trouble?'

Arianwen tilted her head, sizing up Roel and his wolf. 'Well, this is a surprise. A mágissa with a dual-nature familiar.' Her eyes narrowed, but she smiled icily. 'Today is my lucky day. I get to see my child again *and* rid the world of one of your insufferable kind.' She waved her hand lazily in the air, and a crimson sheen covered the Grisharu's hide. 'Kill them,' she spat before focusing her gaze on the staff. The monstrosity hissed and charged towards us. Out of the corner of my eye, I saw Cerberus limping towards Devon and Margie. We needed Silera, but I had no idea where she had disappeared to. My heart squeezed into a tight ball of worry.

'Do you think you can take the Grisharu?' I called to Roel as I made my way to Devon.

Man and wolf both looked at the incoming creature and nodded in unison. Roel's eyes flashed with fiery light, resembling his familiar's own otherworldly gaze. He clenched his fist and punched the air, power radiating from him like a volcano on the verge of erupting. 'Ekrígnymai.'

The wolf's eyes blazed red hot as it grew a foot taller and opened its mouth, spitting a torrent of lava that took the shape of a molten fist floating in mid-air. The fist had sucker-punched the Grisharu right in the kisser, pushing it back half a dozen feet. Of course, he would come up with some cartoony spell. Kid's not right in the head. I'd expected the monster to have half its face burnt away but Arianwen spells seemed to be protecting her creation from the heat.

Devon kissed Margie, still thrashing, and picked up his kukri knife. 'I need you to help me. I can kill her, but not alone.'

I nodded. 'Anything you need.' We turned to face the witch, leaving the wounded Cerberus to guard Margie. I would have felt better with Rela at our side too, but we would have to make do. Alice and Margie didn't have much longer.

We needed to sever their connection to the staff before it drained their life energy completely, and that meant Arianwen had to die. Now.

Devon began to chant in a low voice as he sped towards the witch. I recognised the words as the hymn of Hades, asking for a swift death to his enemies. The blade in his hand shone with black light as if eager to do his bidding. Devon swung it towards the witch as I ran after him. A barrage of roots rose to try and block our way. They withered with a wave of my hand.

Arianwen parried Devon's blade with the paler side of the staff. Sparks ignited when the weapons collided before the witch spun her rod to jab at Devon with the killing edge. Devon's momentum wouldn't allow him to save himself. I swung Fjall at an awkward angle and caught the staff. Thunder roared, and I felt my arm violently wrenched back.

Arianwen's hand glowed with crimson light as she swept it toward me. I raised my broken hand, and the hairs on the back of my neck rose with the twinge of pain. I ignored it and sent a wave of Oregon's magic towards the witch. The two energies collided again, and my feet slid back. The pain in my wrist spiked, but I pushed through, gritting my teeth. I needed to give Devon his opening.

Devon used the distraction to slash with his blade at the witch's throat. Arianwen let out a fierce battle cry and slammed the staff down, sending out another shockwave, making him miss. This time it was weaker, only pushing us back slightly. We landed just feet away, next to Roel.

Roel was frowning as he yelled, 'Erímosi!' His wolf raised its muzzle and let out a thunderous howl as its body glowed with a fiery light. To my surprise, the familiar turned and aimed the blaze right at Roel. Magma covered my friend from head to toe, and my eyes grew round. What the hell was he doing? His form began to shift until a fiery armor shielded his body. The ground around him boiled from the heat, cracks forming in the shape of a burning torch. 'I am Roel Theron, Heart of the Mountain, Bearer of the Sacred Flame, and I will wipe your stain from this world in the name of Hecate!'

# 24

Arianwen spun Lorg Mór at Roel's declaration. The staff turned darker on one side, her death magic fueling it. Alice continued to scream as the light pouring from her fed the staff. Devon and I looked at each other; an understanding crossed the space between us. We ran towards the witch.

Arianwen smirked at our approach. 'As if two suicidal fools could ever hope to kill me when an army couldn't touch the hem of my robes.' An army would have been nice right about now, but we were too far from any cemeteries for Devon to raise one.

'Then how about *three* suicidal fools,' a velvety voice parted the clotted air.

A gust of wind carrying Winter Ice rolled through the woods, blanketing the landscape. The icey flakes coiled together, condensing into sharp spikes that pierced Arianwen, impaling her. A look of surprise flashed through her eyes as she coughed up a mouth full of blood.

Devon and I stopped in our tracks, looking around in confusion until the air between us shimmered, and Rela stumbled through, rubbing her temples. 'Evernight take you. That was unpleasant.'

Relief washed over me at seeing her relatively unharmed. Her timing was impeccable. Gods, how could I not love this murderous woman?

A cackle came from the witch as she spat out another globule of blood. She smiled at us. 'Well, that was certainly unexpected,' she said through labored breath. 'Too bad you wasted your chance. Should've gone for the heart, dear.'

The blood coating the ice began to boil and evaporate until it hung like a red cloud above her head. The cloud split into two and each shaped itself into a facsimile of Arianwen.

Rela swore beside me, making me do a double-take. I could count on one hand the number of times I'd heard Rela swear.

The copies waved their hands, and the ice piercing the original shattered, the wounds healing instantly. Behind us, I could hear the battle between Roel and the Grisharu heating up, but I didn't dare look away from Arianwen.

Arianwen and her clones spoke as one, 'I have been burned at the stake, hanged, shot, stabbed and even had my throat ripped out once, yet here I stand.' The effect of the triple voice made it feel as if she were the three-faced Goddess herself. 'The only way they could stop me was by sealing me away. Even that was only possible because that miserable wretch sacrificed his own life to bind me to page and ink. I don't think you are prepared for such a sacrifice.'

A lance of Rela's signature sapphire flames streaked through the sky towards her, but one of the clones stepped forward. The lance struck, piercing her body, leaving a giant hole where the heart should be but the lance did not leave the other side of the cloud. Arianwen smirked as the hole re-filled itself. 'Well, that was incredibly rude of you. I was speaking.'

'I've had just enough of your endless yapping.' I risked a glance at Rela to see a ball of blue flames floating above her palm, a spiked ring of indigo ice condensed around the sphere. Both forces fought to consume each other and were only held back by Silera's will. My senses went into overdrive. No matter how small that thing looked, it sent every hair on my body on edge. Merging two opposing elements like fire and ice should be all but impossible. Then again, Silera ate impossible for breakfast and spat it back out when she was finished.

Rela launched the sphere. The red clones of Arianwen exploded into a mass of red smoke and streaked through the air, engulfing the sphere in their smoke. They glowed with azure light before contracting back into their original forms.

'I have waited a thousand moons to see my daughter's face again, and I will not be stopped by anyone.' Arianwen twirled the staff around in her hands and rushed at us.

Instinct spurred me forward, and I ran to meet her impending strike. She swung the staff, aiming its killing end at my head. Thunder rolled from Fjall as they connected. I had imagined the force from the blow would break her arms and send the staff flying from her hands, the witch going with it. But in reality, it felt like hitting a mountain.

The staff suddenly jerked to the side, sliding along the edge of Fjall. Arianwen's eyes widened as she fell forward. I thrust my knee into her stomach and slammed my elbow into the side of her face. The witch tumbled to the grass below, a trickle of blood flowed from a cut in her temple. She looked at the staff, horrified. The staff jerked again as if trying to free itself. Arianwen's knuckles turned white from strain as the weapon kept moving. I raised Fjall overhead, crimson light flared from the witch's hands, and the staff stopped its struggle. Striking like a cobra, she swung the staff to meet my blow.

Arianwen's eyes darted behind me, and relief flooded her irises. From the corner of my eye, I saw the clones approaching me. Their arms turned smokey before reforming as sharp spikes. If I moved an inch, the real witch would kill me instantly. She only needed to touch me with the dark end of the staff. But if I didn't, I would be turned into swiss cheese.

As the red spikes loomed closer, I held my breath as my muscles tensed, ready for the inevitable strike. But before they could do any damage, Devon stepped between one of them and sliced it in half with his kukri while Rela blew up the other with a flame lance. As Rela's clone reformed, she prepared to send out another lance, but Devon's kukri flashed with eerie green light, scattering the two halves of his clone. It did not reform. Devon's eyes lit with triumph as the red smoke dissipated. Rela called forth a sword of Winter Ice and slashed at it. But every puncture refilled, and each slice left no mark.

Arianwen pushed herself from the ground with a snarl and pushed me back. Shit.

'Get me close enough, and I can end her!' Devon yelled, the green light from his blade illuminating his face, and I nodded. Arianwen was up and moving, striking out at me as I moved in closer, trying to keep her focus away from Devon. My world narrowed to one purpose: *keep the death stick away from me*. I raised Fjall with my one good hand and clumsily blocked her strikes. I was becoming slower. Wielding so much magic had a price, and it was time for me to pay it in full.

Each blow made thunder roll across the woods as if a giant was flattening a cockroach. Every failed blow made the witch scowl deeper, eyes burning with hatred as a fierce expression overtook her face, and she moved faster. I strived to match her pace. Devon was counting on me. If this was to be Winter's Wolf's final stand, it would be a good one. Our arms became a blur of steel and wood, but I couldn't keep this up for long. A hammer was not meant to be a dueling weapon, and my arm was burning with the effort. If I had my old sword. I might've already had her pinned but that blade was lost somewhere in the Crooked Man's Forest.

Suddenly something changed. A wall of heat surged from behind me, and then all I felt was ice. A stab in my side. Arianwen smiled. My vision blurred, and I could see dark spots dancing along it. I looked back, my eyes widening, Arianwen had pushed me all the way to the edge of the glowing crevasse. I struggled to maintain my balance; one more step and I would fall in. My breath came out in short pants, and my arm ached from wielding Fjall. The hammer slid from my grasp as my fingers numb, and I swayed. Cold pain pulsed through my veins and travelled through my body, but I turned my head, needing to confirm what my body already knew.

On the other side of the crevasse Roel stood gaping at me in horror. His mouth was moving, but I couldn't hear him above the loud pumping of blood in my ears. He stood next to the smoldering corpse of the Grisharu, and I followed his gaze down, past the creature's missing tail, to the barb that stuck out of my side. My knees buckled, and I knelt at Arianwen's feet.

Was my chest always this heavy? Did my heart always beat so slow? My vision narrowed to pinpricks as sweat slid down the side of my face. My hands trembled, slick with sweat or blood, I couldn't see which, as I struggled to yank the stinger out of my body. My strength failed at last with the tide of blood that poured from me, and I fell forward. The slow movement was agony, and I wondered if it would be the last thing I would ever feel. Was this death? This shivering cold that shattered my bones and chilled my blood? Maybe it was fitting to die surrounded by friends as well as enemies. Could I have asked for more? Should I have kissed Rela one last time before heading into battle? I chuckled and spat a mouthful of blood. What waited for me beyond? Mag Mell? Would Manannan mac Lir even allow me to enter?

I felt as something was pressed against my shoulder and pushed me onto my back. I looked up to see the hazy figure of Arianwen, her foot on my chest, holding Lorg Mór in her hands. Above, I thought I could see a feathery shadow with glowing red eyes flying in circles.

Arianwen raised the staff and brought it down on me. I tried to raise my arm to do something, anything. But it didn't respond. I closed my eyes and waited for death to finally take me. Maybe Morrigan would pay me a visit and take my soul somewhere peaceful.

But, suddenly, I was warm, unbearably warm. Was this hell? I struggled to open my eyes; it felt like someone had poured concrete over them. When I finally managed to force them apart, I lay watching the scene continue. Roel's fiery form hung in the air between me and the witch. Two flaming daggers embedded themselves in Arianwen's shoulders, pushing her back. Flames licked her body before they were snuffed out, and her skin began to heal.

I tried to open my mouth to warn him not to let the staff touch him. Could the weapon of an ancient Irish God kill him if his skin was made of magma?

'You and your kind are a plague upon this world that needs to be eradicated!' The witch's eyes flared with crimson light, and her knuckles whitened as she gripped the staff.

Magic rolled off her like a tsunami wanting to devour everything in sight. Though it was numb, my skin prickled, the hairs rising on my arms in a small wave. She ran with preternatural speed towards Roel. He conjured another pair of flame daggers and met her blows with liquid grace. The two figures blurred, and I struggled to breathe as black and white and a myriad of reds bled into one another. The red blur fell to the floor. I closed my eyes, and when I opened them, Arianwen stood over the prone form of Roel. Some of his armor flaked into ash, drifting on the breeze. I thought he was dead until I saw the rise and fall of his chest.

A smirk twisted the witch's face as she moved to strike Roel with Lorg Mór. A killing blow. But it never landed. The smile froze on her face, the staff trembling in the air as the sharp blade of the kukri knife burst through her chest in a shower of blood. Arianwen coughed a mouthful of blood, eyes wide as she turned her head to look at Devon.

'You fool. I was being dramatic when I told you to aim for the heart, *I have no heart.* Nothing can kill me, not anymore.' Yet, Arianwen was turning pale. An ugly green light pulsed over the wound, and Devon smiled for the first time in hours. The sudden silence around the battle-field was deafening now. Where were the girls? I struggled to move my head, but I couldn't. Damn it, I couldn't see or hear them. Were they alright? Were they free? Devon's head turned to look at something behind me, the tension in his shoulders eased a little, and it gave me a small ray of hope. At least this hadn't all been for nothing. The girls were safe – they had to be.

'Maybe,' Devon said and whatever Arianwen saw on his face made her eyes dull and her lips tremble, even as she shook her head. 'If it were a regular blade, you might've survived. This blade, however' – Devon ripped it from her chest in emphasis and smiled again when she screamed – 'was carved from the fang of the immortal Cerberus, guardian of the souls of Hades, forged in the fires of the River Phlegethon and cooled in the waters of the River Acheron. There is *nothing* this blade can't kill.'

The witch's mouth formed a silent 'oh'. Devon raised his arm and gave the final blow, dismembering the witch in a quick motion. Arianwen's head fell to the ground and slowly rolled until it stopped right in front of me. I stared into her blank eyes and felt no remorse. This might once have been just a woman who lost her daughter, but what we had fought was little more than a monster in human flesh.

Devon turned back and disappeared from my field of vision. I blinked, and there he stood again, cradling Margie to his side. Her skin was as pale as a ghost, and her hand shook, her black eyes staring at the corpse of the woman who caused her so much pain. My mouth felt like it was stuffed with cotton, I wanted to speak, but no sound came out.

'You tapped into the darkness of your grandfather's realm, baby, his power now flows within you. Feel the connection to the underworld and bring forth its flames to cleanse the land.'

Margie raised her hand, and in a sonorous voice that didn't fit her small frame, she called out, 'Phlegethon!'

Above her hand, a stream of fire rose from the crevasse, snuggling around her like a pet. She let it cuddle into her before sending it towards the witch's corpse, reducing it to ash.

The red glow that had dominated the skies vanished, leaving behind the calm clouds of a regular Oregon night. I let out a labored breath, and closed my eyes. It was over, finally. Alice and Margie were safe.

Silence claimed the woods, and for a blissful moment, I felt myself drifting away. Death loomed at my periphery like a stalking predator waiting to strike. I didn't have the strength to fight it anymore. I just wanted to be away from the pain. Gods knew how much it hurt. Every single cell of my body felt like it was being pierced by icy cold needles as whatever poison was in that stinger killed me slowly.

'Devon, your wife's water just broke.' Rela's voice sounded urgent yet far away. I fought to stay conscious, but the darkness was now warm, promising an end to the cold.

A commotion suddenly broke out around me. I tried to open my eyes, but they were too heavy and the darkness too complete.

'Hades! I summon you to human form!' I no longer recognised the voice of who was yelling. A distant rumble of thunder detonated, and I felt the earth underneath me tremble for a moment.

A warm sensation touched my chest and flowed all over my body. Something wet fell on my forehead. 'You stupid fool of a man. You only needed to distract her.' The velvet voice sounded strained. 'I did not go through a decade of torture and sorrow only for you leave just when we found each other again. Fight, you damn insensitive bastard. Fight for me. Fight for us.' The voice broke and stirred something within me, something that wanted to stay. To fight one more day. 'Damn it, Nathaniel. I love you. Stay with me, please.'

'Artemis!' A deep voice thundered through the dark fog before it swallowed me whole.

## 25

Death was supposed to be soothing – peaceful, even. That hadn't been my experience so far.

Devon yelled at someone, '*Fix him*. He saved your grandchildren's lives.'

A deep voice answered him. 'His fate belongs to another, Son. Even with my vast array of powers, I could not heal him. Death is my domain, not life.'

Devon growled a curse. 'Ma Dia, what about you? Can't you call on your brother?'

'His fate is not ours to interfere with,' a gentler, throaty voice repeated. 'If this is to be his last hunt then, it was a glorious one.'

A cool sensation washed over me, and the voices stopped.

Until I heard Roel. 'Boss, you better not leave us, you still have a lot of people counting on you, and Julia is so mad at you. She says if you dare to wake up, she'll pin your balls next to the stove.'

A soft whine, followed by a cold, wet sensation skated across my cheek and soothed something restless within me. A small weight fell on my chest and burrowed into my neck.

I opened my eyes. A myriad of scents attacked my senses as the world slowly came into focus. Sabine had been here before but now was nowhere to be seen. I squinted against the soft glow of the lights and sky-blue ceiling. The afterlife looked a lot like a hospital room. Where were the girls in tiny bikinis holding fruity drinks with the little parasols? Or the cozy cabin in the woods with the warm fireplace? Hell, at this point, I would settle for Mufasa's giant floating head.

The room was painted like the ocean in soft blues and greens, and a large window to my left revealed the night sky. I sat up gingerly and groaned at the pain that flared along my ribs and back. Two IVs trailed out of me, pumping me full of Gods knew what – I hoped it was the good stuff at least. I struggled to free my arm from the cocoon of sheets and almost ripped out a line in the process.

*Awake two seconds and already causing trouble for the nurses.* I could practically hear Devon saying the words, but where was he? Where was Rela?

Someone had clearly been visiting, judging by the half-eaten chocolate-sponge cake that had been left on a side table. It looked a lot like one of Julia's Chocolate Surprise Yule Logs. It was placed near enough to my bedside that it was obviously deliberate like someone had tried to use the lure of cake to wake me. Julia baked one of those cakes every year, switching the amount and types of chocolates each time. My favorite so far had been the Quadruple Dark Chocolate Log with chocolate chips and heavy cream that she'd made two years ago, and this one didn't look far off.

It smelled really good, and my stomach growled, demanding that I feed it the clearly delicious food that was nearby. I was on my third attempt to reach the cake when the door to the room suddenly opened. Devon stepped inside, looking haggard and carrying a pitcher of water. He paused abruptly mid-step, and the water in the pitcher sloshed over his shirt. His eyes darted from me to the cake. The upper half of my body remained on the bed whilst my legs stretched through the air, trying to pull the table closer with my foot. My face must've been strained in the valiant attempt not to fall from the bed. His mouth curved upwards, and he started cursing at me in what I assumed was Ancient Greek. He spoke so fast that I only caught one word in five, something about the crows and my stupidity. Good to know he'd missed me.

'I woke up alone, hungry and hurting. Cake was the best medicine for all of that,' I said defensively, wiggling my toes under the edge of the table, but the damn thing was just out of reach. My voice sounded rough as if I had licked all the salt from Julia's cupboards.

Devon scoffed at me, putting the pitcher on the table before helping me sit back up. 'Leave it to your cantankerous ass to wake up the moment I go and refill the water. Couldn't you wait five more seconds?' I tried to pour myself a glass, but the pitcher was so heavy I could barely lift it. Devon growled at me. 'I swear if all living patients are anything like you, then I'm glad I only work with the stiff ones.'

He poured me a drink and sat down on the chair by my bedside. He looked exhausted, but some of the tension had faded from him since sitting down. I drank the water in one gulp before attacking the sponge cake. As soon as the first piece hit my mouth, I moaned in pleasure and didn't care. The cake was filled with dark chocolate chips, triple-layered with milk and dark chocolate. My tastebuds were dancing and by the time I finished the rest of the log, my hands were covered with choco-late syrup, and I was licking them like a three-year-old.

'Well, I'm glad your appetite is back. We've been worried about you,' Devon said when I leaned back. 'You ever scare Margie like that again; I'll have to kill you myself.'

I swallowed another mouthful of water and rested my head on the pillow. 'Honestly? I wasn't planning on dying. I don't remember much after passing out. You killed Arianwen and – am I remembering rightly that your dad showed up?'

Devon nodded and let out a breath. 'Well, your girlfriend played a very large part in all that. If she hadn't been tending to Alice and Margie ... well, it all worked out, right?'

'Where are Alice and Margie now? Are they waiting outside?'

Devon's face dropped as he took a deep breath and all the strength seemed to leave his body. My stomach dropped. 'Alice went into labor. The stress of what that bitch did – we were so far away from any hospital. The only thing I could do was call my father, who summoned my cousin Artemis. The boys were delivered safely thanks to her gifts, but they were too early. The risks were high and we didn't know what effect, if any, Arianwen's magic might have had on them.'

I nodded, concerned as to where this was going.

'Artemis took them to Olympus so that Apollo could keep an eye on them, heal them if necessary. I stayed here with Margie, and to watch your stupid ass, of course. Plus, Zeus isn't really a big fan of me due to his millennia-old feud with Hades. You've been out for a month, and all I've heard from Apollo since then is that they're healing, but it's going to take time.' He rubbed his face tiredly. 'Margie has been crying herself to sleep every night. She misses her mom. I'm doing everything I can to cheer her up but...'

I lay there stunned, digesting all the news. My stomach churned as I thought of Margie's nightly tears, I started to regret eating all that chocolate cake. A month? I'd been in a coma for a whole month. I couldn't believe this. Guilt ran through me hard and fast. We had tried to save Devon and his family, only for him to lose them anyway. I looked at him again, and the dark circles under his eyes and unshaved cheeks made way more sense now. He had to be beyond frustrated but somehow keeping it together for Margie's sake.

I tried to think of some comforting words to say if only to ease his worry momentarily. 'I'm sure Alice and the babies are going to be fine. You literally called on divine intervention, and it answered. If not, as soon as they discharge me we'll storm the gates of Olympus. Guns blazing.'

Devon gave me a weak laugh and shook his head. 'Appreciate the sentiment, bud, but we just got you back. Besides, I trust my cousin to heal them. The bastard owes me. You'd only wind up getting yourself nearly killed. Again. Seems to be your specialty.' Devon leaned back with a roll of his eyes. 'Now that you're awake, I can at least tell the others, and we can all quit worrying. Margie has been asking about you non-stop. Thank the Gods she doesn't remember much of what happened – except when she dreams, I think. Awakening her magic like that was a blessing in disguise. I want her to forget as much about that night as possible. The fewer nightmares my little girl has, the better.'

Sweet, playful Margie summoning a three-headed hound of hell and ordering it to kill wasn't the sort of thing I usually considered a blessing, but beggars couldn't be choosers, I supposed. 'So not a necromancer or a telepath, but a summoner, huh? One with a big weapon in her arsenal. I always thought Cerberus was a rottweiler. And that he'd be bigger.'

Devon snorted. 'You think a ten-year-old would have the power to summon the guardian of Hades? That's cute.' He shook his head. 'She summoned one of Cerberus' pups; he has like a gazillion. She decided to call this one Spots. She's been begging us for a puppy for ages, and I guess since we wouldn't give her one, she went and did something about it herself. Have to applaud her resourcefulness, I guess. And, of course, Cerberus isn't a rottweiler, he's an Espirus Mastiff. I don't know what's going to happen about her magic.' He shrugged. 'Scions like us don't fall under the traditional magical spectrum. Our magic always has some relation to our Godly parents.'

'And in her case, it came in the form of summoning the literal guardian of Hades? What little girl wouldn't want a three-headed puppy?' I laughed and immediately regretted it when my side throbbed. 'What happened to Rela?'

'She saw you go down and worked some healing magic that kept you alive long enough to arrive at Ohsu Hospital. She would've stayed with you, but apparently, there's too much metal in the hospital for her to come in.' He pulled out an envelope with a wax seal and handed it to me. 'She told me to give this to you before she left. The doctors here had a hell of a time keeping you alive. The Grisharu pumped you with so much poison they had a whole team of healers working on you for the first twenty-four hours. Then the gifts started to arrive.'

I took the envelope, wishing that Rela was here instead of the letter. 'Gifts? What gifts?' I asked, perking up.

Devon grinned. 'Well, apparently, you're a very popular patient and have been feeding the staff for the past month. Julia basically bakes a yule log every day and sends Roel or Leann to bring it over, and they, in turn, have been bringing a plate themselves. A pair of EMTs, Bryan Lane and Brittany Hernandez, also dropped by and left you a couple boxes of homemade pizza with a message to contact them as soon as you wake up. Travis has been sending you bacon burgers and coffee. He said the coffee was from him and the bacon from his brother? I didn't know he had one.'

I huffed a soft laugh. Travis didn't have a brother, but he treated his other shifter-half as such even though the animal side of him was an ornery bastard. Devon continued, 'Hope and Russell have been sending you just about every dish in the restaurant. It had the nurses drooling. The leader of the local mountain lion pack found out you were here and has been asking about you every day. He wants to stop by and express his gratitude for saving his daughter.'

I thought about the baby mountain lion we rescued when all of this started and couldn't help the bittersweet feeling that crept up my chest and dampened my eyes. We had avenged the death of her mother, but that wouldn't bring her back. I tried to pour myself another glass of water, but Devon slapped my hand away and did it for me. 'I'm glad she's doing okay.' A thought suddenly occurred to me. 'What happened to the staff?'

Devon's face grew somber. 'Silera said that, by right of conquest, it was mine. She also warned me that if any of the Fae found out that one of their Gods' weapons had resurfaced, they would move heaven and earth to secure it.' His eyes hardened, flashing with green light. 'I couldn't put my family through that, not again. So I did the only logical thing and gifted it to Xaris. He appreciated the 'tribute' as he called it, and told me if I found any more goodies I should send them his way.'

I nearly choked on my water. 'Yeah, that'll do it.' You would have to be insane to try and steal from a dragon. If so much as a penny was stolen from their hoard, they would know about it and relentlessly track down the thief stupid enough to steal from them.

'Elaine stopped by to apologize for not getting the Assembly's help in time. But after an in-depth investigation, she confirmed what we already knew about Arianwen and the killings. She said that the Assembly recognizes your efforts in averting this crisis and would contact you later on for compensation.' He laced his fingers together and sighed, slumping down in his chair like he needed a nap. I knew the feeling, despite only just waking up I was exhausted. 'The dead patches of land coincided with the ley nodes as we suspected. They've had a team crawling over the park ever since the battle – something about magical residue analysis. Elaine also confirmed that the woman we found in the clearing was Makayla. I'm sorry, Nathan.'

That meant the entire Portland Coven had basically been wiped out. The only surviving member was Leann. I clenched my fists as guilt gnawed at me. I took a deep breath. The coven would re-form eventually, and I would be there to help them when it did. If they even wanted my help, that is, so far, I'd been nothing but a curse. 'I just hope that wherever they are, they're at peace knowing their killer is dead.'

Devon nodded and tapped my hand. 'They are, trust me. I spoke with my father ,and the coven will be granted passage to Elysium.' He got up and smiled. 'Try and get some rest. I'll let the doctor know you're awake.'

I watched him walk away, letting out a deep breath and pondering how lucky I was to be alive. The fact that I had survived was miraculous. My magic had acted in ways it never had before, ways that I couldn't even begin to understand. The new runes I had produced were more powerful, but the cost of their use was high. My own energy fuelled them and if I didn't figure out what was causing my powers to fluctuate sooner rather than later, then it was going to get me killed. I never wanted to be left tapped-out like that again, not with the Fae lurking around every corner these days.

I looked at the envelope in my hand and opened it. Inside was a smooth glassy gray stone with a hole in the middle. An adder stone. Silera called it a Hag Stone or Druid's Glass. If you looked through the hole, you could pierce through illusions and glamours. It also served as a protective amulet, able to defend its owner against foreign magic. Inside the envelope, beside the Druid's Glass, was a short note written with delicate penmanship.

*Dear Rún,*

*Important matters demand my attention at home, and I don't know when*

*I will be able to return. Stay strong and don't do anything foolish. This talisman should be able to protect you when you inevitably get into trouble without me.*

*Love eternally,*

*Rela.*

The bottom of the letter was signed with an imprint of a pair of red lips that made me grin despite myself. The scent of primrose slipped through the air as I carefully placed the note back into the envelope. What was so important it made her leave in such a hurry? I closed my eyes, sensing the tether of Oregon's magic, coiled deep inside me and relaxed incrementally. I put the stone on, next to my armor charm. It made me feel like I carried a piece of her with me.

A storm was brewing on the horizon, and I needed to prepare. But first and foremost, I needed more cake.

# EPILOGUE

Silera walked through the frozen hallways of the Winter palace, aware of the many pairs of eyes that followed her. She smiled sharply, knowing what this was about. She had been ready for it since the moment she had decided to make her move. The Fae had forgotten how swift and cold her wrath could be. They needed a reminder that she wasn't someone to be trifled with. Now they scurried away from her as she made her way to the deepest parts of the castle.

She descended the winding staircase and wondered what her lover would think about her behavior. Probably make some kind of mortal reference that she would have to research the meaning of. Aggravating man.

She pushed through the cold black doors to the dungeons and was met with screams that rang through the icy walls. The place was deserted. The air smelled stale except for the subtly copper scent of blood that came from further within. She could hear the rats scurrying about, running from Tundra, as her faithful companion trailed next to her from the shadows. Always vigilant, her precious guardian.

The Fae were not keen on keeping prisoners. They preferred swift justice unless the prisoner was more useful alive than dead. Frost covered the floor, and the only source of light was the sconces. Their indigo flames made the shadows along the floor lengthen into unnatural gnarled shapes. When Nathan had been presumed dead, she had spent a lot of her time down here. But it had been a while since she'd seen these walls.

She reached the end of the hall, where a large wooden door was guarded by a troll. Vicious and strong, the brutes were her mother's favorite enforcers. Personally, she preferred goblins. Small, but ruthless and cunning. Often underestimated. Her lips twisted into an approximation of a smile. The troll regarded her with beady black eyes that were filled with fear, the stink of it filling the hallway.

'Leave us,' she said, her voice echoing. The troll lumbered past her, leaving her alone. She waited for the screams to stop, and the door opened noiselessly. A male stepped out and gave her a short bow after closing the door behind him, motioning for her to move several steps away.

The fae before her was the epitome of male beauty. His wheat colored hair was pulled back into a ponytail, revealing soft ethereal features. He wore a loose white shirt over a slim frame, dampened slightly by sweat. His golden skin was an oddity here amongst the Winter Fae, and the ladies at court found it fascinating. Unfortunately for him, her tastes ran a little rougher.

'My dear Princess, how lovely it is to see you.' He wiped his bloody hands with a piece of cloth and smirked at her. 'I take it things have settled down with the Queen?'

Insufferable male. She motioned towards the door. 'Has he spoken?'

'I'll take that as no then.' He let out a dramatic sigh. 'My lady, you must speak with your mother soon. She might give you more leeway than the rest of us, but she will want an account of this.' He pointed his thumb at the door.

'Robin, how I handle my mother is none of your concern.' She crossed her arms, tapping her finger on her elbow. 'You've had him for days now, is the infamous Hobgoblin losing his touch?'

As a defector from her brother's court after a failed coup, Robin Goodfellow wasn't just a spymaster, he was the best of the best, and he knew it. That's why she made it her business to keep him humble, lest his ego gets the best of him.

Robin appeared insulted. 'Princess, please, he has been singing since the minute you brought him to me.' A look of disgust marred his beautiful face. 'Unfortunately, all he's done is cry for his daddy and how he will make us all pay.' Robin raised his hand, opening it and closing it to mimic a mouth. 'He says he is the son of a court duke, and this an outrage blah, blah, blah.' He rolled his eyes and lowered his hand. 'Had to burn his tongue off just to make him stop.'

She arched an eyebrow at him and he continued. 'Then I healed him and told him that if he mentioned the duke one more time, I would bring his precious father down here so that they could share a room.' Robin's smile was positively deviant. She fought the urge not to grab him by the shoulders and shake him until he told her everything. 'He told me the marginalized would rise to power and topple down their oppressors.' Robin shuddered. 'I hate fanatics. You can never get more than two sentences out of them before their recruitment spiel comes out. I was about to get more out of him when you arrived.'

She began to reply when a loud booming noise echoed from behind her. Someone had thrown open the doors to the dungeon. Silera turned towards the sound; a low feline growl came from the shadows next to her as Tundra assumed her true form, shaking out her snowy white hair. Rela felt immediately better with the big cat watching her back.

Coming down the hall was one of her ladies in waiting, beautiful with dark brown hair framing a heart-shaped face. Sorcha was her closest confidant at court, the sister of the Spring King, banished from court for daring to love and bear a child to a human. She and the exiled Princess had both given their hearts to mortal men.

'My lady, the Queen requests your immediate presence in the throne room,' Sorcha said, her cupid's bow lips arching into a small smile as she curtsied. Her brown eyes darted from Tundra to the prisoner's door as she rose. 'She gave me the impression that any delay would not be welcomed.'

Tundra growled low in her throat before laying at Silera's feet. A snort escaped Rela's nose. Her mother didn't imply anything. She demanded with extreme prejudice. 'Your service is appreciated, Sorcha. I'll see my mother soon.'

'I'll make myself scarce until such a time as you do.' Sorcha smiled and curtsied again. With a flourish, she turned and walked back up the stairs.

Silera turned around to see Robin staring after Sorcha. 'Interested, Robin?'

Robin shook his head,.'Not even if you paid me.' He tapped his chin. 'There are rumors floating around the Floral Court about her. I don't know. Something about her doesn't sit right with me.'

'Robin, you're a spy. There's always something about someone that never sits well with you.' Rela tucked a strand of hair behind her ear as she rolled her eyes. 'It's one of your most annoying qualities but also the reason you're so good at your job.' She paused for a moment. 'Rumors?'

He shook his head. 'Nothing concrete. I've put some feelers out.'

She nodded. There was no point rushing him. A spider needed time to spin his webs. She motioned to the door. 'Open it. I will see him.'

Robin nodded and opened the heavy wooden door. She strode inside, ignoring the stink of blood and piss that permeated the air. The room was bare of windows. The only light came from the sole lit sconce. There was no furniture except for the table made of ice in the middle of the room.

Strapped to it was a naked male. His perfect skin was marred by a series of deep cuts that went all the way to the bone. Salt had been spread through every single one. The pain had to be excruciating. Several daggers perforated the male's arms, six inches from each other, starting at the armpit and finishing at the wrist. His legs bore several burn marks in the shape of handprints. Robin was a vicious, cunning spider and his methods always got the desired results. The prisoner's ash-coloured hair that had been written about in many bards now lay in clumps on the floor beneath a shaved head.

She snorted again. The Fae were so vain that it must've felt like a physical blow to him. His mouth moved but no sound came out. She arched an eyebrow. Leave it to Robin to torture someone and not give him even the reprieve to voice his pain. He had been blindfolded, and his ears had two metal spikes embedded deep in them – total sensory deprivation. Robin was a brutal bastard, and that's why her mother gave him a home in her court.

'I see you haven't lost your touch,' she remarked to Robin.

'Thank you, Princess,' Robin said as he approached.

'Take the blades out.' Robin obeyed, and she moved closer to the body, her hand glowing with orange light. She laid it on his chest, sending a pulse of magic into him.

The cuts and burns began to heal at a rapid pace. She could make her healing completely painless but in this case... Unlike when she healed Nathan, and had only made it hurt a little out of annoyance. This male deserved to feel every cut sealed, every burn flake away. The male's mouth opened wider in a silent scream.

Once he was completely healed, she removed his blindfold and stared into eyes filled with despair. 'You have a choice. Tell me what I want to know and die a swift death, or spend some more time with Robin. I think he has a new dagger he's been meaning to try out.' She paused for a moment. 'Are you going to be smart or stupid, Galesh?' The man's eyes widened, and he closed his jaw stubbornly. Silera smiled. It wasn't a nice smile. 'As you wish, but you will tell me who ordered you to kill Nathan and who is behind this little revolution of yours.'

Robin stepped forward once more. 'Don't worry, Princess. He'll talk.'

Silera nodded at him and walked out, not missing the glint of a blade as she passed him. Talk, he must, because if her gamble failed, then it would cost them more than their lives. Nathaniel might never forgive her.

# ACKNOWLEDGMENTS

The journey from a first draft to a published version of any book is one of twists, turns and lots of fast food stops, and this book really could not have been possible without some amazing and wonderful people. First and foremost, I want to thank my editing team at SmashBear Publishing. You guys are a wonderful source of help, unconditional support and professionalism. Loredana Carini, Zola Copeland, Tazmin Aldiz, Natalia Grzeszkiewicz, and Molly Chell. Thank you, ladies, for the hours and hours you poured into Death's Edge with me to make it into what it is today. I couldn't have done it without you.

To Rachel Hobbs, Brittany Weisrock, and Roel Cisnero for putting up with my late-night ramblings as I sorted out the plot and put words together with duct tape. Your feedback is always welcome, and your friendship is priceless.

A special thanks to my alpha readers, Melissa Tovgaard, and Kerris Humphreys, for sticking with me and reading the jagged edge version of the book; you ladies are amazing.

Thanks to Declan Mullane for helping me with the Gaelic translations, Sophia Maria Nicolipoulos with the Greek translations, and Claire Patterson with the Welsh translations. You guys allow me to give more depth and color to Nathan's world.

As always, my eternal gratitude to Erin Durst, my eyes on the ground and local Portland expert. You will always have a room at Tir na nÓg.

And most importantly, thank you my readers. Without your support and love for Nathan and his friends, any of this couldn't have been possible. The doors of Tir na nÓg will always be open for you guys, and your favorite innkeeper and his loyal hound will serve you with a smile.

# GLOSSARY

Gob Reoites- Frozen Bills

Dóiteán- Fire

Tintreach- Lightning

Oscaíl- Open

A stóirín - My treasure

Talamh- Ground

Rún- my love

Féach- See

Armúr ar- Armor On

Ag Fás- Grow

Gaoth- Wind

Lasair- Flame

Mo ghrá Thú- I love you

Amach- Out

Kourtína neroú- Water curtain

Cheímaros- Torrent

Omíchli- Mist

Klósi Velos- Spinning Arrow

Emfanízomai- Appear

Sikotheite! O gios tou Adi sas diatazei!- Rise! The son of Hades commands you!

Neró lepída: Water Blade

Mágissa- Witch

Ma to aema tis parthenou odigise me stin ikogenia mou- By the Maiden's Blood guide me to my family.

Skotóno- Kill

Ekrígnymai- Erupt

Erímosi- Desolation

Ma Dia- By Zeus

Armis simiae- Armor Simian

Velamen Sphera- Concealment Globe

Psofa- Die

Mewn enw Chraos-Fhiachlach, lladdwyr y Dagda, Rwy'n hawlio'r staff hyn trwy hawliau concwest- In the name of the Voracious, slayer of the Dadga, I lay claim to her enemy's staff, won by right of conquest.

Ilygredig- Corrupt

See where it all started ...

# STORM'S
# CHILD

## THE RUNE CASTER CHRONICLES
## BOOK:1

SMASH BEAR
-PUBLISHING-

# PROLOGUE

*Ten Years Ago*

The forest gave off an oppressive aura. A chill breeze swept between the branches sending shivers down my spine. I ducked beneath the branches of a large pine before moving between a cluster of trees as we slowly made our way through the thicket. The musky scent of the woods permeated the air the deeper we went and, mixed with the copper scent of blood, stung the back of my throat.

We stopped next to a large tree to gather our bearings. Why would she come here? I turned towards the knight beside me. Like many of the Fae he was tall, but he managed to walk through the forest with graceful elegance. His ash-colored hair tied in a ponytail revealed slightly pointed ears, and his intricate silver armor shone like a beacon in the dark forest. Unlike mine, which, whilst simple and less ornate, let me blend in with the darkness around us. Two swords were sheathed across his back and a small dagger tied to his waist.

It had been years since I saw Galesh have so much as a paper cut. Yet now the fae had blood dripping from his face and neck, marring his otherwise perfect complexion. But if there were one knight I would have to guard my back in this godforsaken forest, it would be him.

'Galesh, where did you last leave her?' I palmed the hilt of my sword, ready to draw it at the sign of any movement. 'What the hell were you guys doing here?'

'We were following orders, Nathan,' he answered softly, his gaze darting around. 'She wanted to hunt a boar to clear her mind before the festival preparations started, and she knew you were called away by the Queen, so she brought a squad of knights.' We stepped over a fallen log, careful not to make too much noise before he continued. 'We came upon the tracks of a drake, and the Princess thought it would prove more of a challenge. During the middle of the hunt, about four miles from the base of the mountain, we were besieged by a squad from Summer and chased like dogs to this shit hole.'

'Of course she did. Only she would do something as stupid as switch hunts from a boar to a drake.' I frowned. Something about the story not making sense. Drakes were massive lizards about twelve feet tall at the shoulder and covered in thick scales with huge spiked tails covered in poison. Though they lacked the ability to fly like their wyvern cousin – and thank the gods they couldn't breathe fire or ice like a dragon – they were a savage breed requiring a full squad of knights to hunt.

Drakes were foul-tempered beasts and resistant to magic, not that it stopped moronic nobles from trying to tame them in the hopes of turning them into a cavalry force. I frowned as we moved again, recalling that drakes made their dens in caves and mountains. The peaks outside Fuar Dorcha, the capital of Winter, were perfect for them. The Queen had to keep sending out squads of knights to deal with them. How did Summer's knights cross the border without raising any alarms? I turned to Galesh and looked him straight in the eyes. 'But why would you abandon her?'

'I did not abandon her!' He glared at me. 'Those bastards ran us down. Mihael and Blyte were the first to fall, shot down by arrows just as we made it to the entrance of the forest.' His shoulders shook as he looked down. 'We were being cut down one after the other, and our only choice was to go deeper. She ordered me to get help, and now here we are.' A cohort of Winter's best would be here at any moment. Today I had been preparing for the Bicentennial Kinship Ball, where the monarchs and nobles of all four courts gathered to mingle and tried not to kill each other. Key word being *tried*. It was Queen Mab's time to host, so preparations were already underway, even if the ball wasn't for another decade or so.

Since the point of the ball was to promote friendship between beings that hated each others' guts, violence was forbidden. Not that it stopped any of the Fae from trying to pull one over on the hosting monarch. As a precaution, the host began preparing things a decade or two in advance.

Earlier today, the Queen summoned all her retainers to discuss the upcoming ball. She went into excruciating detail, explaining that if anything went wrong during the ball, heads would roll. At the end of the meeting, she handed a scroll to each captain with their individual assignments. As I was walking to the stables with my scroll in hand, I ran into a wounded Galesh. The fae was bleeding from half a dozen cuts and had branches in his hair.

'Crooked Man's Forest' and 'Princess in danger' were all he needed to say before I pulled the nearest knight and ordered a cohort to mount up before riding ahead with Galesh. The deeper we went, the harder it was to see where we were going. Even with my enhanced vision, I could only see five feet in front of me.

Eventually, we left the horses tied to a nearby tree as they wouldn't be able to carry us any deeper; the foliage was just too thick. Lighting a torch wasn't an option. We were no longer in Winter's lands, and the Crooked Man didn't take kindly to fire in his forest.

'How much farther, Galesh?' I turned just in time to see a flash of steel before I felt a sharp, piercing pain in my side. A pained gasp escaped me as I looked to see my armor pierced by Galesh's dagger. The knight had a smirk on his face as he pulled the dagger out and stabbed me again.

The weapon went through my armor like it wasn't even there – that wasn't supposed to happen. My armor was bespelled to stop knives. As the dagger was plunged deeper into me, I tried to steady myself against a tree, coughing up mouthfuls of blood. I tried to speak, to call my magic to me, but through the blood loss and pain, it was no use. The pain was too much. The magic slipped through my fingers like dry sand. Galesh twisted the dagger before he leaned forward and whispered in my ear,

'The Princess sends her love.'

# CHAPTER 1

**Present Day**

I looked out of the window, noticing how the grey clouds formed a dim atmosphere on the grounds. The satyr father and son duo ran through the rain, rejoicing in the cleansing the fresh water brought. The large windows of the Inn gave the guests a great view whilst enjoying the comfort of chilling by the roaring fire, but it also meant I could see the mud that would be dragged in and require cleaning. Looking at my floors, I regretted not putting the 'wipe your feet if you have them' mat out.

It was a slow morning. The family of centaurs took to the woods at sunrise and wouldn't be back until lunch, which left me with plenty of time to catch up on work. I put one of my favourite records on and the soft tunes of Beirut played in the background as I turned to my current project: reorganizing the living room. I tapped my foot to the beat of the song as I tilted my head, thinking of the best way to improve my guest's comfort. The fireplace sat in a cozy corner with two leather chairs and a small tea table, while on the other side of the room, a black leather couch lay behind an oak wood piano. A fine layer of dust covered the couch, and with winter around the corner, my guests would probably appreciate an extra seat next to the fireplace.

'That's it, I quit,' said a frustrated voice behind me, followed by the absence of music.

I sighed and turned to the bane of my existence. Standing at five-foot-something, Lucas wasn't the first person you imagined as a mage in training. His shabby, short blonde hair and gray overalls made him an unexpected candidate. I sighed again, softly –he wouldn't let me walk by until I heard whatever teenage ailment bothered him now. I could already feel the need for a soothing cup of hot tea.

I ignored him and looked about the living room again; the boy threatened to quit about three times a day since he'd started working at the Inn back in August. He'd lasted a month, which is more than could be said for the several others that came before him.

Maybe if I didn't say anything, he would go away? Then I could finish with the living room and move onto the next chore on the list. I walked to the couch, considering if I moved it a little more to the right, the guests could have a nice view of the woods without getting baked in the afternoon sun ...

'I mean it, Nathan. That beast almost killed me.'

I rolled my eyes. Got to give the kid points for drama, at the very least. Still undecided as to how I wanted the room to look, I grabbed the back of the couch and frowned. Now I wondered if I moved it to the left, the guests would get nice and cozy by the fireplace at night when it gets cold. Decisions, decisions. Woods or Fireplace?

Lucas parked himself in front of me just as I was about to move the couch to the left. 'Nathan, are you even listening?' He had a determined look on his face that told me, this time, he was trying to be serious. 'That thing tried to kill me.'

I looked dubiously towards said thing napping by the fireplace without a care in the world. 'What did you do to her?'

Lucas threw his hands in the air with all the angst a teenage mage in training could muster. 'You *always* take her side over mine.'

I let go of the couch, accepting he wouldn't let me move it until I heard his side of the story. The sooner this was over, the sooner I could make some tea.

'Okay, you have my undivided attention. What happened?'

He took a deep and calming breath before looking at me. 'I just got in from the college and was about to make myself something to eat before getting started on the lunch rush, and she just bolted at me and nearly took my whole damn leg off!' He glared at the aforementioned beast, who was busy kicking her paws at the air while making soft growly noises. 'I told you that if I kept working here, you'd need to keep that demon chained. I'm a mage, for Merlin's sake!'

It was only then I noticed he was missing the bottom half of his pants, hanging in tatters, like a grass skirt around his calf. Today was Friday, so Lucas had probably come straight from his class at the college, which meant he stank of magic and other interesting things that usually set Sabine off.

I raised a finger at him. 'You're not a mage ... yet.' I raised another finger, 'Second, did you shower before coming to work?' I cut him off before he could answer. 'Let me answer that for you; that would be a no. Because if you showered like you were supposed to, this wouldn't have happened.' I pointed towards the fireplace. 'You know Sabine is sensitive to magic, and she's not a demon, a thing or a beast. She's a beagle.'

A look of resentment washed over his face. 'So, it's my fault then?'

I sighed and pinched the bridge of my nose, thinking about every regretful decision that led me to this very moment, all for paying back a favour to Lucas's father, Cassius. He'd helped me out some time ago and now here was my comeuppance. His little bundle of joy got into trouble at school for unauthorized use of magic in the girls' locker room, and he'd rung me asking if I had any jobs lying around to keep the kid busy.

It just so happened my last kitchen boy quit after a near-death experience with my cook for screwing up a guest's order – who knew minotaurs were allergic to peanuts? Lucas was a hard worker, no doubt, but his constant insistence on quitting was draining.

'Lucas, how about you take the rest of the day off and come back tomorrow?'

Lucas crossed his arms over his chest and lifted his chin defiantly.

'I don't need to be in a place where a dog is more appreciated than me.' He spun on his heel and slammed the door on the way out.

Sabine looked up from her spot and wagged her tail at me.

I sighed. 'You see what you did? Now what am I going to tell Julia?'

'Tell Julia what?'

I cringed before turning around to look at the suspicious dryad. 'Er, hey Julia, did you do something new with your hair? I have to say it looks great.'

She stood in the middle of the room and arched an eyebrow at me. 'Don't bullshit me, Nathan, what did you do?'

Of average height and slim build, Julia looked more like a college student than a dryad. She still managed to scare the bejeezus out of me, though, not that I would ever tell her that. Today she wore her hair in a tight ponytail which highlighted her sharp eyes and made her look quite severe.

I took a deep breath and tried to think quickly the best way to explain what just happened. 'Sabine fired Lucas. I tried to stop her but she wouldn't listen to reason.'

Sabine whined behind me.

Julia's eyes swirled and shifted, glowing like liquid steel. She walked towards me, poking my chest with her finger. 'What do you mean Sabine fired him? Wait, don't answer that.' She pinched her nose in frustration and growled. 'What the hell am I going to do now? Lunch is in two hours!'

I gave her my best smile. 'I'm sure you'll figure it out. You always do.'

She rolled her eyes at me in exasperation. 'How in Pan's ass do you stay in business?'

I smiled at her and nodded towards the outside. 'Where else in the world could you see something like that?' The satyr family were playing a mud version of a snowball fight, laughing like idiots. One of the mud balls missed the kid and splattered onto one of the windows. I frowned. That would need a good scrubbing. 'Tír na nÓg is the only inn for supernatural folks, where people feel safe enough to—'

243

'Be their true selves,' she finished and rolled her eyes. I could practically see her counting to ten. 'I didn't ask for the sales pitch. Get your
ass in the kitchen.'

I took a couple of steps back from her. 'Wait, what?'

She crossed her arms over her chest and gave me the stink eye.
'You didn't stop Lucas from quitting, so until you can replace him,
guess what?' She reached over and poked me on the shoulder. 'Tag,
you're it.'

~

B y the time I finished, it was almost midnight. Julia couldn't stand
my incompetence for more than a couple of minutes before
grumpily kicking me out of the kitchen, muttering she was faster by
herself.

Unfortunately, my day didn't stop there. One of the joys of running
an inn for things that go bump in the night was that there was always
something to do. Most of my afternoon was spent replacing the attic
window, which managed to stay relatively intact despite boasting three
arrows, courtesy of the centaurs and their 'target practice'. Xaris, the
dragon who permanently rented the attic, was not amused. I had to
spend the rest of the afternoon convincing him centaurs leave a bad
taste in your mouth.

After that, I'd made my way back towards the living room, where
the couch still sat at an awkward angle next to the piano. The fireplace
crackled with faint dying flames still warming the room. I stood by the
entrance and gave the living room a cursory glance. The record player
stood to my left on top of an eighteenth-century oak table Xaris gifted
the inn to commemorate his fifth year staying here.

I smiled, remembering the dragon making a whole show of it, and
how it was our honor to receive a part of his hoard. To my right stood a
worn bookshelf. I'd bagged it for an absolute steal after a local bookstore closed and sold their furniture. A wine colored rug covered the
wooden floors; it was one of Sabine's favorite spots as she loved to roll
around in it. Across from me were a pair of wooden double doors with

circular windows in the middle. It had taken a bit of elbow grease, but the mud had finally come off.

The windows gave a clear view of the woods, and it was never difficult to see what inspired Shakespeare's 'A Midsummer Night's Dream' on nights like this. I could imagine the Fair Folk dancing between the silver light and the shadows cast by the moonlight shining through the trees.

I started moving the couch towards the doors when the front desk bell rang, announcing the arrival of a new guest. I sighed, letting go of the couch before making my way to the reception hall.

The hall was at the heart of the inn, an open space that connected the downstairs to the upper parts through a wooden staircase. Snuggled between the entrance to the living and dining rooms was my little piece of the kingdom. A dark cherry wood desk sat perfectly in the corner. It had taken me more than two weeks to find it. Funds were tight at the beginning, but it was worth it. The large table and chairs were collecting a fine layer of dust, needing to be cleaned tomorrow. It was rarely used unless we had a big party or a formal gathering. Most guests like to take their meals in their rooms or the upstairs balcony. There was no better spot for going through paperwork and enjoying a cup of peppermint tea.

Sabine was lying down on her bed next to the stairs. The word 'manager' was embroidered on the side of the bed – the guests thought it was cute.

A young man was standing at the desk. He was in his mid-twenties with light brown hair, and his skin had a ruddy tone from spending too much time in the sun. Wearing a tattered jacket with a black shirt and blue jeans that had seen better days, he looked rather worse for wear. Even his shoes looked like they were about to fall apart.

I mentally checked the protective wards. The familiar tingle at the back of my neck gave me a brief pause of relief.

'Welcome to Tír na nÓg. I'm Nathan. How can I help you?' I smiled, extending my hand.

He hesitated before slowly shaking it. 'I heard this is a safe place. Is that true?'

I gave him a reassuring smile. 'As long as guests abide by the inn's laws, it's the safest place in Portland. They have our full protection.'

He shifted his weight from one foot to the other as he let go of my hand. 'What laws?'

I pointed to a small plaque on the wall next to the stairs where a cartoon version of Sabine was reading the text:

'Come in peace. Do not harm the other guests. Don't run out on your bill. Be courteous to the staff.'

Normally guests came to the inn for one of three reasons. Some wanted to escape the mortals oblivious to the darker side of the world and let their supernatural side shine. Some needed a quiet place to rest. Others were running from something big and bad.

The kid wet his chapped lips before nodding to himself as if he was coming to a decision. 'How much for a room?'

I took another look at the prospective guest standing in front of me. He didn't have any luggage to speak of except for a small black leather hip pouch that was in pristine condition, unlike the rest of him. The only jewelry he had on was a small silver ring with a dark blue gem with a faint glow of magic. Now that was odd. Jewelry was usually the first thing to be sold or pawned when someone's this down on their luck. There was a slight tangy, sweet smell wafting from him, reminiscent of when Sabine thought it was a good idea to go dumpster diving. Even if he didn't have the money for a room, I'd at least offer him a shower. Then again, with supernatural folk, appearances are most definitely deceiving. He could be a one thousand-year-old prince with more money than I make in a year just sitting in his pocket.

'It's five gold pieces a night. You can pay up front if you know how long your stay is going to be. If not, then we collect weekly payments on Sundays.' I stood behind the front desk. 'Do you know how long you'll be staying with us?'

Gold was the universal currency of the supernatural world – empires rose and fell every other century, but gold would never devalue. Each piece was the size of a Girl Scout cookie and would go for about $100 dollars each. I didn't think the kid had that much money.

Which meant I was surprised when he pulled out thirty-five gold pieces from his hip pouch and laid them down on the counter.

I nodded and pulled out the registration form. 'Please sign your name on the bottom.' He gave me that same deer in headlights look from before. 'Don't worry. It's not a magical contract. Just your consent of the inn's laws.'

He signed his name. I smiled and took the form back before grabbing one of the keys from inside the desk. 'Okay, Mr...' I looked at the flowing cursive writing. 'Roel. Please follow me.'

Sabine stood up from her bed and shook herself off before bolting for the stairs. Welcoming a new guest was one of her favorite things to do.

As we walked to his room on the second floor, I tried to get a feel for the kid. He didn't have any of the usual smells of a shifter (although it would be difficult to tell considering the only thing I could smell at the moment was garbage) or the unnatural stillness of the undead. He sure as hell wasn't any type of Fae, which my wards would have warned me against.

He did have magic, though. I could sense that much, just not what flavor. The only vibe I got off this kid was that he needed somewhere safe to crash.

I let my magic gather around my thumb and traced a small symbol: two white parallel lines inside a circle at the base of the key. All the keys had different runes that needed to be drawn by me to allow the doors to open. An extra safety measure the guests appreciated, no one but myself and the guest could use the key to access the room. We arrived at his room, where Sabine, as expected, was already waiting impatiently outside the reddish-brown door.

The door opened to reveal a large sandalwood bed in the center of the room, dark blue linens adorning it. A small nightstand stood on either side, both with brass candle holders. At the foot of the bed stood a soft blue lounging chair positioned on woolen gray carpet. Opposite the bed, two large doors lead to a marble-tiled bathroom and walk-in closet. Two arched windows gave a perfect view of the woods outside, while a wooden door led to the second-floor balcony.

I turned towards the kid, and the look of relief in his eyes as I handed him the key made me happy. At least here, he could sleep knowing he would be safe. 'Here you go, Mr Roel. Breakfast is at seven, lunch at noon and dinner just after sunset. You need anything, call me. The number is next to the phone. Have a good night.'

He stood by the door for a good twenty seconds before Sabine let out a small bark of annoyance and sat in the middle of the room, giving the new guest a look. Roel looked at me.

I shrugged. 'She won't feel her job is done until you step inside.'

He chuckled a little, then caught himself and stopped. He walked inside, passing by Sabine and sat on the bed. My little manager gave him a nod before she sneezed in his general direction and walked out of the room.

I waved at the kid and smiled. 'You have a good night.' I closed the door and turned to Sabine, who was giving me the stink eye.

'What?' She looked at the door, sneezed again then looked back at me.

I looked at her, annoyed, as we walked downstairs. 'Don't be a busy-body. His business is none of our business.'

She whined before lying down on her bed.

I ran my hand through my hair, a dark strand falling next to her paws. I still wasn't used to how short it was now. 'No, I'm not making things hard on you. If he feels up to it, he will let us know. If not, then we'll deal with whatever it is when it comes knocking.'

She gave me a small growl of acceptance before laying on her back. I laughed and knelt to give her a belly rub. 'Now you're just being a spoiled brat.'

After Sabine got her fill, she dashed towards the kitchen, probably to beg for some treats off Julia. I walked back towards the couch. 'Okay, time to get you out of the way.'

I bent over to grab the couch, about to move it, when a knock on the door stopped me. I laid my head on the armrest and rolled my eyes. 'You gotta be kidding me.' I gave the couch a glare, mumbling, 'This isn't over,' and made my way towards the door.

I looked through the peephole of the large oak door to see a tall woman standing on my porch. She was probably in her mid-thirties with piercing dark brown eyes with bags beneath them and dark curly hair that fell just below her neck. She was wearing a dark blue pant suit. The glint of a gun could be seen beneath her jacket.

I opened the door and put on my most charming voice. She was either a cop or someone ready to make trouble. Or even worse, a door to door salesman, although I dismissed that idea given the hour and the gun. 'Good evening, Miss, how can I help you?'

'Nathaniel Mercer?' she asked in a stern tone.

From the way she carried herself and spoke, she was definitely a cop. I extended my senses around her and found she was a vanilla human ... lucky me. 'Nathan, please. Nathaniel makes me sound like a grumpy old man.'

The joke bounced off her like dry peas on a wall. She pulled up her credentials confirming my cop suspicion. 'I'm Detective Garcia, Portland PD. Can we speak for a moment?'

A shiver ran down my spine. I ran a mental note of my guests; none of them were of the violent variety – well, except for the dragon in the attic and maybe Roel. But the kid was too new for me to get a read on. I was apprehensive, concerned that I was in for a world of trouble. What could my guests have done?

I stepped outside, closing the door behind me and motioned to a couple of chairs on the porch. 'Sure, Detective. I hope it's okay that we talk outside. As you can see, I run an inn and don't want my guests feeling uncomfortable. I hope you understand.'

The inn sat in the middle of a five hundred acre property west of the Willamette River. It gave enough privacy to my less-than-human guests to shed their disguises while being relatively close to civilization for a nice cup of coffee.

The cool night breeze swept through the front porch, carrying the musky scent of the woods with the undertones of the sweet citrusy red verbena and St. John's wort circling the whole property. Several chairs sat around an ash wooden table. It was a particular favourite spot of the guests, who liked to sit around amongst nature and drink a glass of iced tea. A half-filled ashtray told me Xaris had been sitting here recently.

That dragon enjoyed his cigars a little too much for my liking – not that he'd be too put out if he burned the place down. Being fireproof had its perks. A blue sedan parked next to my truck caught the corner of my eye; must be the detective's.

She gave me a stiff nod before following to the table. I pulled out a chair for her, but she shook her head. 'No, thank you. How long have you known Lucas Gray?'

I frowned at her, a bad feeling slowly creeping up my spine. 'His dad and I have been friends for years. I have known Lucas since he was in grade school. Why? Has he done something?'

She took out a little notepad and began writing on it. 'Was he having trouble at school? History of bullying? Anyone that might want to hurt him?'

What the hell? Did something happen to the kid? Shit. Cassius is going to kill me.

'No, not at all. He started going to college this year, and his dad asked me to look out for him. So, I gave him a job in the kitchen, helping with the meals. He's new to town, so he mostly spends his time here or at school. Detective, what is this about? Is Lucas okay?'

She took a few notes before putting the notebook away. 'Mr Mercer, I'm sorry to say this but we found Lucas floating beneath the Hawthorne Bridge. Paramedics at the scene tried everything they could. I'm sorry.'

SMASH BEAR
-PUBLISHING-

Thank you for supporting
SmashBear Publishing and our
authors.

For more information about our
authors, upcoming releases and
what we publish, you can check out
our website

**www.smashbearpublishing.com**

Or find us on: